DEATH OVER HIS SHOULDER

Decker took three more swallows before returning the canteen to the carrier. With a satisfied sigh, he reached down to retrieve his Pitbull. The weapon was gone. He knelt down, searching the dusty bottom of the shallow foxhole with his starlight viewer. The assault rifle was nowhere to be found.

A strange sensation prickled along the back of Decker's neck. Fear gripped his belly. Slowly he turned his head. There, perched on the rim of the foxhole, was a Masher. The thing squatting above him had a filthy hide that bore many scars. An arching row of bolt heads followed the line of the creature's ridged eyebrows, looking like a rounded M of metallic warpaint across its forehead. Even more horrible than the monster's disfigurement was the fact that it held Decker's Pitbull in its massive hands . . .

VOR: THE MAELSTROM

Vor: *Into the Maelstrom*
by Loren L. Coleman

Vor: *The Playback War*
by Lisa Smedman

Vor: *Island of Power*
by Dean Wesley Smith

Vor: *The Rescue*
by Don Ellis

Vor: *Hell Heart*
by Robert E. Vardeman

Available from Warner Aspect®

OPERATION SIERRA-75

THOMAS S. GRESSMAN

A Time Warner Company

WARNER BOOKS EDITION

Copyright © 2001 by FASA Corporation
All rights reserved. No part of this book may be reproduced in any form or by any electronic or mechanical means, including information storage and retrieval systems, without permission in writing from the publisher, except by a reviewer who may quote brief passages in a review.

Aspect® name and logo are registered trademarks of Warner Books, Inc.

VOR: The Maelstrom and all related characters, slogans, and indicia are trademarks of FASA Corporation.

Cover design by Don Puckey
Cover illustration by Donato
Cover logo design by Jim Nelson

Warner Books, Inc.
1271 Avenue of the Americas
New York, NY 10020

Visit our Web site at
www.twbookmark.com

 A Time Warner Company

Printed in the United States of America

First Printing: January 2001

10 9 8 7 6 5 4 3 2 1
ISBN: 978-0-446-60493-2
ISBN: -0-446-60493-3

For my parents, Thomas B. and Mildred S. Gressman.
I guess you raised me right after all.

Thanks once again to all those who have contributed their time, encouragement, and expertise to the creation of this story. Particular thanks to Donna Ippolito, Jaime Levine, and Wyn Hilty, for their support, guidance, and useful suggestions. I extend my gratitude to those experts who have lent me their aid, and a special thank-you to Bill Kyle, who gave me a bit of insight into the mind of a Marine. Any errors in these pages are mine, alone.

Once again, thanks to Brenda for putting up with me as I labored over this book.

And as always, my thanks to You, Lord, for the abilities you've given me, and the opportunity to exercise them once again.

OPERATION SIERRA-75

Prologue

Mission Control, this is *Cabot*. We have established standard orbit at Sierra Seven-Five, and are beginning preliminary survey."

Lieutenant Colonel Julian LaVree's voice crackled from the overhead speakers, echoing in the hard-walled Mission Control Center. The chamber was one of the largest in the Union's Tycho Crater Moonbase. Communication, telemetry monitoring, and long-range scanner terminals stood in ordered ranks, occupying much of the room's floor space. One wall was taken up by larger, flat-screen monitors.

"Roger, *Cabot*," senior controller Adam Paige responded. "Mission Control awaits your feeds."

Paige logged in *Cabot*'s message, glancing at the largest of the wall-mounted monitors. In the center right of the display, a yellow cursor marked the position of the mission currently under way. The cursor, in the shape of a tiny spaceship, held position over a near-Earth body designated Sierra Seven-Five. In the lower right-hand corner of the display was the mission clock. Bold white characters proclaimed the time and date, 08:38 A.M. 27 March 2114.

No one knew the origins of that planet. That was at least part of the reason *Cabot* had been sent out across the uncertain reaches of the Outer Ring to investigate the seemingly dead world. Unmanned probes suggested that several man-made structures existed on that world, many of them still intact. The lack of major power sources indicated that the beings who had raised these buildings had either died out, or fled their world. In either case, Sierra Seven-Five was yet another victim of the Maelstrom.

The Maelstrom. The word caused a qualm of uneasiness in Paige. No one knew exactly what or even where the Maelstrom was. All that was known for certain was that it was an immeasurably vast area of time and space into which Earth and the moon had been dragged. During the chaos that accompanied Earth's "Induction" into the Maelstrom, as scientists were calling it, incredible "Earth Changes" occurred. Radical shifts in planetary weather patterns led to massive storms. Seismic tremors shook nearly every area of the planet, some laying waste to entire regions. The island nation of Japan was one area to suffer such massive devastation. Alien plants, fungi, and animal life began to appear in those places. Some of these were benign, some hostile. All were frightening. There had been reports of alien creatures actually invading the planet. Many of the surviving humans had put these rumors down to panic and to an increased level of hostility between the Neo-Soviet Empire and the North American Union. In the wake of the Induction, first skirmishes, and then outright battles had been fought between the old enemies, culminating in a limited exchange of nuclear weapons. There were still the occasional scraps between east and west, but things seemed to have settled down for now.

In all the terror and chaos of the Induction, little had been discovered about Terra's new and frightening neighborhood. It had been eight years since the Induction. Now the Union Space Corps was seeking to make up for that failure. It was known that the Maelstrom seemed to be a huge vortex, a pocket universe existing in some other dimension than the one it had been ripped out of. Earth occupied the outermost ring of the Maelstrom, far away from the huge blank disk of the Maw, a writhing, tentacled ball of energy that lay at the center of the Maelstrom. Other planets in the Outer Ring were close enough to be investigated by long-range probes. Sierra Seven-Five was one such world. The fact that the probe detected structures but no signs of life suggested several possibilities. Perhaps the entire population of the planet had died before, during, or after Sierra Seven-Five's Induction, or they had been wiped out by one of the alien races inhabiting the Maelstrom, or they might have found a way to escape through the Veil, the dark, shifting curtain that surrounded the Maelstrom. Survival and escape were the two highest priorities on everyone's minds.

While Paige mused on these unsettling thoughts, Lieutenant Colonel LaVree's voice sounded from the control room's speakers once again.

"*Cabot* to Mission Control, beginning first sensor sweep. Preliminary scans indicate a toxic atmosphere with high concentrations of ammonia and carbon dioxide. Pressure seems to be about the same as Earth. Indications of large bodies of wat—"

A burst of loud static blasted from the speakers, ending abruptly. Then there was silence.

Paige sat upright in his chair.

"*Cabot*, this is Mission Control, say again your last." Paige knew it would take over forty-five minutes for a reply from the survey ship to reach Mission Control. He keyed a command into his computer terminal, calling up the vessel's telemetry feeds. All of the indicators that were relayed back to the control center from *Cabot*'s sensor suite were blank.

"Telemetry, run a diagnostic," Paige barked.

"Already doing it, boss," a technician responded. "We got nothing. No telemetry, no carrier signal, no nothing. *Cabot* is completely off-line."

"Dammit," Paige cursed. "All right, keep trying to reestablish contact. Let me know the second you get anything. I've gotta call the Director."

The senior controller swore again as he reached for the comm-set. In a few moments, a link was established between the lunar control center and the Johnson Space Center on Earth.

"I'm sorry to disturb you, sir," Paige said, as the Director of the Union Space Agency answered. A glance at his console clock revealed it was three in the morning in Texas. "We have a problem. *Cabot* has gone off-line. We're trying to reestablish contact, but I'm afraid she may be down."

1

"C ome in, Captain Taggart. Please sit down." General Keith Andrews gestured at a vacant chair.

"Yessir," Captain Maxwell Taggart responded. A slight turn of his head and a barely perceptible flicker of his eyes directed the tall, ruddy-skinned woman who had entered the room with him to take up a position behind the officer's chair.

Taggart was not what most people would refer to as a handsome man. Standing just over 180 centimeters tall, he was strongly built, with unremarkable brown eyes and equally unremarkable brown hair, worn "high-and-tight" according to UAF regulations. It was the uniform that marked him as a special individual. A gold globe-and-anchor device graced the collar of his drab green dress uniform, balanced by the paired silver bars of a captain. A gold dragon coiled against a scarlet shield graced the shoulder of his drab green uniform jacket. Together the insignia proclaimed him to be an officer of the Third Amphibious Marine Division, the first unit specially trained for spaceborne operations. Officially, Taggart's unit was considered to be a Special Forces platoon in the Union Armed Forces Ground Corps, though their cross training could easily relegate them to the Space Corps as well. Like most of his brothers-in-arms, Taggart considered himself a Marine, even though the old United States Marine Corps had technically been absorbed into the UAF G-Forces. The pride and *esprit de corps* of the Marines was evident in the officer's stance and bearing.

The woman who followed him into the room also wore the insignia of the Third Division, but her uniform bore no officers' bars. In their place were the stripes and crossed rifles of a gunnery sergeant. Again, though the rank of gunnery sergeant technically no longer existed, those of the old Marine Corps were reluctant to give up any of their traditions, or their identity as one of the oldest, and most elite, fighting forces in the UAF.

Taggart dropped easily into the chair Andrews had indicated and placed a small notebook computer on the table. As he waited for Andrews to begin, Taggart glanced around the room. The briefing room, like many of the spaces in the Union's lunar base at Tycho, was small almost to the point of being cramped. Besides the general, there were two others present, a young man wearing the collar flashes of the Union Technical Corps and a dark-haired woman clad in the white dress uniform of the Union Space Corps.

"Two days ago," General Andrews said, "The USS *Cabot*, an Explorer class survey ship, settled into a standard orbit above the near-Earth planet Sierra Seven-Five. Her mission was to investigate that planet, based upon sensor imagery sent back by an H-25-type unmanned probe."

As the general spoke, a chart flashed across a screen set into the briefing room's back wall. Taggart was familiar with the chart. It was the best computer-generated representation of the Maelstrom that the Union's limited sensor, probe, and survey efforts could produce. Only the "near-Earth" area of the Outer Ring was represented in detail. Only a few features, such as the anomalies called the Tangle and the Near Maw Manifestation, were visible in the Central and Inner Rings. The large blank, or sparsely marked, sections of the chart reminded Taggart of the old mariners' charts of Earth, drawn up during the Age of Exploration. Only in this case, the featureless sections of the map before him were missing the inscription "Here there be Monsters."

"The mission controllers tried to reestablish contact with *Cabot* for several hours. Eventually they gave up," the general continued. "Virtually anything could have happened to her. She may have met with some form of accident, she may have been pulled into the Maw. Intelligence reports suggest that the Neo-Soviet Empire has increased its space-exploration efforts. It is possible that *Cabot* may have run into a Neo-Sov mission and been shot down."

Andrews paused briefly, as though reluctant to speak the words that were coming next.

"*Cabot* may have been attacked and destroyed by one of the alien races inhabiting the Maelstrom."

Taggart jerked his eyes up from his notebook computer to stare in shock at the general.

"Excuse me, sir, but you did just say 'alien races,' didn't you?"

"That's right, Captain," Andrews said, his voice flat. "Alien races, plural. We've been keeping this information secret. The people of Earth have been through enough in the past eight years, without the added stressor of learning that there are powerful, sometimes hostile, races out there.

"We've included a précis on each of the races we've encountered so far in your briefing material. Distribute that material to your crew *only* after you've launched. None of this can be allowed to leak out, Captain. I'm afraid, after this mission, you and your entire unit will fall under the Official Secrets Act."

Taggart nodded silently, wanting the general to get on with the briefing. Once again, his perception of reality had been turned inside out. The normalcy of listening to a commander outlining an upcoming mission provided him with a touchstone of reality in the lunatic world of the Maelstrom. As Andrews returned to his theme, Taggart spared Onawa Frost a quick glance. The Mohawk gunnery sergeant stood impassively, her hands clasped behind her. Frost's unflappable nature was a second valuable touchstone to the Marine officer.

"Unable to reestablish contact with *Cabot*," Andrews continued. "And lacking any scanners sensitive enough at long range to detect anything so small as a survey ship, they were forced to give her up as lost.

"Then, less than a day after *Cabot* was listed as 'presumed lost,' this came through on her regular communication channel."

The general stopped and gestured to a civilian technician seated at a computer terminal in the corner of the room. The tech entered a command on his machine and a hissing crackle filled the room. Almost buried in the clutter of cosmic noise, was a brief, garbled message.

". . . ission Control . . . s *Cabot*. We're down. I say ag . . . *bot* is down on Sierra Seven-Five. Coordinates . . . east. Can't last long. They . . . ight come again. For God's sake hurry!"

Despite being broken by the crack and hiss of static, there was a clear note of rising fear in the speaker's voice.

"That, Captain," General Andrews resumed once the recording ran out, "was the voice of *Cabot*'s third officer,

Ensign Walter Michelli. His profile says he is a good, steady officer, *cool under fire* as they say. In spite of that assessment, you can plainly tell the man is on the ragged edge of panic.

"We've played that message, and the records of the ship's last telemetry readings, backward and forward and we still have no idea what brought *Cabot* down. What we do know is that there is at least one of her crew still alive. You, Captain, are to take your platoon to Sierra Seven-Five and pull him out."

"Begging the general's pardon," Taggart said in a pleasant baritone. "Why us? We're combat Marines, not a rescue team."

"Precisely, Captain. We don't know what happened to the ship. She may have suffered an accident, but then again, she may have been shot down either by the Neo-Soviets or by some of the aliens. In any case, I really don't want to send an unarmed rescue team and have them run afoul of the same bad guys who brought *Cabot* down. Your platoon will be providing cover for the rescuers."

Andrews gestured to the female Space Corps officer, who until that time had been sitting quietly at the general's right, tapping notes into her own palm-top.

"Captain, this is Dr. Lieutenant Rebecca Cortez, of the Mexican Contribution Force. She is a trauma surgeon, specializing in space-related injuries. She will be leading the rescue team."

Cortez rose slightly from her chair and greeted Taggart, a courtesy he returned, albeit somewhat stiffly.

"General, I have a question," Taggart said quietly, the stiff formality still in his voice. "As Dr. Cortez is an S-Corps lieutenant, that puts us equal in rank. Who will have overall command of this operation?"

"Since it is a rescue mission, I had assumed I would." Cortez spoke before the general could reply.

"I might be inclined to agree with you, *Doctor*," Taggart shot back, stressing her civilian title, rather than her military rank, "if you had any experience at leading troops in the field. But you don't, do you? You're a medic, not a professional soldier."

Unlike many officers in the Union Armed Forces, Maxwell Taggart had no preconceived hatred or distrust of the Mexican Contribution Forces. Rather, his crustiness came from a strong concern for his men. As a professional soldier, he was loath to turn command of his platoon over to another officer, especially if that officer was a doctor who was what he viewed as essentially a civilian dressed up as a soldier.

"If *Cabot* was a victim of hostile action, as your recording would seem to suggest, this is a military matter, just the same as it would be if we were rescuing a fighter pilot shot down behind enemy lines."

Cortez frowned as she leaned forward, placing her elbows on the edge of the briefing-room table. The doctor glared at Taggart as though she were designating him for a laser-guided missile strike. Something ugly flashed in her eyes.

"General, I . . ." Cortez began, but Andrews cut her off.

"That's enough, Doctor. I have to agree with Captain Taggart. He is an experienced combat officer. He and his platoon have been serving as ship's Marines aboard our security cutters ever since the Induction. He will have operational control of the mission. You may overrule him in matters of medical necessity, but only so long as it does not endanger the mission or the rescue team.

"Your cutter is being prepped now. I've assigned you the

best, most veteran crew we've got available. You shouldn't have any worries in that department. The yeoman here has chip copies of all briefing and background materials you should need. You and your people should be ready to move out in twenty-four hours.

"Dismissed."

Taggart got to his feet, saluted, and headed for the door, followed by his gunnery sergeant. Almost predictably, he arrived at the door at precisely the same moment as Rebecca Cortez.

"After you, Doctor," the Marine captain said, stepping back slightly.

"Don't patronize me, Taggart," Cortez shot back. "I may not be a trained killer like you, but I'm still an officer. So let's put aside all this 'professional courtesy' crap, and call things like they really are. I don't give a damn if you like me or not, but you had damn well better give me the respect I deserve."

With that she turned on her heel and stormed out of the briefing room.

"Now what the hell was that all about?" Gunnery Sergeant Onawa Frost said over Taggart's shoulder, her features darkening in anger.

"C'mon, Gunny, you know damn well what that was all about," Taggart said, stepping into the corridor. "She's MCF. There are so many jokers in the Union Armed Forces who despise the Mexican Contribution Forces. And the Corps is certainly not exempt from it. She probably thinks that I think that she can't handle command of the mission 'cause she's MCF."

"I can understand the feelings," Frost snorted. "But not the expression of them."

Taggart stopped and gazed levelly at his senior noncom.

Gunnery Sergeant Frost was a Mohawk, with as pure blood-lines as it was possible to have in America today. Her strong features and coppery skin tone had been the cause and butt of many coarse jokes and the target of many prejudices throughout her career in the Corps. Even now, as a Gunnery Sergeant, she faced old prejudices which refused to die out, though the age that spawned them had long gone by.

Far too often, the objects of those prejudices responded by adopting prejudices of their own, hating others first, before the others had a chance to hate them. Frost was speculating, and to Taggart it seemed correct, that Cortez had adopted such an attitude toward him.

"Yeah, Gunny, I guess you would at that."

"Yeah," Frost echoed. "Just leave her alone for a while, Cap. She'll come around. They all do eventually."

"Yeah," Taggart said, as though relying on the superstition of three-for-luck. "I just hope it's sooner with this one. If she keeps up this hardcase act, it's gonna make things really interesting when we hit Sierra Seven-Five."

2

Tycho Base's main hangar bay smelled like every other hangar bay Captain Taggart had been in. The odors of fresh and burnt fuel, spilled lubricants, paint, hot metal, and human sweat mingled to create a sour aroma like no other. If the stink of Tycho's hangar bay had any distinction, it was the added undertone of staleness that came from recycled air. In the hours since his briefing, Taggart had changed from his dress uniform into the mottled green, brown, and black of standard Battle Dress Utility fatigues issued to every G-Forces trooper, regardless of rank. Only the black embroidered cloth "railroad tracks" sewn to his collar proclaimed him to be an officer.

"Okay, squad leaders," he barked, turning his attention back to the armed men and women standing before him. "We've got two hours before we're due to board the cutter. I want a final equipment check. Make sure we aren't leaving anything behind. If there's any gear you need or think you might need, tell Gunny Frost, and she'll tell me. We'll see if we can't get it for you.

"Any questions? No? Good. Fall 'em out, Gunny."

"Platoon," Frost said in a deep, rasping growl. "Fall out."

As the Marines under his command broke ranks and began checking over their equipment, Captain Taggart turned toward the cutter to which the rescue team had been assigned.

She was a fairly large ship, just over one hundred meters in length and thirty across the widest part of her fuselage. Her wingspan was over seventy-five meters. Much of her hull was taken up by two powerful engines and the fuel needed to power them. Two sets of massive, clamshell-type doors in the ship's midsection stood open. Inside Taggart could see a pair of angular shapes, like fat grasshoppers. The dark olive green machines were military shuttlecraft. Each of the assault boats was about the size of a large, conventional helicopter, minus the rotors, and was capable of carrying a platoon of heavily armed men.

What remained of the cutter once you took engineering and the assault-boat hangars into account was not impressive. It was almost as though her designers had slapped living spaces into the vessel as an afterthought. The result was a big, ungainly-seeming vessel intended more for practicality's sake than the comfort of her crew. Taggart knew from long experience with patrol cutters that this was precisely the designers' intention. The original ships of this type were converted Martian shuttles. Now that Earth had been ripped out of its own solar system, leaving Mars very far behind, the shuttles had been stripped down and refitted into long-range patrol cutters and exploration ships. The missing *Cabot* was one of those vessels. So was the ship before him.

Like many spacecraft in use before the Induction, the cutter had once been painted a spotless white with black accents. Now, in the wake of intensified hostilities with the

Neo-Sovs and contact with alien races, she had been given a coat of dark gray radar-absorbent material. Just beneath the command deck glazing, in black paint, barely perceptible against the smoky RAM, was the vessel's official designation PY-20. Beneath that, in the same black paint, her crew had stenciled the ship's nickname, *Gallatin.*

Captain Taggart watched as a small man wearing dark off-blue coveralls dropped out of the assault-boat bay, landing lightly on the concrete hangar floor. Pinned to the collar of the man's coveralls was a single silver bar. The nametape sewn to the garment's right breast proclaimed his name to be Tamm.

"Lieutenant?" Taggart said, approaching the naval officer. "I'm Captain Maxwell Taggart. Your passengers are just about ready to go."

"Levi Tamm, lieutenant, junior grade." The man smiled broadly and shook Taggart's proffered hand. "I wish I could say the same for the *Gallatin.*"

"How's that?"

Tamm crooked his thumb at the open boat bays. "The old girl wasn't designed with assault boats in mind. Our boat bays were intended for pinnaces or shuttles. Your assault boats are a good bit bigger than we're used to carrying. We had some trouble with the launch and recovery systems. Took all damn night to get the things to work right."

Taggart stepped forward to peer at the big magnetic grapples that held the assault boats fast in the *Gallatin*'s bay. Three oblong pads, each housing a powerful electromagnet, were mounted on extensible arms. When launching or recovering a shuttle, the arms were extended and the magnets turned on or off, as the situation dictated. The simple, but efficient system was usually controlled by computer, but could, in a pinch, be handled manually. The most dicey part of the operation was making sure the shuttle was properly aligned with the boat bay.

"What's the problem?" Taggart asked.

Tamm said, "We had a heck of a time figuring that out ourselves. It seemed like the grapples didn't want to latch on to your boats. We finally figured it out. The system is used to much smaller craft. Your assault boats barely fit the bays. The system judges the space between the bay's bulkheads and the hull of the boat and decides if it's lined up correctly. With so little clearance, the computer kept thinking the boat was out of position in two directions at the same time and refused to grapple. Once we figured that out, it was simply a matter of resetting the parameters of the docking program, and the grapples took hold slick as you please."

Tamm said ruefully, "I know, it sounds simple, and it is. We just kinda had a case of group brain-lock. We never thought about looking at the software. We assumed it was a hardware problem."

Ducking out of the boat bay, Taggart chuckled. Tamm's honesty was refreshing. Even experts sometimes overlook the obvious.

"Do you mind one more question, Lieutenant?"

"Not at all."

"What's with the name?" Taggart asked. "I was under the impression that all patrol cutters were just given a number."

"Officially, that's true," Tamm said, looking up at the black-painted characters. "Officially, we're PY-20—PY for patrol cutter. Yeah, I know the *Y* doesn't make sense, but that's the traditional designation for a cutter. The *C* designation is reserved for cruisers or carriers. I think the Navy came up with all the abbreviations and designations just to confuse civilians and ground pounders. Anyhow, like a lot of crews, we've given the old girl her own name. In this case *Gallatin*, after the first patrol/rescue cutter deployed by the old US Coast Guard. I guess the crew feel she deserves it. After all, we were the first patrol cutter commissioned as such after the Induction."

"I see." As a Marine, Maxwell Taggart understood pride and tradition. Movement on the far side of the cavernous hangar bay caught his attention.

Dr. Lieutenant Rebecca Cortez and her ten-man medical team had finally put in their appearance. The medical personnel were far less burdened than the Marines. Each of the medics carried only one small bag, containing whatever clothing and personal effects they chose to bring aboard the *Gallatin*. Most of their equipment and supplies had already been stowed aboard the cutter by ground crewmen.

Taggart had not seen or spoken to the medic since the chilly end of the briefing session. The lapse in contact was not wholly Taggart's doing, nor, he was forced to admit, was it Cortez's. Both the Marine and the doctor had plenty of things to keep them busy during the scant preparation time; neither had the leisure or the inclination to pay a social call on the other.

In an attempt to smooth the way between them, Taggart caught the doctor's eye and tossed off a friendly wave, which Cortez returned in kind. To the Marine captain, that was a positive sign. Doctors, he knew, could be touchy about who was in charge, but Cortez seemed to have a firm enough grasp on the reality of the situation to defer to the judgment of a superior officer.

"How long 'til I can board my men?" Taggart asked, dragging his attention back to the issue at hand.

"As soon as you like, Captain," Tamm answered. "My

XO is around here somewhere. He can see to getting your troops billeted."

"As soon as you like" was a lot longer than either Captain Taggart, or Lieutenant j.g. Tamm had expected. By the time the Marines finished their final equipment check and had been assigned berthing spaces aboard the *Gallatin*, nearly two hours had elapsed.

"Okay, folks, we're ready for departure. Please assume launch positions," Tamm's cheerful voice sounded through the ship's intercom.

As Taggart strapped himself into a thickly padded acceleration couch, he felt a distinct rumble through the cutter's steel decking. Taggart knew the preferred method for launching the ship in a heavier-gravity environment was vertically, with the aid of a gantry and a belly-mounted scramjet boost vehicle. The cutter, unlike most spacecraft of the past, was capable of level-flight takeoff, rather like a gigantic airplane. The moon's weak gravity and a pair of solid-fuel rocket-assisted takeoff booster packs attached to the *Gallatin*'s aftersection made the task that much easier.

"All personnel, prepare for boost," Tamm's voice came again. "Boost in ten seconds . . . nine . . ."

Taggart tuned out the cutter skipper's droning count, closed his eyes and braced himself for the powerful inertial forces that would shove him back into his seat when the boosters fired.

"Zero . . . launch." There was no hint of excitement in Tamm's voice as the boosters fired. For a long second the *Gallatin* remained in place, as though she refused to move. Then, slowly at first, but rapidly gaining in speed, she started off down the launch track. The expected Newtonian forces felt like a giant hand pressing Taggart into the acceleration couch's synth-leather padding. The whole ship vibrated as the boosters propelled it forward. A new sensation crept into Taggart's awareness, as the *Gallatin* pulled up into its takeoff rotation. Almost reluctantly, the big patrol cutter pointed its nose toward the sky. For several long moments, the cutter streaked down the launch track, its nose in the air, and its after landing gear seemingly refusing to loose their hold on the lunar soil. Then, with a lurch, the ship staggered into the air. The *Gallatin*'s engines cut in, adding their thrust to that of the rapidly depleting RATO packs. Minutes ticked by as the pale blue-gray sky of the terraformed lunar surface around Tycho Crater Moonbase was gradually replaced by the diamond-studded black of space. A pair of heavy thuds rumbled through the cutter's hull as the RATO packs were jettisoned.

"That's it, folks," Lieutenant Tamm said through the intercom. "*Gallatin* is spaceborne, and outbound for Sierra Seven-Five. Major Taggart, would you please come to the control deck?"

Taggart snorted in amusement as he unfastened the thick nylon seat restraints. No matter how many flights he took, he would never get used to the temporary and strictly honorary promotion given to all ground-pounder captains the moment they set foot on a naval vessel. The promotion was another tradition stretching back to the wet-water navies of the last century. Tradition dictated there could be only one captain aboard any one vessel. Though Levi Tamm was officially a lieutenant junior grade, he was the *Gallatin*'s commander, and was therefore called *Captain*. Thus, Taggart would be called *Major* so long as he and his platoon were aboard the cutter.

Unbidden, Onawa Frost released her safety harness and

pulled herself to Taggart's side as he made his way out of the troop bay.

Reaching the command deck, Taggart and Frost were met by Lieutenant Tamm. The cheerful officer quickly laid out the mission's flight plan. The plan called for the *Gallatin* to follow *Cabot*'s original flight path, passing within a few thousand kilometers of three other planet-sized bodies. These planetoids were, according to probes, dead, or at least uninhabited. Tamm wanted to mimic *Cabot*'s outward course, in an attempt to learn what had caused the survey ship to go missing.

"It'll take us a couple of weeks to reach Sierra Seven-Five," Tamm explained. "And that's barring any kind of encounter or incident. Your Marines going to be able to keep themselves occupied that long?"

"I wouldn't worry about it if I were you, Lieutenant." Gunny Frost grinned at the *Gallatin*'s commander. "We've got all sorts of things planned to keep the boys busy."

"That's right," Taggart cut her off with a choppy wave of his right hand. Frost had referred to Levi Tamm by his official rank, rather than *Captain* as his position dictated. While the cheerful S-Corps officer did not seem the type to stand on the regs, Taggart did not want a flare-up of the interservice rivalry that often accompanied close contact between Marines and their "Navy" counterparts. Tamm had let the matter slide, but the *Gallatin*'s crew might not.

"We've got a lot of work to do, familiarizing ourselves with the telemetry recordings *Cabot* sent back before she vanished. If the boys get bored with that, I'm sure we can find something for them to do. Don't worry, Captain," Taggart said, stressing the honorary rank. "We'll stay out of your way."

3

Lieutenant Tamm's estimate of a couple of weeks proved accurate enough. Fifteen days after the *Gallatin* lifted off from Tycho Base, she slid gracefully into a high-altitude orbit over the planetoid designated Sierra Seven-Five.

The trip had been so uneventful that Captain Taggart would have called it boring if not for the constant exercises he and Gunny Frost were putting the platoon through.

Far from being the mindless, barbaric robots that many believed them to be, the Marines displayed an intelligence that would have surprised their detractors. They quickly assimilated the data provided by the Union Space Agency, becoming so familiar with the ship and her layout that any one of them could have made a freehand drawing of the survey ship's deck plan and not been off by more than a meter. They knew the bios of *Cabot*'s officers and senior crewmen almost as well as they knew their own. Each could recite and understand the survey vessel's meager findings regarding Sierra Seven-Five's atmospheric composition, pressure and temperature, gravity and projected hydrographic index.

Only the chilling reports detailing encounters with alien races separated the background data of this mission from that of a more routine operation. Taggart made sure that all of his men, especially his highly trained reconnaissance scouts, were familiar with those sections of the briefing material dealing with the nonhumans.

When the "head-work" threatened to become boringly familiar, Gunny Frost broke the platoon into squads, or fire teams, and took them to the *Gallatin*'s cargo bay, where she ran them through zero-G combat exercises. Still more time was devoted to checking and rechecking equipment, including the two Type 60 assault craft in the cutter's boat bay.

The Type 60s were a relatively new class of assault boat. Measuring twenty-five meters in length and twelve wide, the ships were intended to deliver a full platoon of combat troops to a planet's surface in relative safety. Clumsy fliers at best, the Type 60s were intended for straight in-and-out insertions and extractions. Type 60s were not agile enough to go head-to-head with a fighter or an armed helicopter. Even the paired twenty-millimeter APE chainguns in a remotely controlled turret mounted under the boat's chin didn't give the assault boat much of a chance against a dedicated combat aircraft. All they could do was delay the inevitable. No, the chainguns, similar to those used in Ares heavy-assault suits, were primarily intended to suppress ground fire and to give support to the Marines as they entered or departed a hot landing zone. Likewise, the Type 60s could be fitted with bolt-on weapon packs, carrying SPEAR missile launchers, Harbinger rail guns, or even Lucifer plasma cannon. But again, these were ground-support weapons, and the Type 60s would never be anything but troop transports.

The three-man flight crews assigned to the assault boats

were technically naval personnel, and therefore under Tamm's command. In practice, the pilot, navigator, and gunner answered to the naval lieutenant until the boats entered the atmosphere or until they engaged a ship to be boarded. At that time tactical command of the vessel passed to the Marine officer-in-charge, in this case Captain Maxwell Taggart.

While his men studied and drilled, Taggart had his own set of exercises to which he had to attend. During these sessions with Lieutenants Cortez and Tamm, Taggart pooled his knowledge with theirs in order to formulate an operation plan for searching out the missing survey ship.

"When a spaceship goes down from orbit," Tamm said, "it isn't exactly like a plane crash. It's more like when a wet-water ship sinks, only with a lot more possible problems. Assuming they were not in the atmosphere, and depending upon their delta-V and heading when they went off-line, they might have hit the air at a steep angle and burned up on entry, or they might have skipped off the atmosphere like a stone off a pond. In that case, God knows how far they might have bounced.

"If *Cabot* was under power and under command when whatever happened happened, it's possible they made a safe entry. They might have even been able to manage a reasonably intact landing, if they found smooth, level ground. I'm betting they did, or at least that they crash-landed. If they burned up, they wouldn't have been able to transmit that last shout for help. It's possible they bounced off the atmosphere and are lying dead in space somewhere, waiting to be picked up, but I don't think so. Call it 'spacer's intuition' if you like."

"I'm inclined to agree with you. Though it has nothing

to do with 'spacer's intuition.' That last message you mentioned; as badly broken up as it was, this fella Michelli seemed in a genuine panic. He said 'they might come back,' or at least I think that's what he said. I doubt he meant his crew, don't you? It's my guess he meant whoever shot the ship down, be it Neo-Sovs, Zhykee, or some other race we know nothing about."

"Even if that's so," Cortez put in, "does it automatically mean they're on the ground? I mean, couldn't he have meant a boarding party, or raiders, or something like that?"

"Perhaps, but unlikely," Tamm answered.

"Right," Taggart stepped in. "Raiders or pirates usually hit their target, disable it, board her, and strip her bare all in one operation. They don't often leave anything behind for a second trip. Now, if *Cabot* is on the ground, the bad guys might have boarded and looted her, but may not have had the carrying capacity to haul everything away at once. Besides, Michelli said, '*Cabot* is down.' That indicates, to my mind at least, that she is down on the planet's surface."

"Oh," Cortez said. "So what's your plan for locating the missing ship then, Major?"

"Not mine," Taggart responded, somehow pleased that Cortez had thawed enough to call him by the honorary rank tradition granted him, rather than calling him by his actual title. "No, this is Levi's show."

"I don't know if I'd call it my 'show' exactly," Tamm responded. "After all, no one in the service really has much experience at this sort of thing.

"What I figure on doing is adapting the search techniques used by the wet-water Coast Guard. We've fed the data from *Cabot*'s last telemetry feeds into the navigation computers. That way, we should be able to follow her course fairly closely, at least up to the point she disappeared. After that, it becomes sort of grunt work. Using the area in which she vanished, we'll start a quarter and search pattern. The *Gallatin* is fitted with some fairly sophisticated sensors: ground-scan radar, thermographic imagers, magnetic anomaly detectors, high-resolution video cameras. And we've got the frequencies of *Cabot*'s distress, cockpit voice, and flight data recorder beacons. One way or another, we should be able to find her."

"And how long will that take?" Cortez asked, a touch of acid in her voice. "If I remember the probe reports on this planet correctly, Sierra Seven-Five has a hostile environment. Its atmosphere is predominantly carbon dioxide and ammonia. *Cabot* has been down for eighteen days. What kind of survival gear does she have? Could her crew survive this long? And how much longer can they last?"

"Not only that, Doctor," Taggart put in. "We have to assume the presence of hostiles on Sierra Seven-Five. Remember Michelli's last transmission. 'Can't last long. They might come again. For God's sake, hurry.' I'm worried if we take too long in locating the ship, there may be no one left to rescue."

Tamm's perpetual grin faded a bit as he shrugged. Taggart got the definite impression that this was as close to an expression of despair and resignation as the young lieutenant could come.

"I don't know what more to tell you. We can try to project a flight path based on *Cabot*'s speed and heading at the time of her disappearance, but beyond that, unless we get real lucky, it's going to come down to a standard search program."

Over the next eight hours, it seemed that the rescue party was out of luck. The *Gallatin* followed *Cabot*'s flight path straight to the spot where the survey ship vanished. Trusting to the luck that sometimes favors the bold, Tamm continued on the projected course he had described to Taggart and Cortez. By the time the rescue cutter stood over the spot where Tamm's projections said *Cabot* should have crashed, the *Gallatin*'s sensors had gone off seven times. Each time the readings were inconsistent with the scanner profile of a wrecked spacecraft. Still, each time the cutter was required to stand to while her sensor operators refined their search. Each time, the results were disappointing.

"Dammit," Tamm cursed, slapping the back of the sensor operator's chair. The vigorous action caused him to wobble a bit in the free-fall environment of the bridge. The strain of eight hours' fruitless search was quickly eroding the naval officer's persistent good humor.

"What now?" Taggart looked up sharply from where he was slumped in the corner of the bridge, studying a printout of the surface map the *Gallatin*'s computers had generated from the sensor scans. The unproductive hunt had left Taggart just as worn as Tamm, and he lacked the lieutenant's ingrained cheeriness.

"Now, nothing," Tamm answered, getting his irritation under control. "For the last eight hours though . . ."

He sighed.

"Our biggest problem is the reason *Cabot* was sent to this damn rock in the first place. The planet's surface is dotted with all kind of structures. We can't 'turn down the gain' on the sensors, or we might miss *Cabot* or her wreckage. So, every time we pass over a cluster of those damn buildings, the sensors go off, and we have to stop to check them out. We've had seven hits in the past eight hours." Tamm grinned at last, then shrugged. "It's getting a little frustrating."

"Captain," the sensor operator called out, "I'm getting a new reading, a power source, a big one."

"Where?" Tamm asked, turning to examine the scanner display.

"Fifty miles, at two-eight-six relative," the tech answered. "The contact is fairly strong and constant, no fading in and out."

The *Gallatin*'s skipper peered at the square, flat-screen monitor. A small white dot glowed steadily a few centimeters from the left-hand edge of the display.

"Whaddya think, Mort?"

"Can't say for certain, sir," the sensor operator replied. "This could be it. The contact is certainly big enough to be a ship's power plant. Maybe *Cabot* didn't crash. Maybe she made a hard landing, and her plant is still operational."

"Could be, Mort, could be. Well done." Tamm patted the tech on the shoulder, in a gesture far more congratulatory than his previous annoyed slap on the back of Mort's chair.

"Navigator," he continued, "give me a course toward Mr. Chalom's contact. Major Taggart, you may want to assemble your men. This could be it."

4

L ion, this is Falcon, we are in position and ready to begin our reconnaissance, over."

"Falcon, Lion. Go ahead, Rick, just watch yourselves." Captain Taggart's voice sounded clearly through the helmet-mounted radio transceiver.

"Roger, Lion. Falcon is on the move."

Switching his helmet-mounted radio transceiver to standby mode, Lance Corporal Richard Dade turned to his partner, gave a jerky tilt of his head, and said, "Okay Krista, lead off."

Behind the closed faceplate of her combat environment suit, Private First Class Krista Black grinned broadly. Hefting her Pitbull assault rifle, she slipped from the shadow of the ruined wall beneath which the Marine scout team had been sheltering. As she moved, Black activated the miniature video camera attached to the left side of her helmet. The device, set on a level plane with her eyes and provided with its own audio pickups, would record everything the scouts saw or heard during their reconnaissance.

As it turned out, the power source detected by the *Gal-*

latin's sensors was located close to the center of what had once been an urban area. The closely packed buildings made it impossible to set the assault boats down inside the city, so the Marines had grounded about a kilometer from the easternmost edge of the ruins and hiked in to their target. As the platoon's scouts, Dade and Black led the way.

Krista Black moved carefully along a broad, flat expanse of dust-covered ground that, in any human city, would have been called a street. But this was no human city. Although they seemed to be made of stone or concrete, the buildings had an odd, almost organic quality to them. Though most of the buildings' outer surfaces had been scoured to a clean off-white finish by time and blowing dust, enough pigment remained to suggest that they had once been painted in pleasant shades of green and blue. To the scouts, the ruined structures were still far more beautiful in comparison to the harsh, angular lines and flat grays and metallics of human architecture.

As she passed the yawning darkness of an open entryway, the door of which had long departed from its hinges, she glanced inside. The building's furnishings had the same organic look to them, and seemed to be part of its structure, installed or grown right along with the rest of the squat pale blue edifice.

A house, she decided, with no more evidence than her own intuition. *It has the feeling of someone's home.* With a touch of sadness, she turned her back on the abandoned building and moved on.

Moving only fifty meters or so at a stretch, Black paused briefly to watch and listen. A half dozen meters behind her, on the opposite side of the street, Lance Corporal Dade followed suit. Nothing moved in the ruins except the fine mustard-colored dust, stirred by the faint breeze. No sounds reached their ears other than the faint hissing of grit as it drifted against the abandoned buildings. Whoever had built, or perhaps grown, this fantastic town, they had found some reason to leave it long ago. Nor were there any traces of animal or plant life. The city was dead.

Moving like a hunting cat, Black carefully, instinctively picked places that were firm and would not shift to set her feet. Her eyes were never still. They constantly flicked from side to side, and up and down, searching for any sign of a threat. The muzzle of her Pitbull followed her gaze. At random intervals, she slowed her steps, not quite pausing. In these stretched-out moments, she twisted her head, looking back over her shoulder to make sure her partner was still in his accustomed place behind her and to her right.

As she moved, Krista Black spared one brief glance at the positioning-system display, which was part of the electronics package built into the back of her left gauntlet. Not as sophisticated or precise as the global positioning system she was used to using back on Earth, this system used only basic triangulation to help keep the scout team on track. The unit kept track of the scouts' destination, current position, and the location of their grounded assault boats, and processed the information through the *Gallatin*'s sensor and navigation computers. As long as the assault boats remained grounded in one spot, the scouts could remain on a straight line toward their destination. If they wandered too far off course, the tiny dot that represented their position would diverge from the electronic path drawn on the display screen, prompting them to return to the proper course. The system was far from perfect, but it was better than stumbling around blind, trying to navigate with a map generated from sensor scans and a compass that might not work on this alien world.

According to the positioning system, they were dead on track for the power source that was their goal.

A few hundred meters from the city's edge, Black came to what might have been an intersection. There she paused, dropping back against the base of a graceful, bottle-shaped building. Dade moved quickly into position across the street from her shadowed hide. For long moments, the scouts remained still, searching the cross street for any signs of a threat. Eventually Black nodded at her partner, who returned the gesture. Moving quickly, but without any sign of hurry, Dade writhed sinuously to his feet, and, without a break in that motion, crossed the street in a smooth, easy trot.

Again, the lance corporal dropped into the shadows of an abandoned building, watching and waiting. Nothing moved but the windblown dust. Another pair of quick nods were exchanged, and Krista Black darted across the street. As she moved, Black felt the muscles of her upper back twitch and tighten, almost as though her body had perceived an attack and was taking the useless defensive step of tensing up against the smashing effect of an incoming bullet. But the bullet never came. Black reached the shelter of an elegant spiral violet obelisk. The structure seemed once to have been some sort of artwork or monument, though what it represented or commemorated was a mystery. The upper third of the obelisk lay broken in the street. The scouts could not have reached around the monument's base if they had stretched their arms so far that only their fingertips touched. The stone of the monument, if it was stone, showed a distinct glitter where the pigment had been worn away. Black examined the material closely, seeing small clear blue crystals embedded in the cementlike material. Even in its ruined state the obelisk retained a compelling alien beauty.

Krista Black was a trained scout who was good at her

job and enjoyed it, but this was one assignment that she had always hated, reconnaissance of a city. The hard pavement held little trace of an enemy's passage, and the concrete-and-steel mazes of buildings and streets gave the enemy his choice of hiding places from which he might eliminate opposing troops with little risk to himself. As she crouched in the lee of the spiral monument, the scout berated herself for becoming distracted by the city's alien beauty. That inattention could have cost her life and that of her partner. Black suppressed a shudder at the thought.

Looking across the street, she nodded at Dade, who returned the gesture. Getting to his feet again with that almost-boneless grace, Dade stepped off carefully down the street, taking the lead for this leg of the journey. When he had gone a half dozen meters or so, Black followed, keeping her interval and concentrating on the job at hand.

As the scouts penetrated deeper into the dead alien city, a sense of foreboding began to settle over Krista Black. The city she had once found so strikingly lovely had become strangely hateful to her. Though she was not given to flights of fancy, the graceful lines and organic curves of the buildings began to remind her of fungi and molds. The faint traces of color against the colorless stony material took on the appearance of decaying flesh over bleached bone. No touch of the breeze that stirred the dust at her feet could be felt through the armored environment suits, causing in Black an odd feeling of breathlessness. The overwhelming stillness of the city made her think of an empty tomb.

Perhaps it had been the uncomfortable realization that she had not been one hundred percent attentive to her job, and that such carelessness could have gotten her killed, that had caused the discomfort. It could also have been that odd sixth sense that good recon scouts seem to be born with.

Whatever the reason, an odd prickling sensation ran the length of Black's spine, causing her to freeze in her tracks. Clucking her tongue against the roof of her mouth, she drew Dade's attention via the short-range radio communicator in her helmet.

Her partner froze, turning his head just far enough to see her. Black could imagine the questioning expression on his face. She had seen it enough times both in training and in combat situations. His posture spoke of a coiled readiness either to fight or flee. She could feel a similar tension in her own muscles.

But Black noticed these things only peripherally. Her whole being was focused on her eyes and ears, as she strained to discern what had triggered her heightened state of readiness. Nothing moved around them. Even the faint breeze seemed to have died away. It was almost as though the city itself was watching them.

Then she heard it—a faint, low-pitched moaning sound. At first Black thought maybe it was the breeze muttering around the corner of a ruined building, but there was no breeze. She brought her left hand up, cupping her palm next to her ear, but the gesture wasn't needed. Lance Corporal Dade heard the sound, too, and was scanning the area, straining to locate the source of the oddly musical groan.

Black consulted the positioning system again. According to that instrument, they were less than two hundred meters from the power source. Looking back to Dade, she held out her left hand, palm upward in the age-old gesture meaning, "What now?"

Dade returned the half shrug and gave a short wave forward.

As she advanced, the moaning grew louder. As she got

closer, Black could tell that the sound was not a constant note, but it rose and dropped in pitch in a random pattern.

Twice more, the Marine scouts crossed intersecting streets as they pressed on toward their goal. One of those intersections boasted a small square, the center of which was clogged with a low pile of rubble, as though a statue had been demolished and the broken shards left where they fell. Each time they crossed a street, the scouts switched off lead and trailing positions. In this way, they would minimize the draining effect on their senses of always being on point.

As they approached a third intersection, Dade, who was in the lead at the time, stopped short. His left arm came up in a clenched fist, signaling Black to do the same.

"Movement," his voice whispered through the helmet communicator. Black looked at her teammate to see the splayed fingers of his left hand pointing to the team's left. Black signaled her acknowledgment and began creeping forward again, as Dade signaled her to join him. With her rifle held at low ready, its buttstock already nestled against her right shoulder, she sidled along the dust-covered street until she drew even with her partner. While she moved, Dade had brought his Pitbull to his shoulder and was covering her end of the cross street. Blanketing every sound she made, and seeming to blend with them, was that damnable moaning.

Black set her back against the flowing curve of a building's cracked and dust-scoured wall, her muscles tensed for action and her senses straining to filter out the ever-present howl. She looked across the street at Dade, waiting for his signal.

Dade gave a short, jerky nod. Black pivoted around the corner, dropping to her right knee as she moved. Her rifle came up into firing position, its elevated sight-rail aligning with her visor-shielded right eye. Before her was a broad, open square, larger than any they had passed before. In the center of the square was a large, intricate-looking sculpture.

The object stood well over three meters tall, and seemed to be constructed entirely of metal, which appeared to have been anodized in pleasing, soft shades of green and gold. Several windmills of different sizes turned in the faint breeze. This had been the motion that had first attracted Dade's keyed-up attention. As they spun, the vaned wheels operated elaborate sets of chain pulleys, which in turn caused a series of wheels to turn against thin sheets of metal. The friction of wheel against metal sheet created the haunting moan that had been setting the scouts' teeth on edge.

Krista Black examined the sculpture closely, using her helmet minicam to record the alien artifact for later review. The recording system in the camera had enough digital memory to record sixty minutes of action before it would have to be downloaded into a permanent storage medium. If the data was not saved, the camera would record over the previous images.

A few pieces had fallen away, apparently the result of age, weathering, and neglect. What remained intact seemed to be in near-new condition. Black plucked a scrap of green metal from the dust at the object's base. Though as long as her hand, two centimeters wide and half a centimeter thick, the fragment weighed almost nothing. The faded green color seemed to go all the way through the metal's thickness. Her curiosity piqued, she tried to bend the green metallic strip, but found that, even exerting all her strength, she could barely flex the shard a few degrees. When she tried the tip of her heavy Ka-Bar combat knife against the fragment, she discovered that the knife's cryogenically hardened edge barely scratched the surface.

Suddenly, the off-key moaning stopped.

*   *   *

Private Black dropped the metal shard and clutched at her Pitbull, where it hung from a cross-chest assault sling. At the edge of her vision, she saw Lance Corporal Dade doing the same.

"What is it?" Dade whispered harshly.

"I don't know," Black answered, apprehension and curiosity mixed in her voice. "The noise stopped."

"You bet it did," Dade laughed.

As she turned to look at her partner, she saw him rise from his crouch behind the sculpture's stone base. He gestured to an axle in the central part of the object's works. A large chunk of stone was wedged between the spindle and a thick golden chain.

"Dammit, Rick! Why the hell did you do that?" Black spat. "You scared the hell out of me!"

Dade blinked in surprise at her uncharacteristic outburst. In all the time the scouts had been working together, he had never known Krista Black to raise her voice. Now here she was ripping him a new orifice over the insignificant matter of his jamming up the sculpture. Truthfully, he wasn't certain why he had done it.

"Look, Krista," he said apologetically, "that noise was beginning to get on my nerves. In fact, this whole damn city is getting on my nerves. What the hell happened here? Where is everybody? We haven't seen a soul. Fer cryin' out loud, we haven't even seen a body. What? Did the whole population of this God-cursed rock wake up one morning and decide to leave? And then there's *that*."

Black came around the sculpture to look closely at the stone her partner had wedged into the statue's works. Two sides of the elongated pyramidal rock were featureless and rough, suggesting that the dark gray shard had been chipped out of a larger stone. The third was finely carved. A strangely human-looking face was carved in the midst of odd, squiggling figures which could have been some kind of writing. But the face, so beautiful and lifelike, wasn't human. In the place where a human's eyes would be, there writhed two pockets of short, bright green, tentacle-like antennae. Black stepped back, feeling a faint twinge of revulsion.

"Oh, that's ugly," she said, blowing out a long breath. "Do me a favor, Rick. If you're gonna do anything like that again, just let me know first. This whole mission's spooky enough. I don't need any more thrills."

"Hmm," Dade grunted. Without saying another word, he moved away from the now-silent sculpture, toward the recon team's goal of the unknown power source.

5

As the scouts left the odd, "musical" sculpture behind, Private Krista Black began to feel better. She was forced to admit that Dade had been right about the eerie, discordant moaning the object generated. Something in the pitch or frequency of the low, mournful groan had scraped along her nerves like broken glass. Now that it had been silenced, she seemed a bit more relaxed and able to concentrate on the task at hand.

Ten meters ahead, Lance Corporal Rick Dade stopped, dropping to one knee in the shelter of a high-arched doorway, his Pitbull assault rifle held at low ready. Black faded back a half step, slipping quietly into a similar entryway on the opposite side of the street from the scout team's point man.

Dade held his place, remaining still. Krista Black mirrored her partner's motionless stance. Only her eyes swept from side to side, carefully searching the area for a potential threat. Twice she spared a glance for her positioning unit. According to the tracking device, Dade should be right on top of the mysterious power source.

Long seconds ticked by, stretching into minutes, and still Dade held his position. Eventually, he half turned to face her. Bringing up his left hand, he shaped his fingers and thumb into a large *O*, following the gesture by pointing off down the street. Black nodded, understanding the gesture to mean "objective in sight."

"Lion, this is Falcon," she said, quietly switching her communicator over to the platoon's tactical frequency. "We have reached the objective."

"Falcon, this is Lion," Taggart responded. "Any signs of our people?"

"Negative, Lion," Dade answered for her. "Objective is not, I repeat *not*, *Cabot*. Objective appears to be an industrial building. Falcon requests instructions. Suggest you allow us to go inside and check it out. Could be that some of the survivors are sheltering inside."

"Lion concurs, Falcon," Taggart said a few moments later. Clearly the captain had been considering the scout's request, perhaps even discussing the wisdom of entering the unknown building with Gunny Frost. "Just be careful. I don't want to lose anybody, especially if this is a false alarm."

"You got it, boss," Dade said. "Okay, Krista, let's move in."

Black moved up to cover her partner, as he stepped out. At first glance the building Dade was approaching was unimpressive, unlike all of the buildings the scouts had seen so far in the abandoned city. The windowless structure was long and low, roughly rectangular in shape, instead of having the soft, almost-organic form they had come to expect. It lacked the pastel colors of the other structures. Instead it was painted a flat gray. Overall, its appearance reminded

Black of an ammunition storage bunker or a hardened air-craft shelter.

Dade reached the structure's only visible door without incident and motioned for Black to join him. As she moved across the narrow open space between her last hiding place and the bunker's shadowed doorway, she felt that sensation again. Taking one long step, she turned around in mid-motion, walking backwards a few steps, searching for the enemy sniper her disquieted intuition told her had to be there. She saw nothing other than the tall, spiral, and fluted buildings she had been seeing ever since they entered the city.

"Dammit," she cursed, reaching Dade's position without incident. "This is getting out of hand. Let's just check this frigging building and get the hell out of Dodge."

Black stopped short, surprised by the vehemence of her tone. Whatever it was about the deserted city that had caused Rick Dade to disable the sculpture was beginning to affect her, and she didn't like it.

"Right." Dade nodded. Hefting his assault rifle, he reached out with his left hand and gave the bunker's black-ened metal door an easy shove. Much to Black's surprise, the panel yielded to the gentle pressure and swung wide without a hint of squeaking hinges. The space inside was dark. In the weak light filtering in from outside the scouts could see indistinct, rectangular shapes, some of which gleamed or shone with reflected light.

Dade brought his weapon to his shoulder, as Black drew a small, powerful flashlight from her environment suit's right breast pocket. She held the light at shoulder level, as far away from her body as she could reach. Black knew if anyone was inside the darkened building, they would be more likely to shoot at the light than anywhere else; thus, she kept the flashlight as far away from her vital areas as she could. The light's powerful beam pierced the gloom, falling on some sort of control panel. Shining the light around as much as she could without leaving the partial protection of the doorjamb, she ascertained that there were no living creatures, hostile or not, inside the bunker, at least none that she could see.

Cautiously, Black slipped around the jamb, moving quickly to keep from being silhouetted against the brightness outside. She moved to her left, putting her back against the structure's outer wall, scanning the space within. The bunker contained one large room, dominated by hulking, shadowed devices, the purpose of which she could only guess. Nothing moved in the darkness.

"Clear," she called to Dade, who moved through the door quickly and smoothly, sweeping to the right, as she had swept to the left. The combined illumination of their flashlights banished the worst of the shadows. Aside from the Marines, there was no sign of any being, living or dead, inside the structure. Krista Black crossed and recrossed the bunker's single room, searching for a door, or passageway, or basement, but found only alien machinery and dust.

"Rick, what do you suppose all this stuff is?" she asked at last, jerking her thumb at a pair of big cylindrical devices in the center of the room.

"If I had to take a guess?" Dade responded. "I'd guess this is a power station, probably geothermal."

"Really," Black shot back acidly. "And how did you figure that one out?"

"Well, I may be wrong, but I don't think so. Y'see, my dad used to work in a geothermal station, back before everything went to hell. He took me to the plant a couple of times, and it looked an awful lot like this. Those cylinders over there are probably the generators themselves. If they are, they might be still in operation. That might account for the power source the *Gallatin*'s sensors picked up. But if they're running, they're running awful quiet.

"And that's not the funniest thing about this whole place," Dade said, gesturing for Black to join him at the control panel he'd been examining. "Look here. I have no idea what these gauges indicate. What's strange is the fact that they are *gauges*. Not digital readouts, or computer displays, but plain, old-fashioned needle-and-dial gauges. But all the controls seem to be touch pads. And here? This looks like a palm reader of some kind. Advanced control units, but antique gauges to monitor the system. Weird."

"This whole bloody planet is weird if you ask me," Black said, leaning closer to look at the devices her partner indicated. The control panel was covered with more of the odd, scrawling lines that crisscrossed the rock Dade had used to jam the sculpture. Some of the character strings reminded Black of Celtic knotwork; others seemed to be almost-hieroglyphic representations of people, plants, and animals. The device Dade called a palm-reader was in the center of an otherwise unadorned panel. Made of some kind of black plasticlike substance, the reader was almost the size of a dinner plate. The hand outline in the center of the device had six overlong fingers and two opposable thumbs.

"Yeah, weird," she said, straightening up from the panel. "Ain't nobody here, Rick."

"Yep, I guess you're right." Dade agreed. He opened a communications channel.

"Lion, this is Falcon. No joy. I say again, no joy. I think what we've got here is some kind of power-generating station. That must be what the *Gallatin*'s sensors picked up on.

There is no sign of life here, Captain. This place has been deserted for an awful long time."

"Falcon, Lion copies co . . ."

The rest of Captain Taggart's message went unheard. Alerted by some sixth sense possessed by all reconnaissance scouts, Dade and Black dropped into virtually identical defensive crouches back-to-back, pointing their rifles into the deep gloom of the station. It did not take long for the Marines to realize what had triggered their combat-honed responses.

A thin, low-toned moaning came from outside the station.

"I thought you jammed that blasted thing," Black hissed.

"I did," Dade shot back. "Somebody must have unjammed it." He said quietly, "Lion? Falcon. Are any of your people in the city?"

"Negative, Falcon," Taggart said, sounding surprised. "Nobody left the rally point while you were running your recon. Why?"

"Stand by, Lion," Dade replied. "We may not be alone here."

After checking the doorway and the area immediately outside the power station, the scouts scuttled out of the long, low bunker, moving one at a time, covering each other's back as they crossed the fivescore meters between the generating station and the large square, wherein stood the musical sculpture.

From her position behind a low, pastel blue stone wall on the edge of the square, Krista Black could see the sculpture easily. Its windmills were once again turning in the faint breeze, the thin sheet-metal panels setting up their low, keening wail. Nothing else in the square was moving.

Cautiously, the Marines crossed the open plaza, eyes and ears alert. No trace of any living creature could be seen. When they reached the sculpture, they found no tracks in the thin dust other than their own. Dade looked around for the rock he had jammed into the mechanism, but could find no trace of it.

"C'mon, Rick, it can't be. There's no tracks. Even with what little breeze there is, there hasn't been enough time to cover our tracks, let alone anyone else's. No one came in here and took your rock away," Black said, gesturing at the yellowish dust, innocent of any footprints save their own. "It must have just worked itself loose and fallen down."

"No way, I had it wedged in there good," Dade shot back. "Even if it did fall out, where is it? Remember that face? None of the other rocks around here have carvings like that. None of the rocks around here are that color. So where did it come from in the first place, and where is it now?"

"Rick, look for yourself. There ain't nobody here but us. It had to have just fallen out," Black said again. Despite her assertions, she felt a qualm. She knew that, if the rock had simply fallen out of the sculpture's works, it should be lying in the dust beneath it. Yet there was no trace of the stone. That meant someone had intentionally pulled the rock out of the mechanism, but why? And who? The absence of tracks in the thin yellow dust immediately conjured up visions of noncorporeal beings who passed by with no trace, and yet could affect physical objects.

"We better call this in," Dade said, and opened a channel.

"Are you certain?" Captain Taggart asked after listening to Dade's story.

"Yessir, I am," Dade answered. "There's something going on out here. We are not alone."

"All right, run a sweep," the captain said. "Search a five-hundred-meter radius from the sculpture, but don't dawdle. If you're right, I don't want you two poking around in there after nightfall."

Two hours later, Dade and Black were on the final leg of their sweep. The scouts had checked every avenue of approach to the square and had examined a dozen possible signs, but had found no trace of any being. Both Marines were about to concede that the stone might have fallen from the mechanism by itself and gotten lost in a dust drift, when something caught Krista Black's attention.

"Rick, I've got a track here."

Dade stepped over to where Black crouched at the base of a pale orange building. In the thick mustard-colored dust drifted against the structure's curving wall was a large, shallow depression.

"Footprint?" he asked.

"I think so," Black replied, gesturing at the track with her Ka-Bar. "See the shape? Here's the heel and the toe. It's been here a while though. Look how eroded the edges of the print are. I'd say it's at least a day old, maybe two or three."

"Could one of *Cabot*'s crew have made it?"

"Maybe, but it looks like whoever made this track was barefoot. I can't say that for certain. It's just my gut instinct." Black sheathed her knife and looked up at her partner. "This is the first solid lead we've had. See if the boss wants us to keep up the search."

"Negative, Falcon." Captain Taggart replied to Dade's request for more search time. "I trust Black's instincts. If she says it wasn't a survivor, we're gonna have to move on. Romeo-Tango-Bravo."

"Falcon copies Lion," Dade answered. "Return to base. Will comply. Falcon out."

"Sorry, Krista, no go. The old man wants us back at the shuttle ASAP."

"Well, one thing's for certain anyhow," Black said.

"How's that?"

"Survivors or no survivors, we aren't alone on this rock."

6

Captain Taggart gripped the back of the sensor operator's padded seat, looking over the woman's shoulder at the softly glowing display.

"Are you sure about this one?" he asked the technician.

"Yessir," the tech drawled, the piney woods of east Texas plain in her voice. "That last target was just a power source. We had no indications of large masses of metal, nor nothin' like that. Now here?" She pointed at the display. "Look here. That's a MAD trace, a fair-sized one. And this?" She tapped a control, bringing up another sensor display. The image was that of a fuzzy, slightly bent arrowhead amid a jumble of small fuzzy dots. "This is ground-scan radar. We're having a hard time resolving the image, but that might be your missing survey ship."

Taggart straightened and rubbed his eyes.

"Uh-huh," he said skeptically. "Why did we miss it on the last pass?"

"Hard to say, sir," the tech shrugged. "Could be any number of reasons. My guess is something out there is messing with the sensors."

"Even if we did miss it before, we found it now," Levi Tamm put in. "According to the scanners, we've got a large metallic object, with a mass, composition, and general outline that suggest that what we're looking at here is *Cabot*."

Taggart shrugged in response. A computer-generated map display showed the location of this most recent possible crash site. The blinking white dot indicating the contact's position was centered in what appeared to be a range of hills about one hundred kilometers northeast of the abandoned city. The scanners suggested that the hills were high, steep, and rocky, which would make traveling difficult. If *Cabot* had indeed gone down in those hills, and if any of her crew survived, it was better than even money that they'd still be at the crash site.

If it *was* the crash site.

When his platoon returned to the *Gallatin* after failing to locate *Cabot* or her crew, the mood of the rescue mission had darkened. The reports filed by his scout team had inevitably filtered back to the rest of the platoon, and thence to the rescue cutter's crew. Sierra Seven-Five was not so uninhabited as they had been led to believe. The evidence of an alien race on the planet added a thread of apprehension to the crew's frustration. Many of the rescuers, spacers, Marines, and medics among them were skeptical about the reports and briefings they had been given regarding alien races. The strange, abandoned city provided irrefutable proof that nonhuman creatures did indeed inhabit the Maelstrom.

Then, there was the indication that the rescue party was not alone at Sierra Seven-Five. Dade and Black were firmly convinced that someone, or some*thing* had removed the stone wedging the sculpture's works. Whether that had been the Neo-Sovs, or some alien creature, they were staying remarkably well hidden. An unseen enemy is always a source of fear.

"Well," the Marine captain said at last, "we can't pick and choose our contacts, now can we? All right. Gunny Frost, assemble the platoon. We're going out again."

The Type 60 assault boat lurched, catching a downdraft as it crossed a jagged, gap-toothed ridgeline. Half a second later the shuttle pitched again as an updraft flung it skyward.

Strapped into the observer's seat on the boat's small flight deck, Taggart fought his stomach as the cursing pilot fought the controls. Though he was an experienced combat Marine officer, there was little he could do to control his own physiology. He gulped down a large draft of air, willing his rising gorge to settle down. Beside him he heard a soft feminine chuckle. Apparently, Dr. Lieutenant Rebecca Cortez, who seemed to be immune to the stomach-churning effects of the pitching assault boat, was taking a perverse delight in his intense discomfort.

"Sorry about that, Captain," the pilot, a chief petty officer named Marco Foy, said as he got the ship back under control. "Damn winds are worse than any I've ever seen. Feels like I'm flying inside the granddaddy of all cyclones."

"That's okay, Chief." Taggart could not quite bring himself to smile, nor could he quite believe what he was about to say. "Can you take her back across the site one more time?"

"Sure thing, Cap," the pilot said breezily. "Question is, can you and your people stand it?"

"Just overfly the sight again, Chief, and never mind us."

Foy nodded, and pulled the Type 60 around in a broad arc. Though he gave the impression that he looked upon the unpredictable winds as the perfect flying weather, he was an experienced enough assault boat pilot to know that the rapidly shifting air currents made even the most basic maneuvers difficult and the more complex ones downright dangerous. As if to punctuate the hazards of flying one of the boxy assault craft under such conditions, a sudden gust jolted the ship as she pulled out of her turn.

"There she is, Captain," Foy said, pointing through the boat's heavily glazed windscreen.

Taggart craned his neck to see over the shoulder of the men in the pilot and copilot's seats. Cortez did likewise.

Lying to one side of a deep, steep-sided valley was the off-gray-painted shape of a Union spaceship.

"Bloody hell," Taggart cursed softly. "Her whole aftersection is gone."

"Yeah," Cortez agreed. "And there are no signs of survivors either. Not that we'd be able to see them from three thousand meters. Can you take us any lower?"

"Sure I can take us lower," Foy said with a grim humor. "I can take us lower, right into the ground. I'm sorry, Lieutenant, but, if I get too much lower and we catch a downdraft, or a wind shear in this valley . . . Well, they'll have to send out a rescue party for *us*."

"Does that mean you can't set us down at the crash site?"

"That's exactly what it means, Lieutenant," Foy told her. "I've done a lot of crazy things in my day, but I'm not so crazy as to try to land this pig in that valley, not under these conditions."

Another jolting gust of turbulent air hit the assault boat as though to punctuate his statement.

"Maybe if we had good weather, and calm winds, then maybe, *maybe*, I'd try it. But even then, that valley is awful narrow. The book says I'm not supposed to land this ship in an area less than four hundred meters by sixty, and that's with a Pathfinder already on the ground. Like I said, if we had calm winds, I might give it a shot, even without a Pathfinder. But in this? Not a chance. I'd likely kill us all if I tried it."

"I think you're right, Chief," Taggart said, taking a last look at the downed ship. "We're gonna have to find a safe place to land and hump our way overland to the wreck."

He looked at the chart the assault boat's computers had created based upon sensor readings taken during their overflight of the wreck.

"How about this flat ground about seven kilometers to the east?"

"Well, that'll do for a landing zone," Chief Foy agreed, glancing at the spot Taggart was indicating on the map. "But it looks like there are some steep hills between there and the crash site. It's gonna be tough going for your rescue team."

The ship gave a final lurch as Foy pulled it up into a gentle climb.

"That's okay, Chief," Taggart replied. "You just get us on solid ground, and I'll be happy to carry the team the rest of the way in."

The assault boat landed fifteen minutes later. Chief Foy brought the blocky, fifteen-ton ship down on its powerful V/STOL thrusters with only the gentlest of bumps.

As soon as the ship had pulled up out of the valley, the turbulent winds began to diminish, almost as though some malevolent force had been creating them and was satisfied by the rescue team's withdrawal. Here on the plain beyond the hills only a gentle, intermittent breeze stirred the long, turquoise-colored grass. But another type of storm was brewing.

"Listen, Captain, I don't think you appreciate the situation."

"You better believe I do, *Doctor*," Captain Taggart snapped at Cortez. "We're seven kilometers from our objective. We've got a range of steep, rocky hills between this LZ and the crash site. I think that sums it up pretty well, don't you?"

"I don't think so, Captain," Cortez shot back, heat creeping into her voice.

"No? Well, let's go a bit farther then." Taggart jerked a thumb in the direction of the hills. His tone began to be infected by Cortez's anger. "Those seven kilometers between the LZ and the wreck are some of the worst terrain I've ever seen. Weren't you looking when Foy brought us in over those hills? God in Heaven, woman, they're straight up and down in places. It's going to be difficult, hazardous going, and it's probably going to involve at least some mountaineering. Are your people prepared for that?

"Let my people go in first. We'll make good time to the site if we don't have your medics in tow. Then, if we find any survivors, we can call you in. I'd rather not risk you and your people on another power-generating station or an alien art gallery."

"Is that the real reason?"

"What?" Cortez's muttered response made it difficult for Taggart to be sure of what the doctor had just said.

"Listen, Captain," Cortez went on as though neither of them had spoken. "I understand what you're saying, and I appreciate your concern, but we have to go. If that is *Cabot* over there, and if there are survivors, they've already gone without medical attention for several weeks. If there is anyone left alive at the wreck, what little hope they have lies with my medical team, not your Marines."

"Sir, as much as I hate to contradict you, I have to agree with Dr. Cortez."

Taggart turned to gaze in surprise at Gunnery Sergeant Frost.

"You do, Gunny?"

"Yes, sir," Frost replied coolly. "I understand your position. I don't like the risk of getting noncombatants greased any more than you do. But, for all we know, we've got a dozen survivors over there who may not last until we get there. Even if they do, I doubt they'd last long enough for our people to get back here and fetch the doctor and her people."

"Thank you, Gunny," Cortez said with a note of triumph in her voice.

"I'm not doing this for you, ma'am." Frost's voice was even and inflectionless. "It really galls me to have to go against my captain, a man I've know his whole career in the Corps. It especially galls me because it seems to support whatever agenda you've got going here. But our first concern has to be those survivors. You two officers can argue things out to your hearts' content, *after* we complete this rescue, but until then, we've got to work together."

"I don't have an agenda, Sergeant," Cortez shot back. "Or if I do, it's simply to do my job and rescue those survivors."

"If you say so, ma'am."

"Take it easy, Gunny," Taggart said, laying a hand on Frost's shoulder. "All right, Doctor, maybe your team had better come along. Get them prepped and ready to move out in one hour.

"Gunnery Sergeant Frost, I'd like a word with you, if you please."

Taggart turned and walked away from the doctor,

moving away from the bulk of the rescue party. He didn't look back to see if Frost was following him. He knew she would be. When he'd gone a few dozen meters the captain stopped and turned to face his subordinate.

"Gunny, what the hell was that all about?"

"Sir?"

"First off, I really don't appreciate your contradicting me in front of Cortez. We've got enough problems on account of her attitude without you giving her any more ammunition.

"Second, your reasons for supporting Dr. Cortez's wanting to go along on this little hike were good enough. I understand that. But why did you feel it necessary to cut her a new belly button? She may be S-Corps, but she's an officer, and I damn well expect you to treat her with the respect her rank deserves." When Frost didn't answer, Taggart laid a gloved hand on her shoulder, and said quietly, "Look, Onawa, I know something about Cortez has been bothering you from the minute she was assigned to this mission. What is it?"

"Permission to speak freely, sir?"

"You know you don't have to ask that, Gunny."

"Sir, it isn't so much that I don't like Cortez, as it is she doesn't like you," Frost answered. "The minute General Andrews introduced her, I could see that she was carrying around a king-size chip on her shoulder, and most of that attitude seemed to be directed at you."

"Yeah, I kinda noticed that," Taggart said quietly.

"I can't say for certain, sir, I think it might be that 're-verse bigotry' thing again. When you said that her medics aren't welcome on this little hike, she hears you saying that *she* isn't welcome on the hike. The whole thing kinda confirms her mistaken notion.

"And, pardon me for saying this, sir, you have been kinda rough on her, maybe not in fact, but in attitude at least."

Taggart stared at the noncom for a long moment, his mind reviewing the limited contacts he'd had with Dr. Lieutenant Rebecca Cortez. Frost was right, Taggart realized. He had avoided Cortez whenever possible. He usually referred to her as *doctor*, rather than calling her by her rank. In his heart, Taggart knew his attitude stemmed, not from racial bigotry, but from the knowledge that he had spent four years in Annapolis and six years in the field to gain the rank of captain in the United States Marine Corps. Cortez, on the other hand, had been *given* the rank of lieutenant, the naval equivalent of a Marine captain, when she joined the Union Navy, simply because she was a doctor. He had never reckoned on his dislike for "ninety-day wonders" being mistaken for racial prejudice.

"Hmm, maybe you're right, Gunny," Taggart said at last. "Maybe I have been a little rough on her. Let me ask you this, do *you* think it's because she's Mexican?"

"No sir, I think you dislike her for the same reason I do," Frost replied. "She got the rank just because she's a doctor."

Taggart nodded. "Well then, Gunny, I guess we're both going to have to watch our attitude toward the good doctor, eh? And if she doesn't like us, well, I guess that's her own lookout."

7

Captain Maxwell Taggart sat on the lower coaming of the hatchway leading to the assault boat's flight deck, studying a hard-copy map spread out on his environment-suited knees. Occasionally he looked up as a good-natured curse or bray of laughter echoed in the boat's troop bay.

The terrain mapped out by the Type 60 assault boat's sensors had been rendered into a rough topographic map. In some ways the chart reminded Taggart of the old, hand-drawn maps he had seen reproduced in some of his textbooks back at the Academy. Many areas of the chart were blank. The rugged hills were drawn in a sketchy fashion, with contour lines beginning and ending for no readily apparent reason, giving the map a ragged, unfinished appearance. There did appear to be long stretches of clear ground in the hills. In these places the contour lines bent uphill toward themselves in a way that, on a good topographic map, would suggest a watercourse. If there were streams in the hills, there might well be trails along their banks, or if the watercourses were dry streambeds, then the empty channels might serve the rescue party as well as a beaten track. Twenty kilometers to the south of the platoon's landing zone, near what appeared to be a dry lake, an irregular oval labeled "LZ 2" marked the rescue team's fallback position. Taggart knew that the assault boats would abandon the primary landing zone only if forced to do so. The secondary position was only a precaution.

Carefully folding the map, Taggart slipped it into a pocket of his combat environment suit. A variant of the standard Union combat fatigues, the CES had been developed specifically for combat activities in low-pressure or hostile atmospheres. The original versions of the suits had been issued to the Army forces garrisoning the various lunar bases. Later, improved variants had been constructed. These were tested by, and later issued to, the Third Marine Division. On this particular mission, both his Marines and Dr. Cortez's medical team would be wearing the bulky protective outfits.

The suits were coverall-type garments constructed of heavy, tear-resistant cloth, in standard camouflage patterns, lined with a protective layer of kevlon armor cloth. At the collar and cuffs, the suit was equipped with pressure fittings that allowed it to be mated with specially designed boots, gauntlets, and helmet. When the whole suit was properly worn and fitted, it provided its wearer with a completely sealed barrier against a hostile environment. The helmet, again a variant of the standard-issue kevlon pot, was fitted with a movable visor, and could be mated with a respirator, filter, or combination mask. If circumstances called for operations in a low-atmospheric-pressure environment, or where pressure might be lost, such as shipboard combat, the whole suit could be fitted with a small, backpack unit that could pressurize the suit in less than a second, assuming, of course, the wearer had all the parts and pieces in place and properly sealed.

Most Marines, Captain Taggart included, seldom wore all the pieces of the combat environment suit. A sealed CES, with boots, gauntlets, and helmet in place was hot and uncomfortable. If the wearer engaged in vigorous physical activity, the odor of his own sweat could become overwhelming.

Another feature of the suits that most Marines disliked was the small digital video camera mounted on the right side of the helmet. The device was linked to a small digital recorder and liquid crystal display attached to the wearer's combat harness.

A goodly number of Marines looked upon the camera as an unwanted hitchhiker at best, and at worst a "Big-Brotherish" intrusion by those they called rear echelon muck flingers. Knowing that any move they made might be scrutinized by officers with backsides the shape of their office chairs tended to make experienced combat troops resentful of the tiny cameras. Generally, they disabled the device almost as soon as they were out of the officer's line of sight.

Though Taggart agreed with his troops' sentiments regarding both the cameras and sealing the suits, on this mission he would brook no playing fast and loose with the regs. Sierra Seven-Five had a hostile atmosphere consisting of a toxic soup of nonbreathable gases. If any of his men or Cortez's medics got a lungful of this planet's "air," little could be done except to dig a grave.

He also made certain that his troops would not disable their helmet-mounted cameras. Theirs was the first Union expedition to land on Sierra Seven-Five, intentionally anyway. Taggart and the powers that be back home both wanted as much of a visual record of the mission as they could get.

In addition, there was still no evidence as to whether the Neo-Soviet Empire had been involved in the downing of the survey ship *Cabot*. If the Sovs were on-planet, and if they had shot down an unarmed survey ship, they were likely to try to prevent a rescue of that ship's surviving crew. Visual evidence of the Soviets' involvement in or innocence of *Cabot*'s downing would be useful should the issue ever come to a bargaining table.

After ensuring that his suit was properly sealed save the connection between the suit's collar and the two-kilo helmet that still lay on the bench beside him, Taggart reached for his weapon. Officially, the weapon was designated Rifle, Assault, M-18. Unofficially, the troops called it the Pitbull for its vicious effectiveness in combat and its consistent reliability under harsh conditions. Following that line of reasoning, the standard infantry sidearm hanging from his belt was generally referred to as a Pug, rather than by its official designation, Pistol, M-43.

In each of his eight-man squads, five men were armed with the Pitbull. Two others carried the slightly heavier Bulldog support rifle, which was a modified Pitbull with a powerful grenade launcher attached over the 5.56 mm rifle barrel. The remaining Marine, the biggest man in each squad, carried a heavy M-11 Rottweiler light machine gun. Every man in the platoon carried several fragmentation grenades, as well as an updated version of the Ka-Bar Marine combat knife. Only Gunnery Sergeant Frost was the exception to the uniformity of the platoon's armament. In place of either Pitbull or Bulldog, Frost carried a short-barreled, 12-gauge Jackal combat shotgun.

At the extreme aft end of the assault boat's troop bay, the medical team stood in a tight cluster, chatting quietly, in stark contrast to the Marines' boisterousness. In addition to their individual equipment and medical supplies, each of the medics carried a sidearm. Though the lightweight pistols might not stop a Growler, or Zhykee, the Pugs would be effective enough to buy time to allow a more heavily armed Marine to intervene.

"Boss? We're about ready to go," Gunny Frost said, stepping up to her commander. Beside her was William Stowe, Third Squad's leading sergeant.

"Captain, are you sure you want to leave us here?" Stowe asked.

"It isn't that I want to, Bill, I have to," Taggart replied. "I hate the notion of cutting my strength by a third. If there *are* Neo-Sovs on this planet, and if we run into them, we're going to need all the firepower we can muster. At the same time, I can't risk losing the assault boats. If the Sovs find them, you know they're going to try to capture them or to destroy them. Either way, I want a security team here to protect the boats."

"You could just dust them off, and call them back in when we need them," Stowe countered.

"Yeah, I thought of that. Problem is, we passed over the wreck site twice before the *Gallatin*'s sensors picked it up. It may have been a hiccup in the ship's scanners, or it may have been some anomaly peculiar to this planet. I don't know if we can trust ground-to-space communications. I'd hate to need a hot extraction and not be able to get in touch with the cavalry."

"One other thing, Bill," Taggart continued, laying a fatherly hand on the sergeant's shoulder. "If the Neo-Sovs do spot this ship, and they come up in greater strength than you can handle, I want you to dust off and move to the alternate landing zone. If you can't hold there, *then* you run for the ship. I won't take any arguments on this one, you hear?"

"Yes, sir," Stowe answered, plainly not agreeing with Taggart's order, but determined to obey it just the same. "The only thing is, sir, it feels like we'd be leaving you behind."

"I know. It feels like that to me, too, like I'll be leaving your squad behind, sitting on the biggest Union target on this planet." Taggart shrugged. "Unfortunately, that's how it's got to be. If the Neo-Sovs are here and they capture the assault boats, they might use them to attack the *Gallatin*, or they might just destroy them. In either case, we'd all be stranded on this rock, and I'd rather not have that happen, if it's all the same to you, Sarge.

"Look, if you have to displace, we know where you're going." Taggart gestured toward the southern horizon. "You can get a message through to us easily enough, and we'll meet you at the secondary LZ. Twenty klicks is a bit of a hike, but we should be able to manage it. Try not to worry too much about it, Sergeant. Either way, we aren't leaving *anybody* behind on this trip."

8

L ance Corporal Dade looked at his watch for the tenth time since leaving the rescue team's landing zone. Nearly two hours had elapsed, and the Marines had yet to locate a viable path through the hills. Many of the possible roads detected by the assault boat's ground-scan sensors turned out to be false trails. The supposed paths were either not there, or were deemed by the scouts to be too dangerous and difficult for the untrained medical team to negotiate.

Dade was beginning to think that the rescue party might have to return to the shuttle and either try to find another landing zone or attempt a landing in the narrow rift valley where the supposed wreck of the survey ship lay.

"Rick, I think I've got something here," Krista Black's alto voice said in his helmet-mounted communicator. Dade looked up to see his partner beckoning him toward her position, thirty meters to the south.

"Coming, Mother," he quipped wearily. Breaking into a trot, he reached her side in a few seconds.

In an area where the assault boats' scanners said there should be no path, there was a path.

No, Dade thought. *Not a path, more like a road, a Roman road.*

"Falcon One to Lion," Dade said, bringing his communicator on-line. "I think we've found a way through the hills. It's not a footpath either, sir. It looks like a regular road."

"Falcon, this is Lion. Sit tight, Corporal, we're on our way," Taggart answered.

"Sir, Falcon requests permission to recon the road for a hundred meters or so. It looks intact, but there's no sense in getting all excited about it, only to have the dang thing vanish in a klick or so."

Taggart replied, "All right, Falcon. Mark your spot with a recognition panel, then go ahead and check out the road. Don't go more than a couple hundred meters. I don't want to lose contact with you. And remember, we aren't exactly in a position to give you much support if you run into trouble."

"Understood, boss," Dade answered, grinning behind his faceplate. "Mark position, and no more than a few hundred meters. Falcon will comply."

As he spoke, Dade watched Krista Black rummage around in her small combat pack. A few seconds later, she extracted a packet of blaze orange nylon cloth. Black spread the one-meter-square panel on the ground, weighting it with rocks. The panels were a standard part of the Marines' kit, and were frequently used to mark friendly positions for aircraft. In this case, the scouts were using it to denote the head of the trail they were about to explore.

"Ready?" Black asked as she straightened, recovering her Pitbull.

"Ready." Dade nodded. "You wanna lead off?"

Black nodded, and started cautiously up the trail. As Dade waited for his partner to move the normal five-meter interval, he studied the construction of the road. The path was broad and level. It was paved with large, flat, off-white flagstones, which looked like Terran marble. The stones had been fitted with exquisite craftsmanship. If not for the joints, which were too even and regular to be stress or impact cracks, Dade might have believed the road to have been poured in place, like a concrete highway back on Earth. There were stone-lined drainage channels, each a handspan deep and wide, on either side of the road. The whole thing reminded Dade powerfully of the illustrations and photographs he had seen of the roads built centuries before by the Caesars.

The road sloped gently up into the hills going thirty meters in a straight line before coming to a gentle, sweeping double-back. At that turning, Dade could see the terracing beneath the road. It was difficult to see at first, for the supporting walls and buttresses seemed to be made of natural rock. But a closer examination revealed a graceful organic quality that stone cannot acquire by nature. The same style of architecture seemed to be present in the buttresses and terraces supporting the road as was visible in the rotting buildings in the abandoned city. He felt a chill at that thought.

"Rick, I've got a building here," Krista Black called over the communicator.

Looking up, Dade saw his partner crouching in the shelter of a pile of dark red-brown rock that seemed to have broken loose from the cliff face above the road. Ten meters to her front, at the point of a switchback, was a small dome-shaped structure. The building was about five meters in diameter, and it had the same organic appearance as the buildings in the empty city, but it had the off-white gleam of the road's paving stones. A single low, arched doorway between two round windows gave the structure the appearance of a gigantic skull, half-sunken in the earth.

"Sit tight, Krista, and keep an eye on the place." Dade switched communications channels and informed his superior officer of the situation.

"We've just reached your marker now, Corporal," Taggart said. "Keep the building under surveillance, but do not approach it until the rest of the team is in position to support you."

"Falcon will comply, Lion," Dade replied. "PFC Black reports no movement from the structure, and no sign that anyone has passed this way in a long time."

"Understood, Falcon, but my order stands. Keep an eye on the place and wait for us."

Ten minutes later the balance of the rescue team was in place. Captain Taggart deployed First Squad along the road where they could have a reasonably clear field of fire on the igloolike structure. Second Squad and the medics were stationed a bit downhill, away from the immediate area, but still close enough to respond should the situation demand either extra firepower or medical attention. The task of actually approaching the stone hut fell to Black, Dade, and two other Marines from First Squad.

Dade and Black led the approach while the others covered them.

If there's anybody home, Dade thought, *they don't seem to be interested in us, at all.*

The scouts reached the ovoid structure with no incident.

Black pressed her back against the curving white wall, her rifle trained on the black arch of the doorway.

"There can't be anybody in there," she hissed to her partner. "If there was, they'd have spotted us a long time before this."

"Yep." Dade's tone was equally hushed. "But we gotta play this out like there was a whole squad of Neo-Sovs in there."

"Yeah," Black snorted. She pulled a small signal mirror from her combat environment suit's breast pocket and held it low to the ground, just inside the hut's open doorway. Angling the rectangular section of reflectorized polymer plastic, she scanned the building's interior. It was difficult to see inside the building, given the relative darkness beyond its egg-shaped walls. The mirror revealed no signs of life. For a few more seconds, she searched the shadows for movement, or a reflection that might betray an aggressor's position, but found none. Withdrawing the mirror, she glanced back at her partner with a short, negative shake of the head. Dade nodded his understanding. Using hand signs, he instructed Black to be ready to enter the hut. By pointing at her and moving his hand in a short arc to the left he indicated that he wanted her to enter the structure and sweep to her left. He signaled that he would follow her inside and move to the right.

Black nodded once, and set herself for the move, her Pitbull at her shoulder, with the weapon's blunt, ugly muzzle pointed at the ground. Dade mimicked her pose and stepped close to her, with his chest almost touching her back in what was often called a pinch-up formation.

"Go," Dade said quietly, and Krista Black exploded into motion. She took one long fast step through the door, bringing her rifle up in line with her eye as she moved. Nothing in the dim interior of the hut responded to her sudden movement. She swept her weapon to her left and quickly moved out of Rick Dade's path as he entered the building, dodging to his right the moment he cleared the doorway.

"Clear," Black said.

"Clear," Dade echoed.

Keeping the Pitbull at his shoulder, Dade reached down with his left hand and pulled a small, powerful flashlight from a thigh pocket. A touch of a button, and the gloomy interior of the stone hut was illuminated with a broad white beam of light. Dade quartered the building's single room carefully with the flashlight's beam. There was no sign to indicate the building was inhabited, or had been in the last hundred years.

A thick layer of yellow-brown dust covered every horizontal surface and drifted like snow against the upward-curving walls. Shelves molded into the stonework and a single stone bench were the only furnishings. It appeared that the dust hadn't been disturbed for decades. Against the wall farthest from the door was a knee-high stone fence. Dade stepped carefully up to the low barrier and shined his light over the wall. A black hole about a meter across gaped in the floor. Dade's light would not reach the bottom.

"Whaddya got?" Black asked.

"Not sure," Dade answered with a shrug. "It looks like it might have been a well, or maybe a latrine." He picked a loose stone from the top of the wall and dropped it into the inky blackness. The rock ricocheted from the pit's stone side with a loud clack. Dade wasn't sure if he heard it hit bottom or not.

"Whatever it is, it's deep."

"Boss," Dade called, switching communications channels. "This place has been empty since before I was born. If

I had to guess, I'd say it was a shelter for travelers using the road."

"Okay, Rick," Taggart answered. "I'm bringing the rest of the platoon up to the house. We'll take a ten and then Charlie Mike."

Ten minutes later the rescue party continued the mission, "Charlie Mike" as Marine slang would have it.

A few kilometers uphill from the stone hut, located at the apex of yet another switchback, the Marines came across a series of low stone boxes. Each was about two meters in length and one wide and deep. Each exhibited the sinuous, flowing construction the team had come to expect. The boxes were open to the sky, with a thick layer of dust coating their bottoms.

"They remind me of flower boxes," Lieutenant Cortez offered.

Dade forced himself to smother a laugh, but a second later he found himself agreeing with the Navy doctor's assessment of the boxes.

From that point on, the team ran across the "flower boxes" every few hundred meters, and one of the stone huts every kilometer or so. Each was as deserted as the first. But the scouts found signs in the road that suggested the huts were sometimes occupied.

Eight kilometers from the point where the rescue team began to follow the road, Dade suddenly signaled his partner to stop. Looking around for any signs of a hostile presence and finding none, he dropped lightly to one knee. A deep gouge surrounded by a number of shallower, parallel scrapes marred the surface of a large paving stone. The central groove was as long as his forearm, and a finger joint in depth. He could feel the roughness of the stone where the gouging implement had scraped along its surface. Slight traces of silvery gray material clung to the inner surfaces of the notch.

A few meters away, another stone was defaced by a similar pattern of scratches. Dade found a third set of virtually identical scars a couple of paces beyond those. Each set of scrapes and gouges lined up with the rest. To Dade, the overall appearance of the scratches suggested that something heavy and metallic had been dragged along the road. The roughness inside the scratches, and the traces of metal still clinging to the scars, indicated that they had been made as recently as a day ago.

As he knelt to examine the last set of scratches, something caught his eye. Under any other circumstances, he might have missed the object, or mistaken it for a stone. Resting on the edge of the right-hand drainage ditch was a fifteen-centimeter-long billet of rusted iron. One end of the round bar tapered to a point.

"What have you got there, Rick?" Black asked from her overwatch position ten meters behind him.

"I'm not sure. It looks like a climber's piton," Dade answered. "But the thing is so badly rusted that I can't say for certain."

When the scouts reported their findings to Captain Taggart, the platoon leader acknowledged the report, and unnecessarily advised Dade and Black to remain alert.

"Stay alert?" Black said with a short, bitter chuckle. "What does he think we've been doing? Sniffing all these pretty flowers?" She waved her hand at the ugly, barren red-brown rock and dusty soil lining the trail.

"I know, Krista." Dade cocked his head to one side as he spoke. "So does he. I guess the boss is just worried about us. Nice ain't it, to have someone so concerned for our well-being?"

"Yeah, Rick, whatever you say." Black gave a second chuckle, as rueful as the first. "I'll lead off this time."

9

What do you think, Gunny?" Captain Taggart asked Onawa Frost.

"Well, sir," the Mohawk gunnery sergeant replied, with a shrug. "I don't know. All the preliminary reports we got about this planet said it was uninhabited. Our intelligence boys say that the Neo-Sovs have kinda pulled back on their space-exploration efforts. And it looks like both reports are wrong."

"Go on," Taggart prompted.

The Marine officer and his senior noncom stopped their upward climb, motioning the troops behind them to continue along the trail. Gunny Frost rested her left foot on a low parapet overlooking a narrow gorge, her Jackal combat shotgun braced across her knee, her arms folded atop the weapon's receiver. Taggart slung his rifle, shoving it behind him, and mimicked her pose. Leaning forward, he picked up a handful of small white pebbles. To his eye, the stones seemed to be made of the same material as the flagstones of the road.

Gunny Frost's thoughtful expression was barely visible

behind the environment suit's masking faceplate. Characteristically, she took a long moment to digest the available information before rendering an opinion. Taggart tossed a few pebbles into the gorge while he waited for Frost to speak.

"If I remember right, we got a report about six months back that said the Neo-Sovs were working on some kind of surface-to-space antiship missile, didn't we?"

"That's right," Taggart said. "Designated SS-N-25 'Grappler.' "

"That's the one. Now, what if the Intel boys were wrong about the Neo-Sovs and exploration?" Frost suggested. "What if *Cabot* was brought down by a Grappler? And those tracks that Dade and Black found. Those could easily have been made by a Cyclops or some other kind of Neo-Sov mutant."

"I was thinking the same thing, Gunny." Taggart nodded. "That would mean that the Neo-Sovs are up to something pretty important on this rock. Grapplers are big, expensive pieces of equipment. They wouldn't move a launcher all the way out here unless they had a powerful reason for doing so."

"Uh-huh. That means we've got . . ." Frost broke off in mid-sentence. "Now that's odd, sir." She put her hand up to shade her eyes. "We've got fog rising in the heat of the day."

Taggart straightened from his resting slouch. His eyes followed Gunny Frost's line of sight. About thirty meters uphill of their position a thin gray mist began blowing across the trail. The lead elements of their platoon had almost reached the wispy gray wall.

"It is kinda unusual, Gunny," Taggart agreed. "But then, what isn't unusual about this planet? Right now, though, we've got more important things to think about than fog."

"Captain Taggart," Dr. Cortez called, making her way

to where the Marines stood. "I want to show you something. One of my medics found this in the drainage ditch."

Cortez held out her hand, displaying a metal circlet nearly twice the size of the palm of her hand. The hoop appeared to be made of gold, but when she passed it to Taggart, he discovered that the object had nearly no weight. He examined the object closely, and was able to pick out strange, scrawling markings on both its inner and outer surfaces.

"Gunny? Any ideas?" he asked, holding out the ring to Onawa Frost.

Frost didn't reply, and made no move to take the object. Instead, she remained stiffly in place, staring at the mist on the trail in front of them.

No, it isn't simply gathering, Taggart realized. *It's rolling downhill toward us.*

"Gunny." Taggart laid a hand on Frost's shoulder. Even through the environment suit, he could feel the rigidity in her muscles. He gently shook her, as though trying to rouse her from sleep. "Gunny Frost."

Then Taggart felt the first touch of the gathering mist. Unlike normal Terran fog, the gray floating vapor was warm. A faint, bitter scent of dry dust, like ancient paper, filtered through the suit's mask. Taggart felt an odd itching sensation run from the base of his spine to the top of his skull. Beneath his thick kevlon helmet, he felt his scalp tighten.

As the mist reached out to envelop the three of them, Taggart heard Gunny Frost gasp. The doctor's words suddenly slurred and sped up as though on a tape being played back at high speed.

Then sudden pain spiked into his hands like a red-hot needle, and the mist enveloped them all. The pain writhed up Taggart's arms to the elbows, sending thin tendrils of liquid fire along his upper arms and across his shoulders. Then, as suddenly as it had begun, the burning pain was gone, leaving only a dull ache. Taggart looked around for Lieutenant Cortez, but he couldn't see either her or Gunnery Sergeant Frost. Nor was there any trace of his platoon or Cortez's rescue medics. All Taggart could see was the thin gray mist and the small portion of the road upon which he stood.

"Lion Three, this is Lion Six, come in," Taggart called, trying to reach Gunny Frost via radio communicator. A high-pitched keening, like a high wind in the rocks, blanketed every frequency, though Taggart was certain he could hear words in the odd, electronic screeching.

They can't have left me here, Taggart told himself.

Oh no, smart guy? Then where are they? An inner voice seemed to mock him.

"Only one way to go," he said aloud. His voice sounded flat, distorted in the swirling gray mist.

He moved the Pitbull assault rifle in front of his body, one aching hand wrapped around the weapon's firing grip. The other hand grasped its forestock. Captain Taggart turned away from the low stone parapet and began moving uphill. A faint stirring of fear roiled through his guts. He was alone in a blind fog, on a mostly unmapped and demonstrably hostile planet. He prayed that he would not meet the Neo-Soviet troops who he was convinced were on Sierra Seven-Five. He resolved that, should he run into the enemy, he would not be taken alive, though with only two hundred seventy rounds for his Pitbull and forty-five for his Pug, he wouldn't be fighting much of a pitched battle. The best he could hope for was to take a few of them with him.

Unable to see more than a few feet in front of him, Taggart moved in a cautious foot-shuffling walk. He probed the ground ahead of him with his toes, only moving forward when he was convinced that there was no hazard to trip over. The slow pace was grueling. After the first twenty minutes or so, Taggart's leg muscles began to ache from the odd gait. After two hours, he was in agony from cramps brought on by the bent-kneed posture. Still the fog refused to lift or thin out. Every hour or so, he would stop, sitting on the edge of the drainage channel for a few minutes to ease his knotted muscles. During those stops, he would try to contact either the rescue team, the assault boats, or the *Gallatin*, but every call went unanswered, save for the high-pitched warbling shriek blanketing the communication channels.

How long he went on like that Taggart could not say. Then, as suddenly as it had come, the mist vanished.

Glancing wildly about in the strangely clear air, Taggart saw that he had caught up with his platoon without knowing it.

No, something was distinctly wrong. He knew he had been climbing the steep grade for hours—the aches in his muscles confirmed that—but the dim shadows cast by the odd light of the Maw were in exactly the same place as they had been when the mist set in. Gunny Frost was still leaning on the leg she had propped up on the parapet, an odd mixture of bafflement and fear plain in her stance and visor-shielded eyes. Dr. Cortez was prattling on about the odd metal ring her medic had found. The rest of the platoon had come to a halt, almost every man appearing confused. Only a few looked as though nothing had happened.

"All right, what the hell was that?" Frost growled, recovering her voice.

"What was what, Sergeant?" Cortez asked in confusion.

"We've been on the trail for hours," Frost snapped.

"And now, we're right back in the same damn place we were eight hours ago."

"No, Gunny," Taggart said, stepping up to Frost and Cortez. "It's only been three hours or so, four at the most. And where the hell were all of you? What did you do, switch all the communicators in the platoon off? Why didn't you answer my calls? Hell, why did you leave me behind in the first place?"

"Leave you behind?" Frost stared at him. "Boss, we didn't leave anybody behind. You were right beside me the whole time."

"What are you two talking about?" Cortez yelled. "Nothing happened. Nothing but a little bit of fog rolling across the trail. You both stopped talking for a second or so, and now you're acting like half a day's gone by."

"It *has*, Lieutenant," Frost snapped, holding up her left wrist. "Look at my chrono. We've been marching in circles for eight hours."

"Let me see that, Gunny," Taggart said, taking her arm. He held Frost's left wrist close to his own. The digital chronograph, part of the small electronics package built into the back of her environment suit's left gauntlet plainly showed that eight hours *had* elapsed since they had stopped to talk about the possible presence of Neo-Sov troops on Sierra Seven-Five. But Taggart's chrono showed four hours had gone by. Cortez held her timepiece out for comparison. According to her chrono, no significant time had elapsed.

"Dammit," Taggart swore under his breath. Then, keying in the platoon's tactical channel, he called out, "Platoon halt. Form up on me."

"What about us, boss?" Dade's voice broke from the headset. "You want us to come in?"

"Negative, Falcon," the captain replied. "Question:

Have you or Black noticed anything odd in the last few minutes?"

"No sir. Well, not other than a little bit of mist that passed between your position and ours. Did you see it, sir?"

"Affirmative," Taggart said. "Falcon, what time does your chrono show?"

"Sir?"

"What time is it, Lance Corporal?"

"Sir, my chrono shows one-three-hundred, Zulu." Dade answered. His tone suggested that he was wondering if his captain had suddenly gone mad.

"Falcon, confirm your last, current time is one-three-hundred, Zulu time?" Taggart said, looking at Cortez's chrono. Dade's report matched her digital display perfectly. Both devices proclaimed the time to be one o'clock in the afternoon Greenwich Mean Time.

"Falcon confirms, current time is one-three-hundred," Dade paused before asking, "Sir? What's this all about?"

"Stand by, Falcon, I'll give you an update presently." Turning to Gunny Frost, he instructed her to check with the rest of the platoon to see if anyone else had experienced a loss of time.

When Frost returned, she informed the captain that almost three-quarters of the platoon had lost between one and ten hours, an anomaly confirmed by each man's chrono. Two men, one a Marine and one a burn specialist on Dr. Cortez's medical team, had not lost, but gained time. The Marine's chrono was running forty-five minutes slow, while the doctor's was a full ten hours behind. No one reported any persistent physical symptoms other than sore, aching muscles, and a jet-lagged feeling.

"You know," Cortez said after listening to Gunny Frost's report. "I've heard of this sort of thing occurring once or twice since the Induction. Always to the crew of a space vessel. The experts are calling it time displacement or time distortion, although that's all they know about it. As far as I know, this is the first time it has ever happened to someone on the ground.

"Some people are wondering if the same phenomenon might not be responsible for lost time in supposed alien abductions."

"And what do you think, Doctor?" Gunny Frost asked sharply.

"I don't know what to think, Gunnery Sergeant." Cortez shook her head and shrugged. "It is difficult to study a temporal phenomenon like time distortion when you're not ready for it to happen."

"All right, whatever it was, it looks like nobody is the worse for wear," Taggart cut in. "Doctor, I want you and your team to check everybody out. Make sure there are no ill effects other than this hungover feeling. Then we're gonna reset everybody's chrono to yours." Taggart squinted at the pale gleaming disk of the Maw where it sat low on the western horizon. It was almost nightfall, regardless of Greenwich Mean Time. "And then, we're all gonna get some rest, so that those of us who were affected by this time distortion of yours can recover a bit. We'll start off again first thing in the morning."

10

"Bloody frigging, hell," Marine Private First Class Leo Kowalski swore under his breath, as he stood beneath the lip of an overhanging rock outcropping. Above him one of Cortez's damn medics scrabbled at the scree, kicking loose a small torrent of red-brown dust and marble-sized pebbles. Kowalski turned his face away from the miniature avalanche, momentarily taking his eyes off the man he'd been assigned to baby-sit.

Fifty meters or so behind the spot where the cursing PFC stood, the "Roman road" came to an abrupt end. Since the team had resumed the climb through the rough hills, some eight hours earlier, they had encountered a handful of places where ancient landslides had damaged the flat paved trail. One of those slides had torn away the rock supporting the paving stones, causing them to collapse into the gorge below. Fortunately, the gap in the road was only a few meters across. While it had presented an obstacle which had to be bypassed by climbing, traversing the chasm required only basic mountaineering techniques. This time, it was different.

Here the road ended in a steep slope of broken, rocky

ground. No sign of the white paving stones could be seen anywhere along the hundred-meter-long expanse of loose, broken, red-brown rock. Dotting the ancient slide area were outcroppings of multicolored crystalline rock, which seemed to grow from the crevices between the boulders like diamond, ruby, and sapphire bushes. At the top of the slope was a sheer escarpment about ten meters high, with a jutting overhang of pavement-capped rock at the top of the precipice. There was no clear evidence as to what had happened to the road at that point. The consensus was that an earthquake, such as those which shook Earth when it was "inducted" into the Maelstrom, must have twisted the fabric of the planet, tearing the road asunder, and erecting the cliff-like obstruction.

Whatever the reason for the break in the road, it caused the rescue team a significant delay. Captain Taggart had been unwilling to expose any of the team to unnecessary risks. So the platoon's strongest climbers went first, stringing a safety line along the steep rockslide's treacherous slope. Then they had to climb the escarpment, which, though only ten meters high, was still a challenge to climb without an overhead belay, especially taking into account the half-meter wide overhang the climbers had to get around. Once the ropes and belays had been strung, the team began the ascent once more. A Marine with climbing experience had been detailed to watch over each of the medics. The entire operation had cost the rescue team forty-five minutes, and they weren't done yet. Kowalski glanced at his chrono: 1156 Zulu. That meant about ninety minutes until local nightfall. Captain Taggart had decided to scale the low escarpment and bivouac at the top. Kowalski snorted in disgust. Though they would have been spending this night in the open along the narrow mountain trail, the Marine private regarded the time spent overcoming this latest obstacle as yet another delay in getting away from this godforsaken planet. With another sigh of displeasure, Kowalski returned his attention to the man he was supposed to be baby-sitting.

PFC Kowalski, a fair hand at mountaineering, had been assigned to keep an eye on Dr. Nicholas Ziwi, one of Cortez's trauma specialists.

Well, he's strong enough, Kowalski thought, dodging another mini-avalanche. *But the man has absolutely no clue when it comes to climbing.* Above him, Ziwi's feet finally vanished over the outcropping.

"Climber coming up," Kowalski called.

"On belay," a voice from above answered. "Come ahead."

"Okay. Climbing now."

Shifting his heavy Bulldog support rifle into a comfortable muzzle-down position across his back, Kowalski tied himself into the climbing rope by means of the strong steel carabinier attached to his combat harness's web belt. This stretch of the climb wasn't especially challenging, not technically anyway, but the sheer rock face required brute strength to haul oneself up the vertical face and across the jutting lip of the overhang.

For a moment, Kowalski paused to catch his breath. He locked the safety rope in tight and reached up with his right hand to grasp the lip of the overhang, steadying himself, and arresting the sway that climbers often ignored until the pendulum-like motion wore through their supporting ropes. Though Kowalski, like all Marines, was in excellent physical condition, the short, vertical climb, combined with the weight of his gear and the closed combat environment suit left him a bit winded. Once his breathing calmed a bit, he was ready to continue.

"I'm at the overhang," he said. "Ready to go on."

"On belay," came the reply. "Come ahead. Just watch yourself. The surface is getting kinda loose."

"Okay, thanks," Kowalski said. "Climbing now."

Unlocking the brake, Kowalski reached out with his left hand and caught a narrow ledge of rock with his finger-tips. With a muscle-cracking effort, he pulled himself up, hand over hand, until he could see the top of the lip. Lance Corporal Tim Henry stood a meter or so back, hanging on to the belay line. The climber grinned at his platoon mates and reached out with his left hand for the next rung of the rocky ladder.

Then Kowalski's right hand was suddenly empty, except for a fistful of thin, crumbling flakes of red-brown rock. The young Marine felt his combat harness catch momentarily on a projection just below the upper rim of the overhang. In the slow-motion world known only to accident victims, Kowalski saw Captain Taggart, Gunny Frost, and Dr. Ziwi, all lunge for his outstretched hands. Ziwi actually managed to touch his fingers. At that moment, the plastic quick-release buckle of Kowalski's thick nylon combat harness gave way. The safety line held momentarily, allowing him to drop in relative safety back across the overhang. Kowalski spun and swung in space for a moment, then slammed sideways into the rock face. A rending pop in his left knee sent a galvanic wave of pain through his body. For a second, Kowalski felt he had survived the worst of it. But with the harness no longer firmly buckled around his body, the jarring impact of a ninety-kilo man carrying fourteen kilos of weapon and gear smashing into the escarpment was too much for the unfastened rig to bear.

Kowalski dropped free of his compromised harness and fell the remaining five meters to the rocks below. He screamed as his injured knee was hammered into the ground.

That impact caused the loose ground beneath the escarpment to give way, tumbling him down slope in a miniature landslide of head-sized rocks. He didn't know how far he slid, but his downhill plunge was only arrested when he slammed into one of the crystalline formations dotting the broken ground. An intense wave of pain washed over him from his mangled knee. He barely noticed the sound of his arm snapping as he landed with his right biceps trapped between his body and the jagged, gemlike growth. Then shock came down like a steel curtain between him and the searing torment of his injuries.

The next thing he knew, Gunny Frost and Captain Taggart were at his side.

"Corpsman!" Frost barked, in a moment of crisis reverting to Marine tradition. "Corpsman!"

Taggart laid a hand on Kowalski's shoulder, saying, "Lie still, Private, lie still and wait for the docs."

Almost before the captain had finished speaking, another environment-suited figure leaned over the injured man. Through the helmet's narrow faceplate, Kowalski saw the dark brown eyes and dark skin belonging to Dr. Lieutenant Rebecca Cortez.

"Take it easy, Private," Cortez said. "I'm here, and we're gonna take good care of you. First, can you feel your feet? Can you wiggle your feet for me?"

Kowalski gritted his teeth against the pain and complied with the doctor's request.

"That's good, Leo," Cortez smiled encouragingly through her visor. "Now how 'bout your fingers? Can you move your fingers?"

"M' right arm's broke," he said, surprised at the thickness in his voice. He gamely wiggled the fingers of his undamaged right hand at the doctor.

"That's good. Now, where does it hurt?" Not waiting for him to reply, Cortez began running her hands over Kowalski's body. In a few moments, Kowalski saw, rather than heard, her sigh of relief.

"You're going to be fine, Leo," Cortez said. "Your right arm is broken, but it doesn't look too bad. I think your left knee is badly sprained, but it doesn't look like the neurovascular bundle has been compromised. You sit tight for a moment, and we'll get you patched up."

Cortez straightened and waved to two of her medics, who moved in immediately to treat Kowalski's injuries. As the medics went to work, Kowalski saw the doctor separate herself from the rest of the team. She motioned for Taggart and Frost to join her.

The pair of medics working on Kowalski quickly erected a small tentlike structure, placed the wounded Marine inside, and then crawled in after him. The tent was necessary to perform emergency medical treatment in the field when the atmosphere was hostile to human life. It was pressurized, and had an independent supply of breathable air, allowing the medics to work in relative comfort.

As the medics broke the seals on Kowalski's combat environment suit, one muttered, "Thank God his suit wasn't ripped."

Kowalski shuddered at the very thought of having his suit compromised.

"How bad is it?" he asked.

"Ah, not too bad," the medic replied. "Sprained left knee and a simple fracture of the right humerus, not to mention numerous scrapes and bruises. You'll be fine. I'm afraid you're out of this game, though."

"No," Kowalski struggled to sit up, but the pain of his fractured right arm prevented the precipitous action. "I'm not gonna leave my buddies."

"I'm sorry, Private." There was sympathy in the doctor's voice. "You're gonna have to. Otherwise, someone is going to have to carry you, and you're too big for that."

"Don't worry," the second man said as he laid out a flimsy-looking array of plastic sheeting and tubes, which Kowalski recognized as an air splint. "We'll take good care of your friends."

Treating Kowalski's injuries was not difficult. A metal-reinforced brace went over the sprained left knee, to support and immobilize the joint. The broken arm required the doctors to administer a painkiller before reducing the fracture and setting it with the inflatable cast. With luck, neither injury would put Kowalski out of the Corps.

"Well that's it," the first medic said once they had finished. "You just lie there and take it easy for a minute, and we'll let your captain know that you're all right."

An hour later, Leo Kowalski was on his feet and preparing to leave his platoon mates behind. Captain Taggart, at Lieutenant Cortez's urging, had decided to send the injured man back to the landing zone. Abraham Ake, one of the doctors assigned to the rescue party, had climbing experience, and was going to escort Kowalski down the hill. Taggart also contacted the Marine squad left to guard the LZ and instructed Sergeant Stowe to send a couple of men up the trail to meet Ake and his charge.

"Take good care of my boy, there, Doc," Taggart said, in a tone both light and serious at the same time.

"Will do, Captain." Ake smiled reassuringly behind his

visor. "But he's more my boy than yours right now. You can have him back in a couple of weeks."

"Okay." The captain nodded. "And you, Private, do what the doc tells you. I want you back in the platoon ASAP."

"Uh-huh, and when you do come back," Gunny Frost added, her face expressionless, "we're gonna have a little refresher course in basic combat mountaineering."

"Well, that's it," Taggart said, taking Kowalski by his uninjured left hand. The captain looked up at the darkening sky. The Maw had reached the far horizon while the medics were working to patch Kowalski back together. Even now, the shadows on the east side of the hill had darkened almost into night. "Be careful going down the hill, and we'll see you when we get back."

With that, the Marines turned away and continued on their march. Ake laid a gentle hand on Kowalski's left shoulder, and said, "Well, come on, Marine, we've got a long way to walk."

"Right, Doc, just let me pick up my rifle," Kowalski said. "Did you see where they put it?"

"No, I didn't," Ake replied, looking around. "I don't see it. They wouldn't have taken it with them, would they?"

"No, sir, they wouldn't," Kowalski answered. "Look, Doc, I'm financially responsible for that weapon. I can't leave it here. Help me look for it, okay?"

"All right, Private, calm down," Ake said as soothingly. "You stay put, I'll see if I can't find it for you."

Ake, started moving up the scree-covered slope, hunting for the lost weapon with the aid of a powerful flashlight. He had only gone ten meters or so when he froze in place.

Kowalski, too, pricked up his ears, listening. A soft scuttling noise, like thick leather being dragged across a concrete floor, reached his ears. Apparently Dr. Ake had heard it, too, because he turned his light in the direction of the sound. Something pale gleamed briefly in the beam of Ake's light.

Then there was a loud, hollow pop. Ake dropped his flashlight with a gasp, staggered back, clutching at his chest. His heel slipped in the treacherous soil and he tumbled over backwards, rolling down the steep, rocky slope.

As the doctor's lifeless body tumbled past him, Kowalski thought he saw a heavy steel spike protruding from the center of the man's chest.

Something moved in the shadow of a boulder. Kowalski scrabbled left-handed for the heavy Pug automatic pistol holstered on his left hip, cursing at the pneumatic cast immobilizing his gun hand.

Before he could drag the weapon free, a misshapen humanoid figure stepped from the gloom into the fading light. The creature was holding Kowalski's Bulldog support rifle. The weapon's over-and-under assault-rifle and grenade-launcher barrels seemed to glare balefully at their former owner. So steadily did the being hold the heavy combination weapon that it seemed to have become part of the creature's right arm.

At last the holster flap gave way, and Kowalski dragged the big pistol clear of its nylon case.

The creature seemed to shrug. A lance of flame reached out from the Bulldog's muzzle and plunged Kowalski into darkness.

11

"Cover!" Taggart and Frost yelled in unison as a short, rolling burst of fire echoed through the hills. Marines and medical personnel scrambled for what slight concealment they could find along the undamaged section of road.

"Lion Six to Kowalski," Taggart called, opening a general command channel. "Kowalski, respond."

"Nothing," Frost said at the captain's side. "Something's wrong."

"Yeah. First Squad over the edge, find out what the hell's going on," Taggart barked. "Second Squad, set up a perimeter here."

Gunnery Sergeant Frost rolled out of the drainage channel and eased her way toward the top of the wall the platoon had just ascended. Dropping prone, she crawled to the edge of the precipice and peered into the gathering darkness below.

"Still nothing," she said. "Not even on infrared. Henry, let's rig the ropes. First Section, you're the lead group. Second Section will cover. Let's go."

Moments later Frost and five Marines from First Squad, First Section stood on the rocky slope below the wall. The troops fanned out, forming a shallow defensive arc facing downhill, as the rest of their squad mates rappelled down to join them.

"Kowalski," Frost called again. "Ake, do you copy?"

Silence.

"All right, fan out by twos. Standard search pattern," Frost said brusquely. "We might have two people down, and I want them found, *now*."

Quickly the Marines paired off and began searching the treacherous, stony hill for their missing companions. Conducting a search in the deepening gloom could be a chancy thing, even when employing light amplification and infrared detection gear such as that mounted in the environment suits' helmets. The uneven ground below the ten-meter escarpment would make things even more difficult.

Frost paired off with Corporal Henry and moved carefully behind the center of the searching line. Onawa Frost knew that sometimes a good leader must lead from behind. While her eyes were as sharp as any Marine's in her squad, she knew the best thing she could do was hang back a bit and coordinate the search.

"Stay sharp, people," Frost said quietly. "There's somebody other than us on this damn rock. Let's not make it too easy for them."

The Marines moved cautiously, their rifles held at low ready.

Frost knew that her men had switched on the integral starlight systems set into their visors as she had. The electronic light-amplification unit gave limited range and rendered the scene before her as a nightmare vista of green, gray, and white. Using it for an extended period of time would cause eyestrain and a stabbing headache. But the benefit of being able to see in the dark made the inconveniences worth it.

"Gunny, I've got something here," a Marine called, beckoning Frost closer. "Looks like a blood trail, but I can't tell through the starlight. Request permission to use my flash."

"Negative, Parks," Frost shot back. "You know better than that. If there's bad guys out there, they'll see your light and use it as an aiming point. Just stay there a minute. I'm coming over."

"Okay, Sarge," Parks replied.

When Frost reached Parks's position, she saw the black smears against the dark green of the rocks. It was impossible to discern the actual color of the stains because of the monochrome nature of the low-light viewer. Briefly, she flicked the system off. In the deep shadows, she could not even see the discoloration. For a moment she considered the situation.

"All right you guys, spread out," she ordered the small cluster of Marines. "I guess I'll have to risk the light. I don't wanna risk you guys if the Sovs see the light and decide to take a little target practice. And turn off your starlights. I don't want anybody getting dazzled when I turn the light on."

After waiting for the Marines to move away a short distance, Frost pulled her small, powerful flashlight from the breast pocket of her environment suit. Hooding the lens with her hand, she leaned forward over the spot where Parks had spotted the dark smear and thumbed the switch. In the sudden glare, Frost saw a thick smear of blood. Someone who was bleeding had crawled or been dragged across this spot. Moving carefully, Frost followed the blood trail for a meter or so in each direction, then snapped off the light.

"Captain, we definitely have a blood trail here," Frost

informed her superior. "I'm gonna split my squad and have them backtrack it both directions. How far downslope do you want me to proceed?"

"No more than two hundred meters from your present position, Gunny," Taggart answered.

Frost opened her mouth to confirm the captain's orders, but a call from one of her men interrupted her.

"Gunny, I've got some spent five-five-six shell casings here."

Looking around, Frost saw the man waving to her.

"And what looks like a big puddle of blood. Hang on . . . Gunny, there's a Pug pistol lying here, too. The mag is full, and there's one in the chamber."

"Captain, did you copy?" Frost asked.

"Affirmative, Gunny," Taggart answered. "How does that position relate to your blood trails?"

"Direct line uphill, and a bit across, sir," Frost answered. "Looks like it's downhill for us."

"Right. But stick to the two-hundred-meter limit. Kowalski was too badly injured to have gone much farther than that, and I doubt Ake would have left him." The tinny-sounding headset speakers could not mask the tension in Taggart's voice.

"Roger, sir. Two hundred meters it is." Frost switched her attention back to her squad. "All right, you guys, spread out. You heard the man, two hundred meters. Let's go find them."

"Sarge, we've gotta stop," Tim Henry had switched off his communications set and leaned in close to Gunnery Sergeant Frost's helmeted head to urge her to halt. What he had to say, he didn't want going out over the open communications channel. "We're *way* past two hundred meters, and there's been no sign of either of them. The boss said . . ."

"I know what the boss said," Frost snapped back. Her voice was a sharp growl that Corporal Henry could barely hear, because she had turned her own communicator off. "But you don't think he'd be out here with us if he could?"

For the past fifteen minutes, Frost and Henry had been quartering the gleaming white pavement of the intact section of road below the rockslide, without discovering any trace of the missing men. The blood trail ran only a dozen meters farther downhill from the place where PFC Parks had discovered the thick dark smears. No more shell casings were found, in either the 5.56 millimeter used by Union forces or the bigger 7.62 round favored by the Neo-Soviets. Nor were there any signs of anyone else being hit. Then the trail ended abruptly. Twice, Gunny Frost thought she saw a faint depression in the rocky soil that might have been a footprint. But it was too hard to tell. Even risking a second's worth of illumination from her flashlight did nothing to alleviate the mystery. If the impressions were footprints, she had no way of knowing if they had been left by the platoon as it made its way up the slope earlier that day, or by the unknown assailants who had spirited away PFC Kowalski and Dr. Ake.

"Sarge, we gotta go back." Henry was insistent, and Frost had to admit that he was right.

"Okay, we go back," she said with a heavy sigh.

"Lion Six, this is Lion Three," she called, switching her communicator back on. "Sir, we haven't seen any trace of Kowalski or Ake since we lost the blood trail. Suggest you recall the scouts and see if they have any better luck. Dade is a helluva lot better tracker than I'll ever be."

At the temporary command post he had set up above the cliff face and broken rocky slope, Captain Taggart considered Gunny Frost's request.

"I think you're right, Gunny," he said. "Mark the spots where you lost the trail and where you found the shell casings. We aren't going to find much in the dark. We'll bivouac here and resume the search in the morning."

As soon as it was light enough for the scouts to follow the faint marks left by whoever or whatever had attacked Kowalski and Ake the night before, Dade and Black took up the search. Gunny Frost and two of the men from First Squad accompanied the recon specialists, keeping well back so as not to spoil any signs.

Frost watched with great interest and open admiration as the scouts followed the unseen enemy beyond the point where she had lost the trail the previous evening. Dade and Black seemed to spot signs invisible to the naked eye, keeping the search party on a straight course downhill.

Just over an hour after the searchers left the platoon's bivouac, Dade came to a sudden halt. Gunny Frost snapped her Jackal combat shotgun up into firing position, searching for an enemy. Then she read the young man's stance as one of sadness and despair, rather than one of a warrior ready for battle.

"What is it, Rick?" she called.

"C'mon up, Gunny," Dade replied quietly.

Approaching the scout, Frost saw the object that had attracted his attention. Wedged in a crevice between two torso-sized boulders was the helmet of a standard-issue combat environment suit. The headgear's faceplate was shattered and smeared with blood. A string of small black characters stenciled across the back of the battered kevlon read *Ake*.

"Understood, Gunny," Taggart said flatly. "Have your trackers seen any sign of Kowalski?"

"Negative, sir," Frost answered hollowly. "What do you want us to do? Should we continue the search?"

"That's right, Gunny, continue the search."

Lieutenant Cortez, who had been sitting next to Taggart on the rim of one of the "flower boxes," let out a strangled gasp and shot to her feet. The doctor stood over him, fists on her hips, glaring.

"Stand by, Lion Three," Taggart said, realizing that Cortez was about to take exception to his decision. "All right, *Doctor*, what is it this time?"

"Captain, I understand your concern for your man. I'm worried about him too, *and* Dr. Ake. But I'm even more concerned for the survivors at the crash site. From what Sergeant Frost says, it sounds like they're both dead. One or both of them has lost a helluva lot of blood, and Ake lost his helmet. There is no way he could have survived this long without it. I'm sorry to put it that bluntly, Captain, but that's the way it sounds to me."

"So what do you want me to do, Lieutenant?" Taggart asked sharply. "Just walk away and leave them without knowing if they're dead, wounded, captured, or whatever? Is that what you'd want me to do if it was you lying back there alone, maybe bleeding to death, maybe captured by the Neo-Sovs? I thought you were a doctor. I thought you had a responsibility to the people under your care. What about that, Lieutenant? Isn't Kowalski a patient of yours?"

"Dammit, Captain. You know that's not it," Cortez shot back, her eyes blazing. "You may not like me, but don't you dare tell me I don't care about those men. I'm not running away from this just because I'm Mexican."

"Mexican? What does that . . ."

"I care about those men more than you'll ever know, Captain." Cortez ran on as though she hadn't heard his startled interruption. "But as much as I care about Ake and Kowalski, I care far more about the people who have been down on this hellhole of a planet for two weeks now.

"Ake and Kowalski are dead, you know that as well as I do. But those people over there might still be alive. We can't risk all of them for two men. Once we reach *Cabot* and pull out her survivors, we'll be coming back this way, right? We can look for the bodies then. But for now, we cannot delay this mission any longer."

Captain Taggart felt a slow burn of anger creeping up the back of his neck. No one had given him a dressing down like that since he was a first-year midshipman at Annapolis. And Cortez's half-stated accusation of racism merely added fuel to the fire.

To Captain Maxwell Taggart, there was no difference. So long as a person did their job and earned their way, without special consideration for race, nationality, or position, then everything ran smoothly. What he hated was favoritism of any kind.

Taking a few breaths to control the anger that was rising in his throat, Taggart grudgingly realized that Cortez was right. Kowalski could not have gone far on his own, and Dr. Ake could not have survived more than a minute or so without the protection of his environment suit's helmet; nor would he have voluntarily left his charge.

"Sergeant Frost." He paused and sighed. "Gunny, bring your squad in. As much as I hate to do it, we're gonna have to call Ake and Kowalski missing. We can't hold up the mission any longer."

12

An odd scuttling sound, like mice moving across the loose rocky soil, caught Rick Dade's attention. He held up his left hand in a signal for Krista Black to halt, but she had already frozen in place. Her tense posture showed an anxiousness that was far from normal for her. Dade searched the deep, shadowed crevices that bordered the trail, straining to discover the source of the noise.

A kilometer or so above the cliff where Abraham Ake and Leo Kowalski had vanished, the "Roman road" came to an abrupt end. The heavy paving flags gave way to a footpath beaten into the dark red-brown soil. Loose rocks, ranging in size from that of Dade's gloved fist to small, flat, coin-sized wafers, dotted the trail.

Leaving the paved road seemed to be a signal to the scouts' subconscious. Barely a hundred meters past the end of the road, Black spun in a quarter circle, snapping up her Pitbull to cover a deeply shadowed niche in the rock face. She claimed to have seen something move in the gloomy recess, but when the scouts investigated it, they found nothing but an empty, shallow crack in the rock. In the two hours since that first, anxious false alarm, Dade and Black had been brought up short by a half dozen other nonexistent contacts.

At first, Dade had been willing to write off their disquiet as a reaction to the mysterious disappearance of their teammates. Until now.

"Rick . . ." Black began, but Dade waved her to silence. The Maw stood high overhead, a bit past its zenith. The strange light it gave cast odd shadows, in some places faint, in others deep. He could see a hulking black shape in the deeper gloom beneath a house-sized boulder that nearly closed off the trail fifteen meters ahead of him. At first he thought the form was just another rock, strangely weathered by whatever natural forces this ugly planet had. But the longer he gazed at the shape, the more certain he became that it had moved, and that movement had caused the odd rustling sound he had heard.

Dade carefully brought up his assault rifle. He settled the front post over the dark mass, centering it in the ghostly ring of his rear peep sight, but kept his finger off the weapon's trigger. For three long breaths he waited for the shape to react, but the shadowy figure remained still. A prickling sensation on the back of his neck told him that Krista Black had finally spotted his target and had brought her rifle up to cover it.

Without lowering his weapon, Dade began moving forward. Slowly, carefully he moved one foot, searching with his toes to make certain his footing would be good before transferring his weight to that leg. All of his senses seemed to be in high gear. He could see the dark shape as a slightly blacker patch in the gloom of the boulder's shadow. He could hear the crunch of stones shifting under his weight, smell and taste the slightly stale flavor of his environment suit's respirator mask, feel the uneven surface beneath his feet and the reassuring weight of his rifle stock in his hands. He had never felt more alive, and yet he felt the presence of death in that lurking shadow.

Dade had gone three steps when the shape moved. It didn't move much, or far, but it most definitely moved. And, there had been a faint gleam in the heart of the darkness, like moonlight on a naked steel knife blade. The scout dropped to his knees. The sharp clatter of scattering pebbles mingled with a rapid, soft, thudding sound. Under the other noises Dade was able to make out a flat hissing growl that might have been a voice gabbling curses. The shape vanished into the hills beyond the huge rock. In a single uncoiling motion, Dade was on his feet, moving quickly as he darted for the shadow of the boulder. Behind him, Krista Black moved into position to cover his advance.

Dade slammed to a stop and put his back against the boulder. The jolt of flesh hitting rock was almost a joyful feeling to the Marine. It meant he was alive and engaged in the very activity he seemed to have been created for. A quick glance at Krista Black to ensure that she was ready to cover his play, and Dade spun around the corner of the huge rock, his rifle coming up into the firing position.

Beyond the boulder lay a broad expanse of relatively level ground. Rocks the size of small bushes dotted the plateau. Nothing moved in the rocky, open ground.

"Rick?"

"Yeah, Krista," Dade said, putting up his gun. "It's clear over here."

"I'm coming up."

"Come ahead." Though to an outsider, the exchange might have seemed silly, or condescending on Dade's part, it served an important purpose. In scouts' heightened state of readiness and awareness, the unexpected appearance of even his partner at Dade's side might have triggered an attack.

"What the hell was that?" Black's voice had taken on an almost-waspish hum. Dade knew his partner was naturally curious, and took mysteries of any kind as a challenge to be solved. These traits contributed to her success as a scout, but often made her seem short-tempered when thwarted.

"I dunno, Krista," Dade answered, scanning the plain once again. "Whatever it was, it vanished into thin air."

As he turned to face his partner, something drew his attention toward the ground.

"Krista, take a look at this." Dade stooped and gestured at a faint impression in a thin layer of loose dust that had built up at the base of the rock.

Black dropped to one knee and leaned over the spot Dade indicated.

"Rick, that's impossible." Black leaned in a bit closer to examine the single footprint.

"What is?" Dade knew the answer, but felt reluctant to say it.

"We've got a bare human footprint. But humans can't go barefoot on this rock because of the atmosphere," Black responded. "But then again, I doubt that he's human. Look at this guy. His feet are absolutely flat. The print has no arch whatsoever. He's got five toes, and they show no signs of separation or crowding. I'd bet he never wore any kind of foot gear. Sandals would separate the toes where the thongs went, and shoes, even well-fitting ones, tend to crowd the toes a bit.

"Besides, look here." Black gestured with her knife. "I don't think our boy ever clipped his toenails. See these gouges. They were left by his nails, or should I say his claws?"

Dade looked closely at the print as Black described it. "Any ideas?"

"Well, at first I thought it might have been a Zhykee," she replied. "But the briefing materials we've seen suggest that they've got long, narrow feet. Naw, this doesn't feel like Zhykee."

"Growlers, then, maybe a pup?"

"Again, no. If it was a Growler that left this track, it would be a heck of a lot deeper. Those critters are big and heavy. They wouldn't leave such a shallow track." Black shook her head. "Even if it was a pup, they've only got three toes, and the claw marks would be far more pronounced. In any event, I doubt that a Growler, even a pup, would have run away from just the two of us."

"So what do you think?"

"Well, Rick, if the captain is right about the Neo-Sovs," Black said, straightening from her crouch. "I think what we're looking at here might be a Cyclops's track. It doesn't really match the 'standard-issue Cyclops,' but I'd guess the Sovs might be field testing a 'new model' or something like that. Either that, or we're dealing with some new kind of alien critter."

"Yeah." Dade sighed. "In either case, we'd better call this one in."

"Record it, and keep moving," Captain Taggart told the scouts. "That's about all we can do until we have something more solid to go on."

"Falcon will comply," Dade said, and switched his communicator to standby.

Kneeling over the track, Dade aimed the small video

camera attached to the right side of his helmet at the foot-print, and held it there for a few seconds before carefully moving around the track so as to provide an all-aspect image. At last he switched the camera off. Pulling a dataclip from a pouch on his combat harness, Dade downloaded the image stored in the recorder's onboard memory into the permanent-storage device. Once the download was complete, Dade ejected and stowed the clip, hefted his rifle, and nodded to Krista Black.

"You wanna go first?"

"Oh thanks, Rick." She chuckled. "That's it, send the girl out first, so if I get wasted by some new Neo-Sov mon-ster, you'll at least have a little bit of warning, right?"

Dade laughed in return. No one in the platoon looked on Krista Black as a "girl," any more than they would con-sider Gunnery Sergeant Frost to be a "girl." To the mind of everyone in the platoon, they, and every other female mem-ber of the outfit, were Marines first. Anything else was sec-ondary. Everyone in Taggart's platoon was treated equally.

"Sure, Krista," Dade answered. "You know you're my chum, don't you?"

Black let out a full-throated laugh at the old running joke between them. She and Rick Dade were indeed friends of the highest degree, but the word had another meaning: the cut-up bloody fish parts used to bait sharks. It was a bit of gallows humor that said that scouts were often used as bait by their fellow Marines. It was a bit of humor that, for the most part, wasn't true.

Shaking her head in amusement, Black hefted her rifle and moved off down the trail.

Half an hour later, she and Dade were once again hunched over another sign that the Marines were not alone, either on the planet or in their use of the mountain trail.

Unlike the previous contact, where only a single track could be found, this latest spoor showed the passage of a number of the barefoot creatures.

Black looked at the ground in front of her. When they encountered the trail, she quickly picked out a set of tracks that was different from the others. The creature that had made those signs must have broken its foot at one time, but the injury had not been properly treated. Thus, when the damage healed, it left the inside of the right foot with an odd bump just behind the toes. She measured the creature's stride and determined it to be around forty-five centimeters, roughly the same as a normal, unburdened human's. From there it was a relatively simple task to mark out a forty-five-centimeter box, using one of the odd tracks as a reference point, and count the tracks which fell within its confines.

"How many?" Dade asked.

"Eight. But there's something else. See these long, skinny marks, here, and here, and here?" Black pointed at the deep gouges in the soil with the tip of her combat knife. "At first I thought those were drag marks, but they're too regular, too well defined. They've gotta be tracks, but I'm not too sure what left them. At least, I don't wanna think about what I think may have left them."

"Krista?" Dade prompted.

"A spider. A big-ass spider. I'm guessing it's some kind of weapon platform, or transport unit with spider legs rather than wheels or tracks."

"The Sovs don't have anything like that in their arsenal, do they?"

"Not that I know of," Black answered as she activated her helmet recorder camera. "Something's going on here Rick, and I don't like it."

13

L ion, this is Falcon. We're at local grid Whiskey-Foxtrot-six-six-three. We've cleared the hills and have visual contact with the wreck."

Captain Taggart lifted his hand to wave Gunnery Sergeant Frost over to him, but the gesture was unnecessary. Frost must have been monitoring the command frequency and was already making her way toward her commanding officer. Lieutenant Cortez was right on Frost's heels. As they made their way along the narrow trail, Taggart pulled from his breast pocket the strip map that had been computer-generated from the assault boat's sensors. The coordinates Dade had given were close to the left-hand edge of the chart and about a kilometer west of the platoon's current position.

"Got it, Falcon. Hold your position until the rest of the platoon catches up. We're about three-zero minutes behind you."

"Roger that," Dade answered laconically.

"Dade and Black have a visual on *Cabot*," he told the women, as they approached him. He touched the chart with a gloved forefinger. "They're just about here, if we can trust these blasted maps."

Frost looked at the chart.

"Y'know, boss, it's gonna be dark soon. It's at least another five klicks from where Dade is to the ship. Suggest we join up with the scouts, bivouac on their position, and start out again in the morning."

"Captain, we've taken almost two days to cross these bloody mountains," Cortez protested. "If we don't press on, it will be at least another full day before we reach the ship. I'm afraid we'll lose the survivors if we wait too long."

"I know all that, Doctor. But I have a few concerns, too," Taggart said wearily. He pointed at the map again. "Look here. See how close those contour lines are? I know map-reading isn't a skill they push in the Navy, but it should be obvious that close contour lines mean a steep slope. This thing is damn near vertical. Descending that slope is going to be dangerous enough in daylight. There is no way we can try it in the dark."

"Besides," Gunny Frost put in, "there are those unknown contacts that Dade and Black have been having. If they're Neo-Sovs, they'll be watching us. We stand a better chance against an ambush if we're in bivouac, with sentries, than we would making a night march, especially over bad terrain."

"That's only part of it, Gunny," Taggart cut in. "I'm more concerned about the actual descent. So far, we've had it pretty easy on this climb. We've only had a couple of really rough spots. But this"—he tapped the chart again—"this is going to be hard going. My troops could manage it, and maybe a few of your medics. The bulk of your people are going to need all the help they can get, and descending this slope in the dark isn't going to be any help to them at all. I'm sorry, Doctor, but my decision stands. We bivouac on Dade's position, and start out at first light."

"Yes, sir," Cortez snapped sarcastically, plainly unhappy with Taggart's ruling and with her inability to reason him out of his decision.

"Y'know something, boss?" Frost said, watching Cortez stalk away. "That woman may be a first-class pain in the butt, but I've got this feeling that, if I ever needed a doc, she'd be the first one I'd want working on me."

"You're probably right, Gunny." Taggart nodded in agreement. "I wouldn't want her in a combat unit, but I'd definitely want her around after the shooting stopped."

He sighed, then said, "All right, Gunny, we've got about an hour before dark. Let's keep 'em moving as quick as we can. I'd like to reach Dade as soon as we can. If we're lucky, we might get a look a the wreck before the light goes completely."

"There she is, sir," Dade said, pointing off to the southwest. Taggart's gaze followed the gesture and fell on a light gray arrow point resting on the valley floor. At a distance of over five thousand meters, he could barely see the vessel with his naked eye, but the powerful electronic binoculars made the details of the wrecked survey vessel frighteningly clear.

Cabot lay right side up on the valley floor. The after third of the vessel was gone, leaving a ragged mass of twisted metal where the massive engines had been. At first look, the rest of the ship seemed to be relatively intact. Then, as Taggart studied the wreck, he could see that she had been twisted along her long axis, and the hull had been split along the spine like a boned fish. Viewing the wreck through the electronic binoculars gave the scene an odd unreal quality. The ruined survey ship looked like a model assembled by a gigantic hobbyist and placed in the narrow valley, rather than a real spacecraft that had crash-landed on an alien world.

The wreck lay in a deep, sheer-sided canyon. Taggart scanned the site, studying every rise and depression in the valley floor. This intense scrutiny was intended to help him pick out an approach route that would afford his platoon and the medics they were escorting the most protection. As a side effect of Taggart's survey of the valley and its curious topography, he came to realize that the canyon before him was a rift valley, a deep gash in the earth caused by some long-ago earthquake. Taggart thought of the huge tear in the African coastline where Nova Cocarada had once been, gouged out by a tendril of energy that accompanied Earth's Induction into the Maelstrom. He wondered if this massive wound in Sierra Seven-Five's surface had been caused by a similar force.

As he surveyed the crash site, Captain Taggart's binoculars caught a faint twinkle of light atop *Cabot*'s ruined hull. He turned the instrument up to its maximum magnification, and was barely able to discern a tiny figure crawling across the twisted metal that had once been the ship's midships hull. Though he could not make out any details at that distance, he got the impression of a man trying to salvage some of the ship's superstructure. Scanning the rest of the crash site, Taggart was able to pick out a half dozen figures similar to the first. All seemed to be working on various parts of the ship as if laboring to remove what bits of the wreckage they found useful.

"Dr. Cortez?" he called. "Take a look at this. There are your survivors."

Cortez took the binoculars from the Marine officer and peered through them. For long moments she gazed at the scene in the valley below. At last she sighed, lowered the instruments, and passed them back to their owner.

"Well, Captain, it looks like you were right," she said quietly. The tone in her voice was a peculiar mixture of relief at the survivors' apparent condition and reluctance to admit that Taggart was right. "I guess we can wait until the morning."

"Yep," the Marine officer answered, taking a last look through the binoculars. The fading light of evening gleamed once again on a piece of wreckage being removed from *Cabot*'s superstructure. "They do seem to be doing all right for themselves."

Night came on quickly. No sooner had the Marines laid out the bivouac's perimeter than the shadows that had been rapidly lengthening across the valley below merged into a solid black shroud.

Only a few small pressurized tents had been erected. The rescue party used these in shifts to rest and eat their cold field rations. When Gunnery Sergeant Frost set the watch, she placed four sentries as opposed to the usual two. The whole arrangement made for grousing among the Marines, especially when one considered that the medical personnel were being exempted from guard duty. Instead of being forced to spend the night either walking a sentry-go, or resting as best they could on the cold hard ground, still wearing their combat environment suits, the medics were allowed the relative ease of the pressure tents. If the Marines had any consolation, it was in the fact that Taggart would only allow three of the small tents to be erected. That would make things awfully crowded, with eleven medics crammed into the shelters' relatively tiny interiors.

The Marines knew the reason the medics were to be afforded even that slim comfort. By the next nightfall, there was a good chance that the medical team would be called upon to render aid to *Cabot*'s injured, possibly dying survivors. The more rest the medics got, the better able they'd be to cope with the trials that lay before them.

Taggart was no more happy about the arrangement than his men were. He sat on a flat stone which reminded him of a torso-sized chunk of red sandstone, wishing for a cup of hot coffee. He might as well have wished the Earth and all its inhabitants out of the Maelstrom. He had given the order for a cold camp himself.

The sight of the wrecked ship in the valley below had combined with the odd sightings, which had multiplied since the team took its first two casualties at the cliff face, to make him feel distinctly uneasy. There had never been direct contact with the beings who seemed to be dogging the rescue party. Taggart hoped it would remain that way, but he knew in the pit of his stomach, in a way known only to combat veterans, that this wish would no more be granted than would his desire for hot coffee.

"Cold, isn't it, sir?"

"Yeah, Gunny, it is." Taggart looked up at his subordinate. "Going to get colder, too."

"Yeah," Frost confirmed. "Well, sir, I've got the watch set. Four men on at a time, two-hour shifts. You want me to deploy remotes, too?"

Taggart considered Frost's proposal to ring the bivouac with remote sensor units.

"No, Gunny, I don't think we need to put out any remotes. Just make sure the sentries stay alert—" He broke off, cocking his head to one side, listening.

A chill wind had suddenly arisen. The breeze seemed to drive long needles of cold through Taggart's gloves and boots into his hands and feet. Accompanying the wind as it snaked its way through the rocky crags, there arose a faint, but audible moaning. Taggart felt his scalp prickle as the sound climbed and fell in pitch. The weird muttering was almost musical, and reminded him of the sound made by the alien sculpture the scouts had discovered in the abandoned city. He had reviewed Black's recording of the statue. Even considering the tinny quality of the sound track, the moaning produced by the alien artifact was enough to make one's flesh crawl. The deep, thin wailing of the wind in the rocks had much the same effect.

He glanced at Sergeant Frost, who had brought her Jackal up in a purely reflexive action.

"Great," she said, with a strange tone in her voice. "That's all we freaking need."

"Easy, Gunny." Taggart got to his feet and laid a hand on her shoulder.

She flinched.

"Onawa, what is it?"

Frost shook her head with a short, bitter laugh of self-deprecation.

"That sound, it goes straight through me." She lowered her shotgun and laughed again. "When I was a child, my grandfather used to tell us stories. Thinking back on them now, I'd say that he probably made them all up, but back then, they scared the pants off of us. He told one about the Manitou, how they'd come in the night and carry off children and eat them. He had one of my older cousins hiding in the darkness with a bullroarer. I don't know how they arranged it, but while he told the story, my cousin would swing the roarer and make this weird muttering sound. Ever since then, that sound just sends chills through me."

Frost laughed again, this time genuinely amused. "Big,

tough gunnery sergeant, eh, getting all unraveled by a little bit of wind."

"Don't sweat it, Gunny," Taggart said somberly. "This whole trip is enough to give anyone the creeps. Sit down a bit. I'll take a look at the sentries."

"No sir," Frost said quickly. "I'm all right."

"Gunny . . ."

"Really, Max," she insisted, calling Taggart by his given name for the first time in his memory. "I'm okay. I'll do my job."

"All right, Gunny," the captain said, knowing that Frost would not allow the demons of a childhood fear to interfere with her duty to her platoon, her commanding officer, or her Corps. "I'm gonna try to get some kip. If nothing happens, wake me in four hours."

Something hard latched on to Taggart's upper left arm and began to worry the limb as a terrier would a rat. He groped at his combat harness, scrambling to find the big Ka-Bar combat knife hanging on his left breast. Another creature, equally strong and hard as the first, grasped his right wrist, pinning it in place.

"Captain! Captain, it's me, Frost."

"What?" Taggart sat up, a qualm of revulsion shaking his body as the Mohawk gunnery sergeant released his wrist and arm.

"Sorry, boss. You told me to wake you in four hours. " She cocked her head to one side. "Nightmare?"

"Gaaaah." Taggart sighed, panting. He tried to rub his face, but his closed helmet visor prohibited such a gesture. "Dunno, Gunny. I don't know. Just feeling weird, I guess. Give me a minute."

It had gotten colder, and the wind had picked up. What

had been a low muttering sound was now the ghastly sob of a dying animal. Was it that sound that had invaded his sleeping mind and transformed Frost's gently shaking hands into a pair of voracious monsters? Taggart shivered again, but not from the cold.

"Okay, Gunny," he said, mastering himself. "What's up?"

"You told me to wake you in four hours, sir," Frost replied, tapping her chrono.

"Aaah, yeah." Taggart found himself wishing again for that cup of coffee, as the last vestiges of the uncomfortable dreams faded from his mind. The dullness that sometimes accompanies a sudden waking was likewise evaporating. "Anything to report?"

"Not really, sir." Frost offered a hand and helped Taggart to his feet. "Well, nothing new anyway. You already know the wind picked up, and it's gotten colder. This damn racket is making it hard to hear anything else, but some of the sentries have been hearing that same scrabbling noise. We can't tell if it's rocks loosened by the wind rattling down the slope, or if there really is something out there."

"Anybody see anything?"

"Nope. Nothing." Frost shook her head and shrugged. "I've had the sentries switching off using their starlight gear, you know, to save their eyes? Even with the low-light stuff, they haven't been able to see a damn thing."

"Something new the boys in Moscow cooked up?" Taggart speculated. "Something that masks a soldier from starlight?"

"I dunno, boss. It doesn't feel that way. Maybe it is the Manitou coming to eat us," she said, half-seriously.

Taggart gave her an old-fashioned look. "Go get some sleep, Gunny. Come morning, you're gonna need it."

14

r. Cortez, oh-six-hundred, Lieutenant. Time to move."

Before Rebecca Cortez was fully conscious, the Marine who had been detailed to wake her was gone. For a moment, she looked suspiciously at the other medics sharing the small pressurized shelter tent. There was an odd tightness in her chest, and the lingering scent of decay in her nostrils. She felt as though she had been locked in a room full of corpses and foul air and was still not certain that this was not the dream, and the charnel house the reality.

She flexed her hands, working the night's stiffness out of them. The fingers were normal flesh-and-blood digits, attached to normal flesh-and-blood hands. Why did she have the feeling that they should have been bone, covered only by a few scraps of ragged flesh?

Cortez shook her head to drive away the last of the sleep-formed cobwebs enshrouding her brain, realizing that the uncomfortable feeling in the pit of her stomach was only the persistent aftereffect of a nightmare. She shook awake the two other medics sharing her tent, eliciting groans of protest from the sleeping doctors. As she groped around the tent, looking for her environment suit's helmet, gloves, and boots, she realized that it was much warmer than it had been when she had fastened the shelter's pressure seal eight hours earlier. The wind had ceased, as well.

"Come on, you two," she said as she fastened her boots. "I want to get moving as quickly as possible today. I don't care what Taggart says. I don't want those survivors to be without aid any longer than possible."

"Yeah, yeah." Barb Moran groaned, sitting up. "We're on it, right, Kate?"

"Yeah, we're on it, Lieutenant," Katherine Howard, a surgical nurse, muttered as she rubbed her eyes.

It took Moran and Howard a few minutes to gather their wits and seal up their environment suits. As Cortez waited for the others to dress, she observed them as carefully as she could without seeming to stare. Though no one said anything, the team's chief medical officer got the distinct impression that neither woman had slept well. Moran, a burn specialist, was her usual grouchy self this morning. Howard was usually so perky, even after a night on the cold ground, that the rest of the team threatened to sedate her until after noon. But there was no good humor about her today.

"Good morning Doctor. Sleep well?" Captain Taggart greeted her as she crawled from the tent. His tone suggested that he knew she hadn't. His bloodshot, dark-circled eyes suggested that he hadn't either.

"No," Cortez growled. "How soon do you want to get moving?"

"Whenever your people are ready."

"All right." Cortez rolled her neck to work out the kinks in her muscles. "I want to do an equipment check before we move down into the valley. I want to be sure that nothing important got broken along the way."

"All right," Taggart said, looking at his chrono. "How long do you figure?"

"An hour, maybe a bit more," Cortez answered.

"All right," he repeated. "What do you need from me?"

"Just have your Marines bring in whatever equipment they were given to carry," Cortez said tersely. "My people will do the rest."

"Do you need the pressure shelters to do your check?"

"Well, it would make things more comfortable, but no," Cortez said, finally mustering a thin smile. "We can do it without the shelters."

"Fine," Taggart said. "Gunny Frost will help you get things squared away. Now if you'll excuse, me, Doctor, I'll see about getting those shelters down, and send my scouts to find us a way down into that valley."

"Dr. Cortez, we have a problem."

"What is it, George?" Cortez looked up from the notebook computer she had been using to check off supplies and equipment as her team inspected their gear.

"Half of our antibiotics and injectable painkillers are missing. So is one of the field surgery kits," Dr. George Grippo, Cortez's first assistant, said angrily.

"Are you sure, George?"

"Of course I'm sure," Grippo snapped. "The surgery kit was in my pack. I checked it before we turned in last night. Now it's gone, along with my watch and my notepad computer. The drugs were in Norwood's pack. He says they were there last night, and now they're gone."

Immediately, the notion came to her that the Marines, spurred by an age-old interservice rivalry between themselves and the Navy, had taken medical supplies. At the same time, she suspected the theft might be an attempt to make her, a Mexican Contribution Force officer, appear to be incompetent, even foolish. From a back corner of her mind, that part of her reason, still unaffected by the suspicious nature she adopted to defend herself from the bigots in the Union Armed Forces, shouted at her.

Why? the silent voice cried out. *Why would they do it?*

Cortez ignored the question, letting a wave of self-righteous anger sweep over her.

"Goddamn jarheads!" Thrusting the notebook computer into Grippo's hands, Cortez barked, "Here, finish the inventory. I'm going to go tear Taggart's head off. This isn't funny."

Without waiting for Grippo to acknowledge her order, Cortez stormed across the small bivouac.

Taggart was leaning over a strip map conferring with Gunnery Sergeant Frost and his scouts. Shouldering Krista Black aside, she grabbed the captain by the arm and snarled, "Just what the hell kind of mental deficients are you people? I understand interservice rivalry, and I understand pranks, but this isn't a prank, Captain, this is stupidity, and it could cost someone their life."

Taggart didn't reply immediately. Instead he snaked his arm over hers, reversing the hold she had on his biceps into a solid grip on her own. He firmly pulled her away from the group. With his free hand he signaled his troops to stay put.

"Now, what the hell are you talking about?" he growled, his voice taking on a dangerous edge.

For a moment Cortez glared at him, uncertain which made her more furious, the theft of her team's supplies, or the way in which Taggart had manhandled her. He seemed to read her thoughts.

"If you're torqued off about being pushed around, don't be. You're an officer, God damn it, one of the senior officers on this team. Try to act like one, not like some jumped-up freaking civilian in an S-Corps uniform. You bloody well ought to know better than to start a fight with another officer, especially in front of enlisteds. Now what the hell are you talking about? What isn't funny?"

"Some of our gear is missing," Cortez blustered to cover her embarrassment. Taggart was right on one point. She knew that she should not have confronted him in front of his troops. "A surgical pack and some drugs. If your goddamn jarheads took them as a joke, it isn't funny. And whoever took them also took Dr. Grippo's watch and personal notepad computer. It's not funny," she repeated.

"Doctor," Taggart said, gritting his teeth. "My men are professionals. They may not be above pulling some bonehead stunts when they're off duty. But when they're in the field, they know lives are on the line, and they don't act like addled fraternity rats.

"May I remind you, *Doctor*, that this isn't the first equipment that's gone missing on this trip?"

"What?" Cortez came up short, confusion warring with anger on her face. Realization won out over both. "The cliff. Your man Kowalski, they never found his rifle, did they?"

"No they didn't," Taggart snapped. "All they found was his pistol, a few spent shell casings and Dr. Ake's helmet, and remember the condition they found *that* in. We've been calling that a climbing accident, when Kowalski got hurt, I mean." Taggart shook his head and sighed. "I'm starting to wonder if it *was* a climbing accident."

"What are you trying to say, Captain, that it was deliberate?"

"That is exactly what I'm saying, Doctor." He gave less

of a sarcastic edge to Cortez's title this time. "I'm starting to wonder if that 'accident' wasn't the result of some kind of booby trap we didn't see. We know we aren't alone on this rock. The footprints Dade and Black have been finding and those shapes in the dark prove that. I'm starting to wonder if whoever else is on-planet killed those two men and took their bodies and their gear. They're probably the same ones who stole your equipment and supplies last night."

"Right," Cortez scoffed. Her heart said he was lying to cover for his men, though her mind told her what he was saying was probably correct. "Are you seriously trying to tell me that some intruder sneaked into this encampment, past armed Marines on sentry duty, stole our stuff, and only our stuff, and then sneaked out again without being noticed? Come on, Captain, I don't buy it."

"Why not? Black and Dade could probably manage it, if conditions were right, and they're only human. What about aliens, eh? According to our briefings, the Zhykee seem to have the ability to move unseen among humans. Is it inconceivable that another race might have developed a similar ability?"

Cortez stared at the Marine captain for a few seconds. What he said made sense, but she didn't like to think that she had misjudged the situation.

"Boss, I hate to bother you, but we've got *another* problem."

There was something in the way Gunnery Sergeant Frost looked at her that made Cortez wonder if the noncom hadn't been listening in on the argument with Taggart.

"What is it, Gunny?" Taggart asked, his eyes never leaving Cortez's.

"Two of my men, Jones and Persio, are missing their weapons," Frost said, her voice a level monotone that carried more accusation than if she had jabbed a finger into the doctor's face. "A couple of the other guys are missing some of their gear and small personal items, too."

Taggart half turned to look at Frost, who was standing two meters behind his left shoulder.

"So, Doctor, what happened here?" he said with a surprising evenness in his voice. "Did your medics steal my guys' guns? Or did my men lose their weapons and then raid your supplies to cover their own stupidity? Or is it possible that someone or something slipped into this bivouac, swiped the missing gear, and then sneaked out again, without being spotted? If you say no, Doctor, then you're an even bigger fool than I thought you were."

For a moment, her temper, which had been waning, flared again, as Taggart touched a raw nerve. She was *not* a fool! Then Rebecca Cortez was forced to agree that the Marine captain was probably correct in his assessment of what happened to the missing equipment.

"All right, Captain," she said wearily. "Now what? I suppose you want to launch a search for whoever stole the stuff?"

"Gunny?"

"Already under way, boss," Frost replied. "I got Dade and Black working on it now. Thing is, there are so damn many of our own footprints around the camp that they don't think they'll be able to turn up much in the way of a trail, unless you want them to widen their search."

"Captain," Cortez cut in. "Our missing gear may be expensive, but it isn't really critical. I planned for redundancy in our supplies and equipment. If you allow your scouts to spend too much time hunting for the stolen equipment, it's going to cost us another day. No matter what we saw, or think we saw, last night, I don't want to leave those people unattended for another twenty-four hours."

"I think the doctor is right, sir," Frost added. "The scouts aren't too hopeful about finding a trail. We might as well get started."

"All right, Doctor. Finish up your equipment check and get your people ready to move as soon as possible." Taggart turned to Frost. "Gunny, tell Jones and Persio I want to see them."

The doctor and the noncom moved off to complete their assigned tasks, while Captain Taggart remained behind. With a sigh, he sat on a large flat stone, and waited.

Privates Winslow Jones and Adrian Persio appeared in short order. Their body language told Taggart that the Marines were feeling a mixture of apprehension, embarrassment, and self-condemning anger. They were professionals; more than that, they were Marines, and every Marine, regardless of his military occupation specialty, was considered a rifleman first. One of the Corps' oldest traditions was that every Marine was expected to take care of his rifle. Losing one's weapon was a serious violation of that tradition.

"Well, gentlemen," Taggart said, as the Marines stood at rigid attention before him. "I'm waiting."

"Sir, we don't know what happened, sir," Persio said. His accent proclaimed him to be a member of the Canadian Contribution Forces. "We both had our weapons when we turned in last night. I don't know how anybody could have stolen them, sir."

"That right, Jones?"

"Sir, that's right, sir," Jones replied, the concrete canyons of New York City echoing in his voice. "Persio 'n' me, we came off guard duty about oh-four-hunnerd. I rolled right inta da' sack. We was both sleepin' onna ground in the open between the south perimeter and the docs' tents." Jones halfheartedly gestured in that direction. "I had my 'bull, right beside me all night long, or at least I t'ought so. When I woke up this mornin', it was gone."

"I see. Well, gentlemen, now what am I supposed to do with you?" Taggart pushed himself up from his stony seat and stood in front of his chagrined troopers. "I have two combat Marines who managed to lose their rifles. What are you two going to do if we run into a firefight, throw rocks? I'd really like to know, gentlemen, because unless you figure out a way to build a couple of M-18s in the next five minutes, you're going to be useless if we run into a spit-storm. No! You'll be worse than useless, you'll be a bloody hazard, 'cause instead of looking out for your buddies, you'll have to look out for yourselves, and the rest of this platoon will *still* have to be looking out for your sorry hides."

"Sir, we still have our Pugs, sir," Persio said hopefully. "And I've got grenades."

"Oh, that's great." Taggart had yet to raise his voice, which somehow made the chewing out sound even worse. The harsh, quiet tone told them he was more disappointed in them than he was angry.

"That's just great," he repeated. "Pistols and hand grenades. And what if we run into something bigger than a cockroach, huh? What if there are Growlers out there, or Zhykee? What if it *is* only the Neo-Soviets, but they really *have* got a Cyclops with them? What good are your Pugs and grenades gonna do then? All right," Taggart snorted and shook his head in disgusted amazement. "You're both on re-port. I'll figure out what to do with you when we make it back to Luna. Meantime, go see Gunny Frost, see if she can't figure out a way to straighten out this damn mess you've gotten us into. Dismissed."

As harsh as the reprimand might seem to a civilian, the situation warranted a response. Taggart might have chewed them out for a lack of vigilance, but whoever stole the rifles and the medical team's supplies had sneaked past the unit's sentries, who hadn't lapsed in their watchfulness. The captain would have bet his life on that.

Jones and Persio snapped him a pair of mirror-image salutes, then the pair executed a crisp about face and went off in search of Gunny Frost. Taggart knew the Gunnery Sergeant would ream them out in a more powerful and colorful manner than he did. He also knew that Frost would come up with a way for the now rifleless men to redeem themselves.

15

It was an hour past dawn by the time Cortez and her medical team completed their equipment check. During that time, Rick Dade and Krista Black had scoured the area around the bivouac, searching both for any traces of the stolen equipment and for an easy way down into the valley below.

The scouts found a number of false leads on both trails. One set of tracks, identical to the single imprint they'd found earlier, led northward into the hills in a straight line. Along that trail, the scouts recovered a drab green case with a black caduceus printed on the surface. The box contained the missing antibiotics. Unfortunately the trail petered out before any more equipment could be recovered.

The scouts had better luck finding a trail down into the valley.

At first, there seemed to be no path leading down the almost-sheer sides of the rift. But after an hour's worth of passing back and forth along the edge of the plateau where the rescue team had spent the night, Rick Dade spotted a steep, narrow path running to the south.

"I'll be a son of a . . ." Dade cursed under his breath. "I can't believe we missed this."

He looked at the trail, assessing it as a pathway into the valley below. Though it was narrow, no more than a meter wide in some places, the grade was not severe, perhaps only ten or twelve percent. An unburdened man might walk it with ease. The burdened Marines and medics of the rescue team would need to exercise caution, but they should have no major problems following the trail.

"What do you think, Rick?" Krista Black asked.

"I think this is our best bet. I can't understand how we missed it. We walked past the dang thing at least four times."

"I know," Black replied. "I'm starting to wonder if the laws of physics apply on this freaking planet."

"I don't know, Krista," Dade said. "That isn't in my department."

The scout switched channels, contacting his platoon leader.

"Lion, this is Falcon. We've got a trailhead about two-zero-zero meters south of the bivouac. It looks like it runs straight down to the valley floor. Should Falcon investigate?"

"Falcon, this is Lion," Taggart replied. "Mark your spot, and then go ahead and take a look. If the trail pans out, advise us, and continue your reconnaissance along the designated route. We'll be about ten minutes behind you."

"Roger, Lion. Falcon will comply." Dade turned to his partner. "Okay, we're on the clock."

Descending the sloping pathway into the valley proved to be easier than the scouts had anticipated. The ten-degree downslope was gentle enough that safety ropes would not be needed. Though there were narrow places, most of the trail was wide enough that even the untrained medics would be able to negotiate it with relative ease. Dade and Black made the descent in less than half an hour.

There was one odd thing. About halfway down the trail, they discovered a patch of light-colored stones. Among the flat, off-beige rocks there lay a dozen or so of a chocolate-brown color. When Black investigated the disparity, she perceived that the darker stones had been kicked out of their original resting places. Though the environment suit's thick gloves prevented her from touching the displaced stones, she felt certain that the dark surface would be cool and slightly moist to the touch. To her skilled tracker's mind, such a trace indicated that the rocks had been kicked over less than twelve hours previously, probably sometime during the night. Otherwise, the heat of the previous day would have dried the dark brown soil clinging to the now exposed underside of the stones to the same tan powder adhering to the surrounding rocks.

"You think it was the guys who raided the camp last night?" Dade asked, already knowing the answer.

"I'd bet on it," Black said, brushing the dust from her knees as she straightened. "If the bad guys are using this trail, I'd say we've got a 'proceed with caution' going here."

"A-ffirmative," Dade said. He spoke quickly into his helmet communicator, apprising Captain Taggart of their find. Then, closing the connection, he addressed his partner. "I gotta tell ya, Krista, this whole mission gives me the creeps. If it was the Neo-Sovs who shot *Cabot* down, why didn't they finish her off? If they're the ones who have been dogging us ever since we landed on this frigging rock, why haven't they ambushed us, instead of pulling all this *Twilight Zone* crud? Why would the Sovs sneak into camp and steal some of our gear instead of greasing us all? I'm telling you, it just doesn't add up."

"You don't think it *might be* the Sovs, using us to test out a new kind of mutant or something like that?"

"It could be," Dade allowed. For a moment he let his rifle hang from its assault sling. He tugged at his combat harness, shifting the nylon straps and pouches into a more comfortable position. "But that's kind of a stretch, don't you think? They set up a base all the way out here, lure in a survey ship, shoot it down, and use it as bait. That's pretty thin, Krista."

"Yeah, but it's happened before," she replied. "Remember the brushfire wars in Southeast Asia? The bad guys there would use captured distress radios to call in rescue birds, and then shoot them down."

"I know all that," Dade said. "But it doesn't feel right. Personally? I think we're in a first-contact situation here, and the bad guys are as curious about us as we are about them."

"And that's why they greased Kowalski and Ake, and then carried off their bodies?"

"Makes sense, doesn't it? I mean, unless they're cannibals."

"Oh thanks for the wonderful image, Rick," Black said with a grim cheerfulness. "Just for that, you can lead off for a while."

Dade chuckled wryly, hefted his Pitbull, and started down the trail.

As the scouts made their way down the narrow trail, Captain Taggart and Dr. Cortez walked to the edge of the small plateau that had been the team's bivouac, to have another look at the wrecked survey ship. *Cabot* looked to be in no better shape by daylight than she did the evening before. Nothing moved in the valley below, reinforcing Taggart's impression of the crash site as little more than a giant diorama.

"Odd, don't you think?" Cortez said, more to herself than to the Marine officer. "Last night there was all sorts of activity down there. Now the site might well be abandoned."

"Yeah," Taggart answered. Then after a brief pause. "Doctor, there is something else that we haven't considered. Up until now, we've been assuming that the figures we saw last night were survivors of *Cabot*'s crew. I think we have to face the possibility that they could have been Neo-Sovs, or they could have been aliens."

Cortez stepped back, lowering her binoculars. Clearly the notion had not occurred to her either.

"But that would mean . . ."

"Yes, Doctor," Taggart agreed grimly. "That would mean that any survivors have been taken prisoner, or there was never anyone left alive down there to rescue."

While Taggart and Cortez looked over the crash site, the scouts descended the narrow sloping pathway without discovering any more traces of the mysterious individuals who seemed to have taken such an interest in the rescue party. They paused briefly to check the strip map Captain Taggart had given them. The route laid out on the narrow, computer-generated chart showed the path they were supposed to follow toward the downed survey ship. The scouts knew that, though the course had been laid out by their commanding officer, they were not obligated to follow it blindly. As highly trained professional warriors whose particular skills gave them an almost instinctive feel for terrain, lines of march, enemy presence and the like, they could leave the predetermined route at their discretion, should circumstances warrant it.

The road Taggart had selected was easy going, a broad, flat section of valley floor that seemed to be relatively free of obstacles or of enclosed places that might conceal an enemy ambush. The scouts moved in an easy, energy-conserving walk. At irregular intervals, one or both of them would pause to look and listen, searching for signs of the presence of an unseen enemy. It was not long before they found such a trace.

Only a kilometer from the bottom of the trail, Dade came to a halt, dropping to one knee. He felt, rather than saw, Krista Black do the same. Looking around, he strained his eyes and ears for sounds or movements that might indicate danger. When he saw none, he held out his left hand, the first two fingers pointed at the ground. He wiggled those digits to indicate a man walking and pointed again at the ground in front of him. Then, with a choppy wave of his hand, he motioned Black to join him.

When his partner arrived, they set themselves back-to-back. Dade knew Krista was marginally the better tracker. He positioned himself to watch the team's back trail. Black knelt behind him, where she could examine the tracks.

"Hmmm. Looks like eight, maybe ten, of those barefoot mutants," Black said. "Tracks are a little scuffed, though. Looks like they might be packing heavy." She touched the long gouges with a gloved forefinger. "Looks like another of those spider-walkers, or else the same one again. I gotta tell you, Rick, the more we see these tracks, the less it feels like the Neo-Sovs. You think we just *might* be in a first-contact situation here?"

"I don't know what to think, Krista, about this whole damn mission." There was an unfamiliar note of anger and frustration in Dade's voice as he got to his feet. "You call it in to the boss. I'll stay on point for a while."

Two kilometers farther on, Dade stopped again. The preplanned course had taken the scouts into an area of soft ground littered with numerous outcroppings of stone. Most of these heaps of white, limestonelike rock were knee-high. A few were taller than a man. Many of the outcroppings were decorated with the fantastic crystalline growths that the Marines had seen all along the "Roman road" through the hills. In the middle of these cairns, the scouts found another set of tracks, similar to those they had encountered earlier. Here there were more of the large bare footprints that had become so aggravatingly familiar. There were also numerous gouges left in the soil by the passage of what Krista Black had dubbed the spider-walker.

"I don't think it's the same bunch as before," Dade said. "There are more tracks here, and look at this." He pointed at a set of walker tracks. "See how these gouges aren't a single channel, but three of them all clustered together? I think we're looking at another machine here."

"I think you're right, Rick," Black agreed. "The spacing between the tracks is wider, too. Unless this guy was moving at speed, we're talking a bigger machi—"

A loud, harsh *pop* echoed among the stones, followed by the muted clang of metal striking metal.

Dade looked up sharply, as his partner broke off. She was twisting her upper body like a cat trying to control its fall. She was barely able to get her hands under her before she landed heavily. Her rifle was caught between the ground and her chest. The weapon's raised-sight/carrying-handle assembly drove into her abdomen, forcing the breath from her lungs in an explosive *whuff* that Dade heard clearly without the aid of a communicator.

Dade dropped to the ground next to his partner, breaking his fall with the butt of his M-18. He tucked the rifle in close to his body and rolled quickly to his left. The move was intended to throw off the aim of anyone who might have been targeting him, as well as to bring him under the shelter of a stone outcropping.

"Krista," he hissed, his attention divided between his stricken partner and the search for an aggressor. "Krista, are you all right?"

His only answer was a whooping gasp.

Something moved among the rocks a few dozen meters away. Instinctively, Dade brought up his rifle and let off a three-round burst. Chips of stone flew from the outcropping where he had seen movement. The shriek of spent and mangled slugs ricocheting off of the rocks was all but blanketed by the echoes of the rifle's stuttering bark.

"Rick," Black rasped out. "Rick, I'm okay. I just got the wind knocked out of me."

"Can you move?" he barked.

"Yeah, I think so."

"Then move, dammit! Get under cover."

Black rolled away from her partner, turning over twice before scuttling forward in a low crawl, to take up position behind a meter-and-a-half-high pile of white stone.

"Lion, Lion, this is Falcon, FLASH! SITREP! Falcon is under attack from an unknown number of hostiles. Request immediate support."

A trio of pneumatic reports split the air. Something ricocheted off the outcropping in front of Dade, shattering one of the delicate crystal "bushes," showering the Marine scout with glittering ruby shards. Black snapped up her rifle and let off a burst. Her attack was rewarded by a sharp, animal yelp of pain. Then, silence.

The exchange of gunfire blanketed Captain Taggart's reply.

Dade rolled right. Carefully, he peered around the edge of his sheltering rock, searching for signs of the enemy. Nothing moved among the stones. He looked across at Black, who shook her head. Either they had driven the enemy off, or he had gone to ground and was waiting for the Marines to make the next move.

"Dade, what the hell is going on down there?" Taggart snarled from Dade's communicator.

"Lion, situation unknown," Dade answered quietly, continuing to scan the area as he spoke. "The enemy may have withdrawn, or he may have just gone to ground. Falcon Two took a round, but seems to be unhurt. C'mon in, Captain, we aren't too proud to ask for help."

Switching his communicator to standby, Dade raised his left hand, snapping his gloved fingers in a silent demand for Black's attention. When she looked toward her partner, he placed the palm of his left hand on top of his head, instructing Black to cover him. She nodded her understanding, and brought her rifle up into firing position. She kept her head raised, looking over the weapon, observing the whole area, rather than just the narrow field of view afforded by the Pitbull's sights.

Dade rolled back to his left and crawled carefully around the end of the outcropping. When he'd crawled a few meters forward and left to the shelter of a waist-high pile of stone, he rolled right and came up on his knees, his rifle at the ready.

The movement seemed to be the cue the unseen enemy was waiting for. Another flurry of reports echoed across the valley. Dade spotted what appeared to be a human head covered with thick shaggy black hair. He snapped his rifle up and touched off two rapid stuttering bursts. The head vanished.

Then Dade realized that though the being he had fired on appeared to be human, it was not wearing an environment suit. Perhaps the target had been some new kind of Neo-Soviet mutant, one created specifically to endure atmospheres hostile to normal humans.

"Krista, did you see that?"

"Yeah, it looked human—well, sort of." Black sounded as confused as he felt.

"Yeah, sort of."

Black's voice became a shout. "Rick, nine o'clock!"

Dade spun to his left, bringing his Pitbull up to his shoulder as he dodged. Less than three meters away, charging at him, was an ugly humanoid creature. A wicked-looking metal club clenched in its fist, the being rushed headlong at the Marine. Dade heard Black cursing, knowing that he was blocking her shot at his attacker.

The creature was upon him before he could bring his rifle to bear. The saw-edged club looped in toward Dade's face. Frantically, he brought the Pitbull up to cross-block the attack. Though his humanoid foe was a full head shorter than Dade, the strength of the blow that smashed into the Pitbull's receiver was astounding. Had the club struck his head, Dade would have died from a crushed skull. Cocking the rifle back over his shoulder, Dade lashed out at the creature with the Pitbull's reinforced plastic stock. The butt stroke should have taken his enemy squarely in the face. But, with surprising speed, the creature slipped aside. The club again licked out. Dade twisted, desperately trying to avoid the blow. If the creature scored a hit, that saw-edged club would rip a hole in Dade's combat environment suit. Death from exposure to the ammonia- and carbon dioxide-laden atmosphere would be neither pretty nor quick.

On the edges of his awareness, Dade heard the stuttering report of Black's assault rifle. He vaguely wondered if she had seen an opening to fire, or if more of the ugly creatures had decided to join the fight.

Dade tried to take a long step backwards so he could fire the rifle. But before he could level the weapon at his attacker, the creature suddenly changed its tactics. The thing made a halfhearted swipe at Dade's face again, which the Marine avoided easily. Lunging forward, the being dropped its club, letting the weapon dangle from a lanyard looped around its wrist. With both hands, the thing seized Dade's rifle, trying to twist the Pitbull from his grasp.

Dade lashed out with his right foot, aiming for the creature's left knee. He missed, catching the thing in its shin. The impact felt as though Dade had kicked a small tree trunk. The creature seemed to sense the Marine's desperation. It gave a mighty heave on the Pitbull, finally tearing it from Dade's clutching fingers.

The thing tipped back its head and let out a guttural snarl of triumph. Dade saw a mouthful of snaggled, rotting teeth. Fighting a qualm of revulsion, the Marine lance corporal yanked his heavy Pug automatic pistol free of its holster. Its trophy secure, the creature was loping off among the rocks. Dade centered the Pug's sights on the thing's back and squeezed the trigger twice in rapid succession.

Both shots went home. The humanoid monster dropped the Pitbull, staggered, and pitched over on its face. From the corner of his eye, Dade saw a shadow bearing down on him. He spun to face it, the big pistol grasped firmly in both hands.

"Rick! Rick, we're clear!" Krista Black shouted as the Pug's sights lined up with her chest.

Dade sighed, and lowered the pistol.

"Krista, you took a hit. Are you okay?"

"Yeah," Black said, still a bit breathless. "Whatever they hit me with tore the heck out of my ruck, but I don't think it got anything important."

"Lemmee take a look."

Black turned and dropped to one knee to allow her partner to examine the damage. The enemy projectile had torn the top flap of her rucksack almost completely away. Some of her gear had spilled out of the gash as she rolled and dodged during the brief firefight.

"Hang on a second. I think . . ." Dade reached into her pack, grasped a shiny sliver of metal, and tugged it free. "Yup, there it is. That's what they hit you with. It was jammed against your pack frame."

Black stared at the heavy metal spike, almost a handspan long and as thick as her gloved finger.

"Dang, if they'd have hit me solid with one of these . . ."

"Even if they'd have grazed you," Dade amended. "The atmosphere would have finished the job. That spike look familiar?"

"Yeah," Black answered. "It's just like those we found along the trail."

"Uh-huh," her partner confirmed. "What in the hell were those things?"

"I don't know." Black shook her head and shrugged. "I think you dropped that last one. Let's go have a look."

When the Marines reached the spot where Dade's attacker had fallen, they found the stolen Pitbull lying next to a pool of dark, reddish purple fluid.

"I would have sworn you killed it," Black said in awe.

Dade retrieved his weapon and examined it closely. The creature's saw-edged club had gouged the metal of the rifle's upper receiver. Dade dropped the magazine and worked the Pitbull's bolt several times. Satisfied that the damage was only superficial, he replaced the curved thirty-round box and chambered a fresh cartridge.

"I thought I killed it, too, Krista," he said. "That's an awful lot of blood if I didn't. Assuming that purple goo *is* that thing's blood. How 'bout you? You drop any of 'em?"

"Yeah, I think so. We'd better check."

A search of the rocky outcroppings yielded several more puddles of reddish purple ooze, and dozens of bare footprints. Next to one of the larger pools of what the Marines assumed was blood, lay what appeared to be a big pneumatic spike driver. It looked like an oversize pistol. The gaping muzzle was big enough to accept the spike Dade had pulled out of Black's backpack.

"What a nasty hell of a weapon!" she said.

"Uh-huh," Dade agreed. "I guess we can be happy they didn't bring up whatever heavy weapons they mount on those spider-walkers."

"Yeah." Black sighed. "I think we'd better call the boss, let him know it's over and we're all right."

16

Captain Taggart reviewed the digital recording of his scouts' firefight with the strange creatures. After watching the video for the third time, he passed the data reader to Gunnery Sergeant Frost. Taggart waited, withholding comment, until she had seen the recordings.

"Well, Dade, Black, do you have anything to add?" he asked in a flat voice.

"No sir," Dade answered. "Everything happened pretty much as you saw it. We took incoming fire, Krista got knocked down, then things hit the fan."

Dr. Cortez, who had watched the recording after Frost finished with it, passed the reader back to Taggart.

"Corporal, are you certain you hit that creature?" she asked.

"Yes, ma'am," Dade replied. "I drew down on his back, center-of-mass. Capped off two rounds. No way I could have missed him at ten meters—not twice."

"You certain about that, Corporal?" Frost growled.

"Yes, Gunny. As sure as I can be." Dade shrugged. "I put two slugs into him. He yelped, and took a header into the ground. If I didn't hit him, where did all that blood come from, and why did he drop my rifle?"

"So where's the body?"

"I dunno, Gunny. We try to recover our casualties whenever possible. Maybe they do it, too."

"That would explain why there are no bodies at all," Taggart said. "Though that kinda makes me wonder. If these critters really *are* some kind of new Neo-Sov mutants, they'd be really anxious to recover any that got damaged both to keep them out of our hands, and to see how they can 'improve' them. The question is, are they really some new kind of mutant, or are we, as Dade puts it, in a first-contact situation?"

"Well, Captain, what I'm about to say isn't going to clear things up any," Cortez said. "Take a look at the tape again. Pay close attention to the creature that your man Dade wrestled with."

Taggart gave the doctor a quizzical look, plugged the data reader back into his recording/playback unit, and swung the display monocle down in front of his eye. When he hit the play command, an image formed on the small viewscreen.

The picture was grainy, badly framed, and jumped around quite a bit. The first was a problem of the recording equipment, while the latter two were results of attaching a camera to a combat soldier's helmet. Still, the image was good enough for Taggart to get a solid idea of what happened to his scouts. When the image smeared to life, he was watching white-gray rock and the business end of Dade's Pitbull assault rifle. He heard the exchanges between his scouts via a link between Dade's helmet communicator and the recording device attached to his belt. Black's warning shout came across loud and clear.

The picture swung just in time to let Taggart see the

wicked saw-edged club leaping out toward the camera. Then the video seemed to focus squarely on the creature that attacked Dade.

The scene jumped again as Dade blocked the thing's attack. For a second, most of the being's body was visible to the camera. Taggart pressed the pause control on his data reader. For a few moments he studied the frozen image of the attacking creature. It was not quite so tall as a man, perhaps five feet overall, but it was broad shouldered and powerful-looking. Matted, unkempt hair fell to its shoulders. Beetled brows drew together, whether by nature or in killing rage, Taggart could not tell. A mouthful of dirty, decaying teeth snarled at him through the vid. Then, as he contemplated the frozen image, he spotted an odd metallic patch on the creature's right forearm. At first he took it to be a vambrace or jewelry. Then he realized that the flat, rusty metal plate was actually set into the being's flesh. He switched his attention to other portions of the image. Along the thing's legs were large metal knobs, like bolt heads, that were, again, embedded in the creature's body. A power cable ran from the big, pistol-shaped weapon hanging across the thing's chest. At first glance the thick wire seemed to attach to the brute's crude rope belt. Closer examination showed that one end of the cable was attached to the weapon's grip, the other was embedded in the thing's abdomen just under its ribs. It was reminiscent of the various cables and tubes that penetrated the flesh of Neo-Soviet Cyclops mutants.

He switched off the recorder and gazed at Dr. Cortez.

"And what is your assessment of that creature's . . . modifications?"

"Well," Cortez replied in a speculative tone. "If I had to render an opinion based solely on the evidence of that video and your scouts' testimony, I'd have to say that what we're looking at is a being that is the slave of a more advanced race. The implants all seem to be rather crude, but I doubt those creatures have the intellect to perform basic surgery, let alone to create a cybernetic interface. We can barely do it in the Union, and every time we attempt it, the interface fails, causing brain damage in the subject."

"But the Sovs do it, don't they, with their Cyclops mutants?"

"That's right," Cortez replied. "And every time Union scientists have had the opportunity to autopsy a dead Cyclops we've discovered that the poor bastard the Sovs twisted into one of those damned killing machines has had such critical damage to his cerebral and cerebellar cortexes, it's a wonder he survived long enough to be killed by our troops."

"So what about these things, then, Doc?" Frost put in. "You think these things *might* be some kind of new version of mutant?"

"They could be, Sergeant," Cortez answered. "We won't know for certain until we get our hands on one. I'd like to take one back alive, but it will probably be easier to grab a dead one."

"Agreed, Doctor," Taggart said. "But, only after we've completed our primary mission here. If we grease any of these ugly buggers, we'll bag him up and bury him until we find out if any of our own people are still alive at the crash site. We may end up having to care for our own wounded and dead. I don't want to be worried about dragging some dead Neo-Soviet mutants along. If we have enough hands on the return trip, you can have your prizes, assuming we run into any more."

"Well, boss," Gunny Frost said with a grim smile. "I don't think we're gonna have to worry on that account. I have a feeling that this is only the beginning."

17

For a moment, the Marines stared silently at Gunnery Sergeant Frost.

"Gunny, I sure hope you're wrong about that," Corporal Henry said at last. "We've got thirty men on this blasted rock, and ten of them are back at the LZ. If the Neo-Sovs really do have a base out here, and if they are testing some kind of new mutant, we could wind up in trouble real fast."

"That's right, Marine," Taggart said, beating Frost to the punch. "Dade, I guess you and Black had better get on the stick and move out. I'm still not certain what we're dealing with here. If, as I'm beginning to suspect, it is a new alien race, we just might have a little more time than we would if we were dealing with the Neo-Sovs. Aliens might sit back a bit and try to analyze what just happened here. If we're quick about it, we can get in to the wreck site, grab whatever survivors there might be, and bounce back across the hills to the LZ before they have much of a chance to react."

"If it *is* the Neo-Sovs, and I'm beginning to doubt that, we know what they'll do. They'll think about it for all of fifteen minutes, then send out a larger, well-equipped force and land on us with both feet. Either way, our best chance at grabbing the survivors and getting off this rock in one piece is for us to get a move on."

"Semper fi," Dade muttered, quoting the abbreviated version of the Marine Corps motto.

"Hoo-rah." Taggart's sarcastic response elicited some laughter from his troops, including Gunnery Sergeant Onawa Frost. "Move out, Dade. We'll go with a five-minute lead time. If you run into trouble, holler, and we'll come in to bail you out."

"Or to give us a decent burial, whichever comes first," Black said.

Without waiting for a response from their commanding officer, the scouts hefted their weapons and started off down the rift valley.

As he watched the scouts picking their way across the valley floor, Taggart motioned Gunny Frost aside.

"Onawa, you notice anything strange about all these trails we've been seeing?"

"Everything about these trails is strange, sir," Frost answered. "You got anything particular in mind?"

"Yeah. We've seen signs of what now, four different walkers, and about a hundred mutants? If it *is* the Neo-Sovs, why haven't we seen any booted feet?" Taggart waved a hand to indicate the unseen Neo-Soviet troops. "They'd have mutant handlers out with these critters, wouldn't they? Every other class of Soviet mutant has at least one handler for every two or three mutants, right? And the handlers are unaltered humans, aren't they? So where are the handlers? Where are the Vanguard troops who'd be protecting an operation like this?"

"I'm beginning to wonder about that myself, sir."

* * *

Moving along the valley floor took longer than the Marines had reckoned on. By the time Dade and Black reported that they had reached the crash site, the shadows were already beginning to lengthen into evening.

"Lion, this is Falcon," Dade called. "Falcon has reached the objective. We are two-zero-zero meters north of the objective. We have no activity in evidence. Request instructions."

"Falcon, Lion," Taggart replied. "Hold position and continue surveillance. I am bringing the rest of the team up. We will hold five-zero meters short of your position."

"Roger, Lion," Dade said. "Falcon will hold position and continue surveillance. If we spot anything, boss, we'll let you know."

"Good enough, Falcon," Taggart said with a thin smile. "Lion will be there shortly."

Thirty minutes later, the platoon, with the medical team in tow, reached the shelter of a shallow defile fifty meters north of the hide selected by the scouts. Taggart ordered his troops to remain in the cover of the defilade while he and Gunnery Sergeant Frost joined Dade and Black.

Taggart and Gunny Frost dropped their heavy combat packs, taking with them only their rifles, sidearms, and the small items of gear clipped to their combat harnesses. Across the narrow defile, Dr. Lieutenant Cortez did likewise. Taggart caught Frost's eye, and jerked his chin toward the Navy medic. Frost glanced at Cortez and shot a questioning look at her commander, who simply shrugged.

"Dr. Cortez?" he called quietly. "I assume you want to go with Gunny Frost and me."

"That's right, Captain," Cortez said challengingly.

"All right, I'm not going to argue with you this time,"

Taggart said. "But make sure you keep your head down and stay quiet. We don't know if the enemy has found *Cabot* yet. If he has, there's a more than even chance that it was his troops and not survivors we saw from the ridge. Let's not give away any more of our advantage than we already have."

Cortez gave no other reply than an icy stare.

Gunny Frost let out a half-amused snort of laughter and slapped Taggart lightly on the back.

"C'mon, sir, I'll take point. You hang back a bit and make sure she doesn't trip over her own feet."

"Listen, Sergeant," Cortez snapped. "I may be a naval officer, and MCF at that, but I can assure you that I went through basic training, the same as you did. I can handle myself if need be."

"Yes, Lieutenant," Frost said, her grin fading into a blank, unreadable expression. "I'm sure you can at that."

Without another word, Frost turned on her heel and crept out of the defile.

Crawling fifty meters on one's belly, while strenuous, is usually not a difficult proposition. When that same distance must be crossed quietly, and unseen, the process can become torturous, both physically and psychologically. Gunnery Sergeant Frost was one of the best in the business. As Taggart watched, she moved from one bit of cover to the next. She cradled her shotgun in her arms, scuttling along the ground on her elbows and hips in what was often called a high crawl. Once she had reached a point of cover a dozen meters away from the platoon's hiding place, Frost paused. She glanced around, making sure no one had seen her moving. Satisfied that she had not been spotted, she gestured sharply at Taggart.

"All right, Doctor, you wanted to come along. Crawl out there and join Gunny Frost. I'll cover you from here."

Cortez gave the Marine captain a cold look, and dropped onto her belly. Unburdened by either rifle or combat harness, she moved more rapidly than did Gunny Frost. Watching the doctor as she wriggled across the gently sloping ground, Taggart found himself mildly impressed with Cortez's reasonably stealthy movement toward the scouts' observation post.

Atop a low rise in the ground, the scouts had located a shallow nest between several large rocks. The reconnaissance team had carefully moved small stones to form a low wall in front of their position. The site overlooked the place where the survey ship *Cabot* had come to rest.

"There she is, sir," Dade said, once Taggart and Frost had ensconced themselves behind the low rock rampart. Taggart brought his electronic binoculars to his eyes and gazed in the direction his scout had indicated. Beside him Onawa Frost did the same.

From two-hundred-odd meters away, Taggart saw that the aftersection of the ship was a mass of twisted metal. The shredded skin and structural members all bore greasy-looking black streaks, as though they had been smeared with dirty engine oil and soot. Many of the steel splinters appeared to be splayed outward, away from the vessel's spine.

"Gunny, you see this? The damage to her aftersection looks like a missile hit, or maybe a fuel or engine explosion," Taggart said quietly.

"Yeah," Frost replied. "And she seems to have had a fire on board too. Look at her for'ard. Her hull is crumpled. I can see a few breaks in her skin, too.

Taggart elevated his glasses to examine the survey ship's forward section. Aside from spatters of mud, plowed up by the ship's long slide along the valley floor, the ship's paint was unmarked by the friction heating that normally occurs with an atmospheric entry.

Taggart said, "Looks like she was under command when she entered the atmosphere. I can't see her belly heat shield, but there doesn't seem to be any reentry charring on her upper works. The pilot must have had enough control to keep her oriented properly for a hot reentry."

Taggart knew that *Cabot* had been designed to make slow, gliding reentries, rather than the straight plunge into the atmosphere that had characterized spacecraft of the previous century. Still, most S-Corps vessels were outfitted with a thick heat shield, protecting their belly and nose, should a hot reentry be necessary.

"What concerns me more is that there is no one moving around down there." Cortez's voice came from above Taggart and to his left. "Do you think we're too late?"

"Dammit," Taggart swore. He caught Dr. Cortez by the belt and yanked her to the ground.

"Listen, Doc. I don't care if you want to take a look at the wreck. The way you were standing there, if there were any bad guys around here, you'd be breathing through another nostril by now, one right between your eyes. Now, you want to get killed, that's your lookout, but I'd rather you didn't get the rest of us greased along with you."

Cortez had the grace to look embarrassed. As a doctor, she hadn't received the same degree of combat training as Taggart and his people. Though she knew in her head that looking over the top of a barrier silhouetted a person against the sky, such a "rule" had not been ingrained in her to the point of a phobia.

"Sorry, Captain," she said in a low, embarrassed tone. "It won't happen again."

"Humph," Taggart snorted. "As to your observation, Doctor, you're right. I didn't see anyone moving around down there. Now, that suggests we're either too late, or the survivors are tucked in for the night. If we are too late, then what about those people we saw crawling all over the wreck last night? Who were they? Neo-Sovs? The critters that attacked our scouts?"

"Could be either, boss," Frost put in. "Or maybe both, if those things *were* a new kind of mutant."

"Right. On the other hand, because of the terrain in this valley, we haven't had a good enough vantage point to have a look at the wreck until now. If there are survivors, it is possible, I suppose, that they are limiting the amount of time they spend outside the ship. It's been a long time since the crash. The life-support packs for their environment suits have got to be almost exhausted. We may have just gotten lucky last night, and caught them outside. We have no way of telling, at least not from here," Taggart said. "We're going to have to move up to the wreck. Gunny, I think we're going to use both squads. First Squad will make the approach. Second Squad will deploy to provide cover."

"Yes, sir. Recommend a roundabout approach." Frost peered through her binoculars. "It looks like we'd have the best cover approaching from the east."

"Concur," Taggart said. "Okay, Gunny, we'll go with your plan. Bring up the platoon."

"Captain, do you think we have time for this roundabout approach?" Cortez asked sharply. "Those people in there have been without aid for a long time. If there is anybody left alive down there, they can't last much longer."

"So what do you recommend, Doctor?" Taggart appreciated what she was saying, but he hoped she wouldn't suggest something that would cause more casualties.

"Leave your Second Squad here as a covering force, but the rest of your platoon and my medics should go straight in, no more wasting time."

"I'm sorry, Doctor, we can't do it that way." Taggart held up a gloved hand to forestall the inevitable protest. "This area is not secure. We've already suffered two attacks on this team that cost us one Marine and one of your doctors. I'd rather not expose the medical team to undue risks. I'll tell you what I will do. Pick three of your people. They can go in with the approach team and start treating desperate cases among the survivors, if anyone is left down there. Then, once we have the area secure, the rest of your people can move up to the wreck with Second Squad. Will that do?"

Cortez gazed at Taggart for a few moments. She wondered how far she should push the matter. Finally, she decided that his plan was sensible.

"All right, Captain, we'll do it your way. Permission to go brief my people?"

"Yeah, go ahead." Taggart was confused. Cortez had given in more easily than he expected. He wondered what she was planning to do next to make his life miserable.

As Cortez vanished back into the defile where the rescue team was concealed, Taggart motioned to his scouts.

"Okay, Dade, Black, here's what I need from you. From the ship, two o'clock, about fifty meters. See that big outcropping? I want you two to go down there. That will give the approach team cover on their right flank."

Dade took out his electronic binoculars and followed Captain Taggart's "clock-ray" directions. Using the wrecked survey vessel as a benchmark, the scout looked to his right, and fifty meters farther down the valley. He located the pile of limestone his commander had designated.

"Got it," he confirmed. "Should take us about thirty

minutes to crawl down there, assuming the bad guys leave us alone."

"All right, move out." Taggart slapped Dade on the shoulder. "And watch yourself, Corporal. I don't want to have to write your mamma when we get back."

"Yessir," Dade said with a deadpan expression. "She'd be real upset with you if you went and got me killed."

Without another word, Dade and his partner slipped from their hide and crawled off into the gathering gloom.

"I've got the boys ready to move. They can step out as soon as you're ready," Frost said quietly, slipping up next to him. "Y'know, sir, we're gonna be in starlight by the time this thing gets under way."

"I know, Gunny, but there's nothing we can do about it." Taggart grimaced. "As much as I hate to agree with Dr. Cortez, she's right on this one. We can't wait another night. Gunny, I want you to take First Squad. Move 'em in as fast as you feel safe. I'll stay here with Second Squad and direct the overall op."

"Yessir," Frost said. She nodded back toward the troop area. "Here come the docs."

Taggart turned to watch as a pair of medical corpsmen, each lugging two heavy medical bags, crawled up the gentle slope toward the hide. Trailing them was Dr. Lieutenant Rebecca Cortez, also heavily burdened.

Taggart shook his head.

"Gunny, if there is one thing I've learned in this man's Corps, it's to pick your battles. This is one I am *not* going to fight."

18

Gunny Frost watched as a four-man section from First Squad moved toward the wreck. The Marines rushed forward a dozen meters or so, then went to ground. The Second Section, under her command, remained in place, providing an overwatch. As soon as the First Section was under cover, the roles reversed. Frost signaled her troops to move up while First Section kept a lookout for the enemy. In order to provide the greatest degree of protection for the noncombatants, Dr. Cortez and her medics were attached to the Second Section.

Frost had been with Captain Taggart a long time, and was impressed with the man's tactical ability and common sense. Many junior officers would have insisted on leading the approach team personally. A platoon leader's place was not on the firing line. Officers belonged in the rear, where they could take in as much of the battlefield as possible. When an officer got down in the mud with the combat troops, he forfeited too much control over directing the men. Being down in the mud was a job for noncoms like herself.

Frost moved toward the wrecked ship in a shuffling run,

keeping her head up and her eyes and ears alert for any sign of the enemy. When she'd gone a dozen long strides, she slashed the flat of her right hand toward the earth, signaling her section to duck and cover. With no wasted motion, she dropped to the ground, breaking her fall with the stock of her shotgun. Quickly, she scuttled into the lee of a small pile of stones.

As Frost's team approached the shattered vessel, they noticed wreckage thinly scattered on the ground east of the crash site. Most of the flotsam seemed to be structural material, but one or two items that seemed to be personal effects were also found. This sparse debris field struck Frost as odd, but she could not quite lay a finger on why.

"Lion Three, this is Six. Be advised, we have contact with an unknown five-five meters south of your position."

"Roger, Six," Frost acknowledged Taggart's message. "You hear that, Koll?"

"A-ffirmative, Gunny," PFC Kevin Koll replied. "I'll keep an eye out."

Frost turned and scanned the area before her. Seeing no opposition, she lifted her right hand, forefinger extended, and gave a short hissing whistle. A second later, she jabbed her extended finger toward the ship.

In response to her signals, the men of the First Section rushed forward. They had only gone a few steps when a yell broke from the communicator.

"Cover!" Taggart shouted. Then, "Decker, take him!"

Marines dived for cover, as the sharp rattle of a three-shot burst from a Pitbull echoed across the rift valley. Frost dropped flat on her belly, using her weapon to break her fall as before. Dr. Cortez landed beside her with a muffled "oof."

"Decker, are we clear?" Taggart called.

"Stand by," came the reply. "I saw one of the bad guys, looked like he was lining up for a shot. I think I got him."

"Gunny, you're clear," the captain said. "Charlie-Mike."

"Roger that, Charlie-Mike," Frost acknowledged. "Koll, you and Scarpetti get over there and make sure we're clear."

"Right, Sarge."

"Section One, keep moving."

The men of the First Section got to their feet and dashed toward *Cabot*. When they grounded, the Marines were only about ten meters from the ship's broken hull.

"Section One, cover," Frost called. "Section Two, move in, straight to the ship, now!"

Marines leapt to their feet and bolted toward the hulk looming before them. Frost ran for the ship alongside them. Cortez and her medics were only a few steps behind.

As she reached the vessel, Gunny Frost stopped with her back against the crumpled outer hull. To her left, the maw of an open cargo bay door yawned blackly. The five-meter-square combination loading ramp and hatch cover had been ripped away from the ship's hull, apparently by the force of the crash.

Cortez was about to bolt headlong into the hulk when Frost grabbed her by the arm and yanked her away from the hatch.

"Wait!" she hissed at the doctor. Then she called aloud over her helmet-mounted communicator. "Koll, are we clear?"

"I guess so, Gunny," the Marine answered. "I don't think Decker got the bad guy. There's no body and no blood. But we have three of those big steel spikes here. Looks like one of those mutant things was getting ready to take a couple shots at us. I guess he got spooked off."

"All right, you and Scarpetti stay there. Keep a watch on our flank," Frost said. "Uschak, Mossier, move up to the ship. Lim, Martinez, stay put and keep us covered."

When the Marines from the First Section joined them at the wreck, Frost called to Taggart.

"Boss, we're ready to go in. Are we clear?"

"Yes, Gunny, you're clear. Go ahead in."

"Right," she answered. "Mossier, you're first, then Uschak, Harris, and deSilva. Lieutenant, you folks stay here."

Anticipating a protest from Cortez, Frost sharpened her tone. "No arguments this time, Doctor. You and your people stay out here until we have a chance to look over the ship. If things go sour on us, we can't worry about wet-nursing a couple of noncombatants when we should be defending ourselves. If you don't like that, go back up to the command post and argue it with the captain."

Cortez glanced anxiously toward the open hatch. Then, looking resigned, she nodded.

"Don't worry about it. You're going to be safer here than you would be in there with us," Frost said gently. "If we come across any survivors, we'll give a yell, and you can come in a-runnin'."

At Frost's gestured command, PFC Mossier squatted to peek into the inky darkness of the cargo bay. He took a quick look, then darted through the hatchway, moving quickly to his left as he entered the bay. The rest of the Marines followed quickly. The last to enter was Gunny Frost, with Cortez and the medics on her heels. A chorus of "clears" echoed muddily in the large bay.

"Lion Six, this is Three. We're in. The cargo bay is

clear. I'm gonna send Mossier and Uschak to engineering. Harris, deSilva and I will take for'ard."

"Six copies. Be careful, Gunny," Taggart answered.

"As always, sir," Frost said matter-of-factly.

"Gunny, I'm not getting much on the starlight here," Mossier said. "Must not be getting enough ambient light from outside. Suggest we go to visible light?"

Frost looked around the cavernous bay and nodded. "Yeah. Starlights off. Entry team, go to visible light."

In a few seconds, five beams of light speared the darkness of the hold. Frost panned her light around a bit, examining the twisted bulkheads and buckled deck of the cargo bay. The hold's aftersection looked like it had suffered fire damage. The thick rubber padding that overlay the bay's deck had been melted into finger-thick blobs of black crusty matter. Soot streaked the overhead. Yellow-white dry chemicals from the automatic firefighting system dusted the bulkheads and deck.

As she examined the ruined cargo bay, Gunny Frost noticed that many of the systems that seemed to have survived the crash had been removed from their mounting brackets. Such measures would make sense, had a salvage team reached the wreck, but the Marine rescue team was the first Union force on the scene.

"All right, Marines, let's do our jobs," Frost said, putting the anomaly out of her mind.

With Jorge deSilva leading the way, Frost's team moved out of the cargo bay and into the crew section of the vessel. Along the way, the Marines noticed that many of the vessel's components, vital or not, had been removed. In several places, the systems seemed to have been ripped from their mounting brackets.

Cabot's interior was dark and cold. The Marines' flashlights seemed to deepen rather than relieve the gloom of the interior. Frost motioned her team to a halt while she quickly checked the deck plan on her palm-top data unit.

"About three meters along, there should be a ladder," she said, pointing her light down the companionway. "Up one deck, then for'ard again, and we should be in the crew's quarters."

The ladder was precisely where Frost said it should be. DeSilva slowly and stiffly climbed the steel rungs. Something ancient must survive in the human mind, a primal fear left over from the days when mankind feared the demons that lurked in the dark, just beyond the light of their fires. That same anxiety, fed on centuries of horror stories about ghost ships and haunted wrecks, was at work in Jorge de-Silva's mind. At the same time, Gunny Frost, who did not believe in the spirits that inhabited her ancestors' folk tales felt some of that same apprehension. But her apprehension had a legitimate source. Someone or something had twice attacked the rescue party, and that same someone or something might well be lurking in the deep shadows aboard *Cabot.*

The hatch at the top of the ladder was open, the hatch cover standing against its retaining latch. Letting his Pitbull hang from its assault sling, the young Mexican PFC reached up and tugged sharply on the heavy steel cover. The latch held. DeSilva left his rifle where it was, instead drawing his Pug autopistol. Cautiously, he poked his head over the hatch coaming, then rolled quickly off the ladder. Frost heard his heavy boots thudding on the deck above.

"We're clear, Gunny," he called in a tight voice.

"Calm down, deSilva," Frost growled, exercising her will to master her own uneasiness. "I'm coming up, and I don't want you to blow my head off the second it clears the coaming."

On *Cabot*'s upper deck, cables hung in disarray from torn overhead conduits. The steel decking was twisted. Litter and debris were everywhere. Frost aimed her light first aft, then forward. Nothing reacted to the beam's illumination.

"Right, let's go," she said, gesturing to deSilva.

The Marine took three steps and froze in place.

"Gunny, I think we've got a survivor."

Frost reached his side in less than a second. DeSilva was pointing to a series of red, yellow, and green indicator lights set into a heavy steel frame against the starboard bulkhead. They indicated a life pod. Frost checked the pod's function monitors. Its life-support systems had been turned down to their minimum operating settings. A ribbon gauge showed that the capsule had less than an hour's worth of breathable air left in its reserve tanks.

"Harris, go back and get the docs, double time," Frost barked. "Tell them we got at least one survivor."

"Yes, Gunny." Harris slid down the ladder and disappeared.

"DeSilva, check the other pods. See if anybody else is alive."

"Right, Gunny." The young Marine's fear had evaporated with the need for action.

Frost put her ear to the life pod door and listened. No sound penetrated the thick metal. Pulling her Ka-Bar combat knife, she hammered on the door with the steel pommel cap, shouting at the top of her voice.

"Hello! We're Union Marines. We're here to rescue you! Hello!"

No response.

"Gunny, all the other pods are wrecked," deSilva said, returning from his assigned task. "Every one of them. If anyone's left alive, they're in there."

Frost nodded grimly and activated her communicator.

"Mossier, Uschak, any sign of life at your end?"

"Not a lick, Gunny," Mossier replied. Interference from *Cabot*'s superstructure crackled across the transmission. "We're in the engine room, or what's left of it. Whatever brought this ship down was big. I doubt any of the 'black-gang' survived."

"All right," Frost said. "Continue your sweep. Let me know if you find anything. Corporal Lim, any signs of life outside?"

"Negative, Gunny. Everything's quiet."

"Copy. Six, this is Three," she called to Taggart. "Whatever happened here, it looks like we missed it, sir. Dr. Cortez is working on an escape pod that may contain survivors."

"Okay, Gunny. Keep your people on their toes." Taggart hesitated for a moment. "We'll call the area secure, though that doesn't mean anyone can relax. I'm moving the rest of the platoon down to the wreck."

19

"Harris, you stay here with the docs," Frost said as she switched her communicator to standby. "DeSilva, you're with me.

"Listen, Doc," the gunnery sergeant said, laying a hand on Cortez's shoulder. "Just 'cause we're calling the area secure don't necessarily make it so. Don't let your people stray until we've had a real good chance to check it out. I'm going to look at the flight deck. We'll be just up this companionway. Anything goes wrong, give a yell and beat it for'ard. Don't take any chances, okay?"

"All right, Sergeant," Cortez said. "We'll be fine."

"Uh-huh," Frost's voice carried a half-skeptical tone. "All right, deSilva, let's move."

As Frost and deSilva picked their way along the companionway toward *Cabot*'s bridge, Dr. Lieutenant Cortez set her heavy medical packs on the twisted deck and began to examine the heavy steel door of the escape pod.

Basically a small spacecraft, the pod was about three meters by one and a half and was designed to keep six people alive, if not especially comfortable, for about a week in space. Sometimes called lifeboats, the pods were equipped with a basic navigation computer and rudimentary engines that would allow them to be steered. The units were also fitted with reentry gear, giving the pod a good chance of safely entering a planetary atmosphere on autopilot.

The entrance to the pod was actually a double door. Not quite an airlock, the inner door sealed the pod itself, while the outer closed tightly to prevent the loss of atmosphere once the pod was launched. Cortez looked up and saw that the massive outer door was still in its retracted position. She knew those doors were held open by explosive bolts that could be closed in less than a second. Once shut, there was no way of reopening the outer doors short of cutting them with a laser torch or blasting them off their tracks.

Several gauges and displays were mounted next to the thick hatch. These were intended to keep track of the pod's state of readiness for an emergency. The gauge monitoring the pod's oxygen reserve barely registered.

Cortez pulled a folding multitool from her combat harness. Selecting a bit, she quickly unscrewed the monitor panel's faceplate. Behind the twenty-centimeter square of steel and gauges, there were a number of receptacles, each with the numerous holes of a computer tie-in. From her pack, the doctor extracted a diagnostic unit. For a few seconds she fiddled with the device, running a self-test program to ensure that the gadget was functioning properly. She extracted a couple of leads, each tipped with a multi-pin plug, which she thrust into the proper jacks.

"Doc, I thought you were in a hurry," PFC Harris said anxiously.

"I am, Marine," Cortez replied absently. "But I'm not in so much of a hurry that I'm going to circumvent procedures. We don't know how many people might be alive in there.

And I'm afraid that, given the low level of the oxygen, some people in there didn't survive. I want to make sure that the pod is functioning properly before we open it."

She broke off as the diagnostic unit squawked, and looked intently at the device. The apparatus confirmed what the pod's monitors told her. There was almost no breathable air left in the lifeboat. The temperature inside the pod was twenty-seven degrees Celsius, with seventy-eight percent humidity. The device also showed pollutants in the air, none of which was life-threatening in the low concentrations present in the pod.

Cortez hit the machine's reset button and keyed in more commands.

"I also want to make sure that there is no viral, bacteriological, chemical or radiological contamination of the pod's interior before we open it up."

The diagnostic system beeped again. Its indicators showed the pod to be uncontaminated.

"Okay, let's get ready to crack it," Cortez said, rapidly unhooking and stowing the device. She turned to one of her medics. "Fritz, break out those extra respirators. A healthy person could take this atmosphere for a few seconds with no worse effect than burning eyes and respiratory irritation, but if there's anybody alive in there and not wearing an environment suit, their systems are going to be compromised enough as it is. We don't need to add poisoning to the mix."

Fritz, the medic, extracted a number of plastic-wrapped packages from his pack. Each package contained one fresh and fully charged emergency respirator. If the occupants of the pod were alive and not wearing environment suits, slapping one of the breathing devices over their nose and mouth as soon as the door was opened might spell the difference between survival and death from atmospheric poisoning. He passed two to Cortez, who handed them to the Marine guard.

"These things are easy to use," she said, taking another pair from Fritz. "You tear open the package, twist the green knob clockwise until you hear the hiss, and then put it over the victim's face. There are five straps. They'll look kind of like an octopus attached to the mask. All you have to do is grab the center of the strap assembly and pull it back over the victim's head. Make sure you pull the straps up tight so that the mask seals. Got it?"

Harris looked at the mask and nodded.

"As soon as the door opens, we rush the pod and get the masks on as many victims as possible. Understand?"

Everyone nodded.

"All right, then. It's showtime."

Cortez pulled back a red-and-white-striped cover printed with the word RESCUE and pulled the lever inside.

Nothing happened.

Cortez stared at the lever, then at the unresponsive door. She rammed the lever back into its starting position and yanked again. The pod door remained shut.

Cursing in Spanish, Cortez worked the lever again, this time so violently that she bent the heavy plastic handle.

Harris stepped forward, passing his masks back to Fritz. He gently slid the frustrated Navy doctor out of his way. For several seconds, he looked over the controls, then stepped back with a disbelieving shake of his head.

"I think they disabled the controls from the inside," he said. "I guess they were more afraid of something out here than they were of not being rescued."

"Dammit, we have got to get this pod open," Cortez snarled. She stepped up to the sealed hatch and repeatedly kicked the heavy steel door.

"Hello! In the pod! We're here to rescue you. Open the door. I'm a doctor. Let me in."

"Take it easy, Doc. That ain't gonna help," the Marine said, laying his hands on her shoulders.

Cortez whirled about, glaring up at the young man, who was half a head taller than she, as though she would like to cut his heart out.

"Okay, Doc, you've got your Pug, you should be safe 'til I get back. Just keep your eyes open," Harris said. "I'm gonna go aft and see if there is anything in engineering we can use to get this door open."

Harris smiled encouragingly and turned away, advising Gunnery Sergeant Frost of his intentions through his communicator.

As Harris vanished down the companionway, Cortez unlimbered her multitool again, she opened another access panel and studied the wires within. Selecting a pair, she cut and stripped the leads, and twisted them together. Again, she tried the "rescue" handle, but to no avail. The door remained sealed.

With an angry, frustrated cry, she threw the multitool to the deck and resumed her physical assault on the door. "Goddammit, open up. We're doctors. We're here to help you."

Fritz and his partner tried to calm their team leader, but she shook off their hands. Rebecca Cortez had become a doctor because she had seen too many people die for lack of help. Her whole career, both as a civilian and as a naval officer, had been dedicated to saving lives. Now, because of a few centimeters of steel, she was unable to help the stricken and dying people in the escape pod.

Giving the door a final, frustrated kick, Cortez slumped forward, resting her head against the steel bulkhead.

"Hurry up, Marine," she said in a hushed, almost-prayerful tone. "They aren't going to last much longer."

Then she heard a sharp, flat *scuff.*

Forgetting all about the hatch, Cortez grabbed for her sidearm. Though lightweight, the weapon felt clumsy as she pointed the pistol down the deeply shadowed companionway. Her right thumb groped for the weapon's safety.

The soft rutching noise repeated itself. She pressed the catch down, readying the big pistol for firing. Taking a deep breath, Cortez brought the Pug up, struggling to hold the weapon still in two trembling hands.

"Take it easy, Doctor. It's me," a familiar baritone voice called out of the gloom.

Cortez let out a deep shuddering breath she hadn't realized she was holding and lowered the pistol. Captain Taggart and two of his men stepped into the circle of light cast by the medics' flashlights. Right behind them was PFC Harris, lugging a portable laser cutter.

Swiftly the young Marine readied the powerful torch, while Captain Taggart called up a schematic of *Cabot*'s escape pods on his palm-top. Using an alcohol marker, he drew a rough circle on the escape pod's hull. Cortez and her medics drew back a bit as Harris powered up the cutter and began burning his way through the tough steel.

It took nearly five minutes for Harris to complete his cut. As he shut down the laser torch, he drew his big Ka-Bar combat knife and prized out the slab of hull plating he had just burned away.

"Ready, Doc?" he asked, as he carefully reached into the rough-edged opening.

Cortez and her medics snatched up their respirator masks. She nodded.

Harris tugged sharply on something, eliciting a loud

thunk from the pod's door. The heavy panel slid partway open, just enough for Dr. Cortez to rush inside.

Dimly, her mind noted the chaos and litter inside the lifeboat. Her attention was focused solely on the prostrate figure lying face-up on the deck.

Dropping to her knees beside the crewman, she ripped the plastic cover from an emergency respirator and strapped it to his face. Only when she was satisfied that the mask was in place and working properly did she look at the patient. He was unconscious, but breathing on his own. Laying two fingers beside the man's larynx, she felt a good carotid pulse. Though both were good signs, it was impossible to say whether they'd reached him in time.

The patient was a young, slight man with dark hair, wearing a Union Space Agency uniform. The nametape sewn to the right breast of his uniform read MICHELLI. This was *Cabot*'s third officer, the man who had sent the distress call.

Cortez glanced about the escape pod and realized that Ensign Michelli had been alone, the sole survivor of a crew of twelve.

20

Captain Taggart leaned into the escape pod in an effort to get a look at the interior of the small vessel while trying to keep out of the medical team's way. He half-expected to see other members of the crew, or at least their lifeless bodies. The sight that met his eyes made him thankful for the closed helmet and respirator of his combat environment suit.

The interior of the escape pod was in a shambles. Survival packs had been piled in every available space. Most of the fluorescent orange rucksacks had been emptied of their contents. A mylar emergency sleeping bag was tossed casually in one corner. The Marine officer could see a long tear in the bag's thin reflectorized fabric. Propped against the bulkhead next to the hatch was a lightweight over-and-under survival gun. Taggart picked up the weapon and hinged open the break-action breach. Both the upper rifle barrel and the lower shotgun tube were empty; so was the compartment in the stock where extra ammunition was normally stored. Taggart had a good idea what Michelli had been shooting at before he sealed himself in the pod. The six rifle and eight shotgun cartridges normally provided for the survival gun would not have allowed the shipwrecked ensign to fight off a serious attack. More likely Michelli had used up the survival gun's limited store of ammunition keeping the enemy at bay while he gathered supplies and sealed himself in the pod.

Used food and water containers littered the rubber-covered steel decking. Oxygen canisters, both the large standard bottles that normally supplied a life pod with breathable air and the smaller emergency size bottles, were roughly stacked against one bulkhead. Judging from the lone survivor's condition, and the pod's monitoring systems, all of those canisters had long since been emptied of their life-giving contents. A dirty environment suit was draped across the top of the canisters. From his vantage point at the pod door, Taggart could see the indicator on the suit's life-support pack. The gauge that measured the level of life-giving oxygen in the suit's reserves indicated that the store of breathable air had been exhausted.

In one back corner partially hidden from view by a blanket duct-taped to the bulkheads was a covered twenty-liter container. Streaky discolorations along the white plastic bucket's sides and rim told Taggart that Ensign Michelli had been using the container as a makeshift latrine.

Opposite the screened-off privy was an untidy pile of blankets, next to an inexpensive videodisk player. The battered entertainment unit and a pile of dog-eared paperbound books seemed to have been Michelli's only means of hanging on to his sanity during his long, self-imposed solitary confinement.

Appalled at the conditions in which the young ensign had been living for the three weeks between crash and rescue, Taggart turned his attention to the doctors struggling to save the survivor's life.

"How's he doing, Doc?"

"Not good," Cortez replied coldly. "He's dehydrated and suffering from borderline malnutrition. So much for those damn survival packs keeping you alive and healthy. He's also suffering the beginning stages of oxygen deprivation. Right now, he's comatose, but he's stable. We're starting him on a glucose IV. That ought to get him hydrated, and take care of some of the malnutrition. We can handle the oxygen deprivation easily enough by stuffing him in a pressure shelter."

"How long until he regains consciousness?"

Cortez glared at him, then turned to her assistant. "Stay with him, George. I'll be right back." Then, motioning for Taggart to follow, she slipped out of the pod.

"I didn't want to say this in front of Michelli. We know a patient in his condition can hear what's being said. We just don't know how much they comprehend. He could wake up in an hour, tomorrow, or never. I just don't know. If he does wake up, I don't know what kind of condition he's going to be in. He's suffering from oxygen deprivation. That means there might be brain damage." Cortez paused as though unsure what to say next. "And you, Captain, may be partly to blame for this."

Taggart looked at the doctor in stunned surprise.

"That's right. You might be responsible for that young man's condition, at least in part." Cortez spat the words at him. "He had the pod's life support system turned down to its minimum operating settings. If he hadn't, I doubt that he'd be alive right now. Even so, he wasn't going to last but a few more hours. If you hadn't been so gung ho on doing things 'the Marine way,' we might have gotten here yesterday, or even the day before that. That might not have made much of a difference in the dehydration, or malnutrition, but he certainly wouldn't have run out of oxygen to the point of risking brain damage."

For a long while, Taggart stared at Dr. Cortez, unsure how to respond to her accusations. Was she overreacting? He had moved the rescue team along as rapidly as he deemed safe, but could he have hurried them more? Had he taken too many precautions, or spent too much time chasing down the mysterious creatures that seemed bent on harrying his small command?

The communicator built into his helmet buzzed sharply, cutting off that line of self-questioning thought. He switched the unit from standby to active.

"This is Lion Six, go ahead."

"Six, this is Three," Onawa Frost's husky contralto said in his ear. "We've finished our sweep of the ship. It's clear. But we've found something you might want to look at."

"What is it, Gunny? Survivors?"

"Sir, you need to see this for yourself." There was an odd note in Frost's normally steady voice, an undertone of revulsion mixed with anger and fear.

"Right. Where are you?"

"About a hundred meters northeast of the ship."

"Very well, I'm on my way," Taggart said, grateful for a reason to leave Dr. Cortez's accusing presence.

When Taggart stepped out of the survey vessel's sprung cargo bay door, he could see Gunnery Sergeant Frost and a small handful of Marines standing on the rim of a shallow gully near the ship. As he made his way across the valley floor toward them, Taggart passed through the debris field that Frost had remarked upon earlier. Taggart noticed that almost all of the debris had come from interior sections of the ship, and none of it seemed to have suffered the kind of damage one would have expected to see had the items been forcibly ejected from the ship. In fact, many of the objects seemed to be components that had been unbolted from their mountings and then simply dropped outside the vessel. The variety of items among the debris field was quite wide. A few meters from *Cabot*'s open cargo bay door, he came across a portable magnetic anomaly detector. A bit farther on, a small plastic case, such as might hold soil samples, lay on a gray-painted steel junction box. The junction box had not been carefully unbolted from its brackets. Short sections of conduit, torn, ragged wires trailing from their twisted and broken ends, were still attached to the hand-sized metal octagon. It seemed to Taggart that all of the items had been removed from the ship, carried a short distance away, and then dropped. There was no sense or reason in the kind or number of objects littering the valley floor.

A few meters short of where Frost awaited him a large black-plastic object caught his attention. A coffeemaker stood upright on the ground, its glass carafe nowhere to be seen. Something odd, beyond the setting in which one would not normally expect to find a coffeemaker, caught Taggart's attention. He knelt next to the appliance and examined it as closely as he could without actually touching the device. A thin shiny layer of dark purple-black material coated the back of the machine. Taggart freed his Ka-Bar from its sheath and lightly probed the foreign substance. The stuff proved be as fragile as spun sugar, flaking away as soon as the knife's hard steel point touched it. Beneath the strange matter, the appliance's housing was shiny and clean. Something about the debris field and the defaced coffeemaker caused an involuntary shudder of disgust along his spine.

Taggart got to his feet, slipping the knife back into its upside-down sheath on his left shoulder. As he crossed the final few meters between him and Frost, he read tension and anger in his normally impassive gunnery sergeant's stance.

"So what is it, Gunny?" he asked quietly.

Frost didn't answer, but gestured sharply at the bottom of the gully. There, in a careless heap, lay a number of human corpses, all clad in the green uniform of the Union Space Corps. A few of his men had climbed down into the gully and were checking the bodies.

Taggart slid rapidly down the uneven slope to the gully floor. He counted six corpses in that narrow defile. All seemed to have been dead before they were tossed into the gully. Though he was no doctor, Captain Taggart had seen enough dead men in his career to know that none of the crewmen had died easily. Many bore the signs of having died in the crash. One, whose collar flashes indicated that he had been *Cabot*'s executive officer, had died of a broken neck. The corpse's head had been twisted at a 180-degree angle to its body. Another, who had once been an attractive young woman, had the cyanotic complexion of someone who had died of asphyxiation. Strangely, her eyelids and lips were puffy and red. None of the bodies seemed to have been abused in any way, though every scrap of metal seemed to have been removed from the corpses. Rings, watches, rank insignia, even belt buckles had been removed.

That last stirred something in Taggart's memory.

"Gunny Frost, turn the recovery operation over to Corporal Henry," he barked. "Tell him to get this all down on tape. I want to document every damn thing about this frigging mission. I want as complete an account as you can give me of where each body was found and what condition they were in when you found them.

"Then, get hold of Dade and Black. Tell them to meet us back at the wreck."

"Okay," Frost answered. "What is it, boss?"

Taggart did not reply but climbed back up the side of the gully. Just short of the rim, he stopped and picked up a small metallic object he saw gleaming in the dirt. Gently he wiped away a bit of mud clinging to the thing. It was a gold Star of David. Turning the bauble over in his fingers, he discovered that it, too, was stained with the odd purple-black substance. But unlike the dry crust on the coffee machine, the stuff coating the back of the six-pointed star was moist and sticky, almost the consistency of half-dried blood.

With a snort of disgust, Taggart wiped both the pendant and his hands clean on the blue-green weeds growing near the lip of the ravine. He shoved the Star into a breast pocket on his environment suit and stalked off toward the ship, with Gunny Frost following close behind him.

"Sir, what is this all about?" Frost asked as they reached *Cabot*. Taggart did not answer, but paced angrily across the gloomy cargo bay. He pulled the Star of David out of his pocket and worried the bauble between his gloved fingers. Why the defiled religious symbol was such a source of anger for him, a backslid Catholic, was a mystery to Maxwell Taggart. It wasn't the fact that the corpses had been looted. He had seen despoiled bodies before. Neo-Soviet troops, especially those in the Rad battalions, were given to stripping the dead, regardless of whose side they were on, of any and all useful or valuable gear. No, this was something different. The corpses tossed so callously into the gully still wore their boots and uniforms. Those two items were usually taken first. Here, the bodies had been plundered of relatively useless accoutrements, like the blackened bronze rank insignia, but clothing and boots were left untouched.

"Captain, what's eating you?" Frost pressed him.

Taggart stopped pacing and shot her a black look, then resumed his measured strides across the cargo bay.

He'd only completed two more laps when Rick Dade stepped inside the empty hold.

"Boss, this is weird. We can't find any trace of the rest of the crew."

"What do you mean, the rest of the crew?" Frost asked.

"I mean the rest of the crew, Gunny. The briefing said there were twelve people aboard *Cabot*, right? Well, we've got six dead in the gully, and one survivor. That leaves five unaccounted for."

"Very well, Corporal," Taggart snapped. The captain surprised himself with the curt tone in his voice, but was unable to moderate it. "Give me the recording you made yesterday when those things attacked you."

Dade glanced at Gunny Frost as he reached into his buttpack to extract the recording. Taggart shoved the disk into his data reader, glaring at the small screen. Images of the previous day's engagement flickered and jumped across the screen. As the recording ran out, he grunted disgustedly.

Taggart handed the unit to Onawa Frost, saying, "Tell me what you see."

Frost played the image file, studying the display carefully. Suddenly she caught her breath, stopped, rewound and restarted the recording, punching pause only a few seconds later.

"That's right, Gunny," Taggart said, as she passed the data unit back to him. "One of those goddam things had a Union Space Force belt buckle implanted in its shoulder, like some kind of frigging trophy. The Sovs aren't exactly given to decorating their mutants, are they?"

"Not that I can remember, sir."

"Gunny, I don't know as how we're dealing with mutants here. At least, not mutants created by the Neo-Sovs. I wonder if we've encountered a new alien race, one that is demonstrably hostile, and bloody dangerous."

21

Corporal Henry," Taggart called through his communicator.

"Right here, boss."

"I want those bodies bagged up for recovery," Taggart instructed. "It's going to be a gruesome job, but we aren't going to leave anyone behind for those bloody grave robbers. And make sure you document everything you see, and I do mean everything, Corporal, is that clear? I'm still not sure what we're dealing with here. I'm starting to think it's a first-contact situation, I want to give the boys in I-Corps every bit of data we can."

"Yessir."

"Good. Then get to it," Taggart said. "And Corporal, tell your men to keep their eyes open. The critters that did this may come back."

Taggart closed the connection and turned to his scouts.

"Dade, you and Black start looking for the bridge voice and data recorders. I want to know what the hell happened to this ship. If you run into any more of those things . . ."

"I know, sir, be careful."

"No, Corporal," Taggart snapped. "If you run into any more of those things, I want you to blow 'em to hell."

"Semper fi," Dade said, and slipped back out of the cargo bay.

"Onawa, you're with me. I want to have a closer look at this ship. We'll start with the bridge."

The platoon leaders headed forward. Instead of merely retracing Frost's steps, they stuck to the vessel's lower deck. The companionway leading forward out of the cargo bay was a shambles. Every square meter of bulkhead space was a ruin of snarled and torn wires, bent metal, and charred plastics. Taggart was struck again by the randomness of the destruction. In one place the thieves had ripped away long sections of conduit, yet in an avionics bay only a few meters along the corridor, the ground-scan radar systems were virtually untouched. An atmospheric testing lab was completely gutted. The aliens, as Taggart was now calling the ugly, misshapen humanoids, had even ripped up the thick rubber pads covering the deck. The next compartment along the corridor, a storage locker for soil and water samples, had been ignored.

Most of the components and instruments had been unbolted, or cut away, apparently with laser torches. One such instrument, its power cells depleted, lay discarded on the deck. Taggart noted that the pistol-shaped tool's grip and part of its housing were coated with the flaky purple-black crust that he had come to think of as dried blood. Other systems seemed to have been ripped out, as the jagged, twisted remains of mounting brackets would suggest.

Reaching the forward end of the corridor, Taggart and Frost mounted a ladder and reached *Cabot*'s upper deck just aft of the flight deck.

The survey ship's bridge was a mess. Nearly every control and panel on the flight deck was smashed. The small, thick, heat-resistant windscreens were nearly opaque because of spiderweb cracks. The steel deck plating was buckled in accordion-like folds just forward of the hatchway leading onto the bridge. Bolts, rivets, and welds had given way under the stress of the vessel's slamming into the floor of the rift valley. One could see through the gap produced by that cave-in to the corridor below. Both the pilot's and flight engineer's acceleration couches had been torn from their moorings and were thickly smeared with the dark reddish brown stains of human blood. Beneath the engineer's console, Taggart caught a glimpse of what might have been an empty boot, but was not. The large coppery smudge on the deck bore witness to that.

Taggart shook his head silently, feeling a deep and genuine sorrow for the men who had died on *Cabot*'s bridge. In his mind's eye, he could see them struggling to keep the big survey ship under control as she plunged toward the rocky surface of the valley floor, too busy fighting to save both ship and shipmates to be afraid for their own lives. Though there was often an interservice rivalry between Ground and Space Forces that stretched back to the time when Marines and blue-water sailors played out the usually good-natured antagonism between their respective military branches, this was no way for two good men to die.

"Let's go, Gunny, We still have the upper decks to look over."

"Sir, what is it you're looking for?" Frost asked, a frown creasing her forehead.

"I don't know, Gunny." Taggart sighed. "I guess I'm just looking. If there *is* something I'm looking for, I suppose I'll know it when I see it."

He squeezed past his subordinate and started aft. A few

meters along the companionway, the Marines came to the life pods. Dr. Cortez was sitting wearily on the deck, her back against the bulkhead. She lifted her head slightly at the Marines' approach, but sagged back against the steel wall and turned her head once she saw who it was. Dr. Grippo was leaning over Ensign Michelli's inert form, studying a medical condition monitor.

"How is he, Doc?" Taggart asked.

"Looks like he'll live, maybe, if we can nurse him along through the next few hours," Grippo answered for his chief. Grippo's tone was far less hostile than Cortez's would have been. Still, it was somewhat lacking in warmth. "Will he recover? I don't know. We have no way of knowing if he's got brain damage."

"All right," Taggart said mildly. "Will you keep us informed on his condition, Doctor?"

"Harrumph." Grippo let out a noncommittal snort.

Taggart noted the hostility being aimed at him from the senior medical staff. He was well aware of the antagonism between Dr. Cortez and himself, but he had had no idea that the feelings were beginning to spread to the rest of the medical team. He looked at Cortez. Her posture convinced Taggart to discard any notion of approaching the doctor to hash out their differences.

"Let's go, Gunny." With another frustrated sigh, the Marine captain jerked a thumb toward the ship's aftersection.

Cabot's upper deck was worse than the lower. Here, crew quarters had been ransacked. Personal effects were strewn about the two gender-segregated cabins. As Taggart and Frost poked through the chaos of ripped clothing and shredded paper, they both noticed that neither one scrap of metal nor a single device more technologically advanced than a pencil remained in either of the living spaces.

In the men's berthing compartment, a thick smear of an alien's purple blood defaced one wall. Beneath the smudge lay a hand-held long-range communicator, minus its power cell. The radio unit was likewise coated with dark, wine-colored flakes.

Gunny Frost squatted on her hams and prodded the communicator with the muzzle of her shotgun.

"Y'know, boss, I've seen a whole truckload of weird stuff since I've been in the Corps, but this is the weirdest. Why in the hell would the aliens cut themselves and smear blood all over everything?"

"I don't think they do, Onawa," Taggart said, kneeling next to her to examine the communicator. "Remember the vids of the one that tried to steal Dade's Pitbull? It had a belt buckle and a couple other bits of metal sort of implanted in its skin."

"Yeah, so?"

"Well, do these things seem smart enough to you to do implant surgery?"

"Not by a long way," Frost said, looking thoughtfully at her commander.

Taggart took a deep breath, hating the stale, rubbery taste of the air provided by his respirator.

"This might seem a little weird. I don't know if it's even possible. Maybe Cortez or one of her medics could tell us, but right now, I don't think they'd be too open to discussion. What if these aliens can somehow absorb things into their bodies?"

"You're right, sir, that's weird."

"Yeah, but think about it for a minute. The Sovs don't even put unit insignia on their mutants, yet these things have 'trophies' implanted in their bodies. That vid Dade took showed some sort of cable running into the creature's body. We figured it was some kind of implant. What if those ugly bastards did the implants by . . . well . . . sort of 'mashing' the stuff into themselves?"

Frost stared at her commanding officer while seconds bled away. "So, do you really think we've got a first-contact situation here?"

Taggart nodded.

Frost gave a rueful shake of her head. "So what are we gonna call 'em? Mashers?"

"That isn't in our department, Gunny, but 'Mashers' is as good a name as any, for now."

"What bothers me the most isn't what to call these creatures, it's more that they exist in the first place." Taggart stood up, and adjusted the ride of his rifle's assault sling. "When we were on the way here, we all studied the briefings about those other alien races, the Growlers, and the Zhykee, right? Then it was just a report, kinda like seeing a flying saucer, or a ghost. But this . . . this is proof. This makes it all real. This forces us to completely redefine reality. And worse, it suggests still more races. How many alien races are out there? How many are hostile? How long will it be before they discover Earth and pay us a visit?"

Taggart stopped shaking his head at the possibilities he had just voiced.

Frost sighed and pushed herself to her feet. She rested her shotgun across her shoulders, and said, "I don't know, boss. The whole thing seems a little weird to me."

"So tell me, Onawa," Taggart said with a bitter smile. "What part of the Maelstrom doesn't seem weird to you?"

"Huh," Frost snorted. "I suppose you're right. Let's go take a look at the rest of the ship."

Immediately aft of *Cabot*'s crew quarters was the survey vessel's galley and wardroom. Oddly, the wardroom, where the ship's crewmen had taken their meals, had barely been touched by the looting aliens. The galley, on the other hand, was even more chaotic than the crew's quarters. Every scrap of metal that was not part of the vessel itself had been taken from its proper place, smeared with the thick purple goo, and then tossed around the compartment as though in some orgiastic ritual.

The room was too small for both environment-suited Marines, so Taggart stood guard in the corridor while Frost searched the disarrayed galley. As Frost poked through the wreckage, she stopped occasionally to prod some bit of cookware with the muzzle of her shotgun. Once or twice she squatted on her heels to get a closer look at some object that caught her attention.

"You ready for another weirdness, boss?" she said, looking at her captain. "There isn't a single knife or cleaver left in the whole place. Come to think of it, that isn't so weird after all. The aliens have been stealing tools. I guess it only makes sense that they'd be stealing cooking knives, too."

Taggart shook his head in disgust, and beckoned Frost back into the companionway.

"Let's keep moving," he said. "We haven't got too many hours of daylight left. I'd like to finish searching the ship before nightfall. I've got a funny feeling the aliens might take another run at us in the dark."

"Holy Mary, Mother of God."

Though she was not a Catholic, the words escaping Gunny Frost's lips carried a tone of awe verging upon reverence.

"Yeah," Taggart seconded. "What a train wreck."

The Marines stood just inside *Cabot*'s engineering compartment, or rather what was left of it. The compartment that had once housed the survey vessel's primary drives and power plant was nothing but a mass of twisted metal, burnt and melted plastics, and shattered composites. The room, which stretched the height of both of *Cabot*'s upper and lower decks, was sheared almost completely through two-thirds of the way back from the forward bulkhead. Along the huge rent in the ship's skin, the hull plates and structural members were bent outward, as though from an explosion inside the engineering compartment. The after bulkhead of the engine room was likewise shattered, almost ripped away. The tattered metal that had once made up the partition between the engineering space and the compartment that actually housed the massive engines was held in place by only a few twisted metal I beams.

Taggart crossed the room and shined his light through the rents in the after bulkhead. The portside engine (what he could see of the enormous drive unit) seemed to be intact, except for several head-sized holes in its outer casing. The starboard engine was gone. A gigantic hole yawned in the deck where it had been.

"Y'know, boss? Back when I was just a baby Marine, I was aboard a wet-navy cruiser, the *Remagen*," Frost said as she flashed her light around the engine room. "We were in that action off Kamchatka. We took a Neo-Sov SS-N-25 in the hull just below the helipad. Missile penetrated the hull and detonated in the engineering spaces. Blew the hell out of the ship, started fires everywhere. The water was too cold to abandon ship, and there were no other vessels close enough to take us off, so we had to try to save her. We kept the old girl afloat for another six hours until the *Porter* came alongside to lend assistance. I was part of the team that went into the engine rooms after the fires were out. That's just what this looks like, only here the damage is more contained. Almost as though the ship was hit by a smaller missile, like a SAM."

"You think the Sovs are building surface-to-space missiles, and testing them on this rock?" Taggart asked, noting a slight blanching of Frost's ruddy complexion as she talked of her lost ship. "Or are you saying those things out there are smarter than they look and are building antispacecraft missiles on their own?"

"I'm not really saying either, sir. It could just as easily been the Zhykee or the Pharon. All I'm saying is that it looks like *Cabot* was hit by a missile. I'm sure once Michelli wakes up, he'll be able to clear things up for us."

"Yeah." Taggart's tone was skeptical.

"Lion Six, this is Falcon." Rick Dade's voice cut into the conversation.

"This is Six. Go ahead, Falcon."

"Boss, we found the bridge voice recorder. It was right were it was supposed to be, in the superstructure. The ship's space frame is pretty badly twisted up here. I don't think we're gonna be able to unbolt it. Think you could send over a couple guys with a cutting torch?"

"Can do, Falcon," Taggart answered. "You sure you can cut it free without screwing up the recorder?"

"That's affirmative, sir." Dade sounded as confident as always. "As long as the guys you send over know which end of the torch is up."

"Stand by, Falcon." Taggart switched off the communicator. "Gunny? You got anybody who knows which end of a torch is up?"

"Yessir," Frost replied, and switched on her own communicator. After a few moments, she said to her commanding officer, "Sir, you can tell Dade I got a couple guys on the way."

"Falcon, Lion. You got a couple of guys heading your way. Please try not to shoot them."

"You got it, boss. Oh, Captain, there is no sign of the flight data recorder. We checked its compartment in the tail section, but it's gone. Looks like it was hacked out of its mountings with a chisel and mallet."

"Very well, Falcon." The captain touched a control, opening a general channel to his men. "Attention to orders. All Marines not specifically assigned to other duties are to begin a detailed search for *Cabot*'s flight data recorder. The operation is to be coordinated through Gunnery Sergeant Frost. Report to her in the cargo bay on the double. Lion Six, out."

"You really think we're gonna find the recorder?" Frost asked.

"I don't know, Gunny," he answered, massaging the back of his neck through the thick, environmentally sealed kevlon of his suit. "I hope so. I'm hoping it was ripped from its moorings by the crash and ejected from the hull. Then again, if that happened, it could be anywhere within two hundred kilometers of here. Or, if, as Dade suspects, it was removed from the superstructure, maybe whoever took it dropped it somewhere along the line, just like the rest of that junk out there in the debris field."

22

---

aggart leaned carefully against the frame of *Cabot*'s sprung cargo bay door, lest a shard of the twisted, jagged metal tear his environment suit. The shadows had begun to deepen into night before he recalled his search teams. In twos and threes his men returned to the wrecked survey ship, all bearing the same report. No one had found the missing flight data recorder. Now only eight of his twenty-two troopers remained outside the vessel: four assigned to sentry duty, his scout team, Gunnery Sergeant Onawa Frost, and Corporal Tim Henry.

As he stood staring at the gathering gloom, a slight scuffling noise reached his ears. He pushed himself away from the doorframe. As he turned toward the sound, his hands dropped to the Pitbull assault rifle hanging under his right arm from its combat sling. Before his fingers closed around the weapon's firing grip, he located the source of the noise. Dr. Cortez had approached him, obviously with something on her mind. Whatever subject she had wanted to discuss had been driven from her mind by the sight of the M-18's stubby flash suppressor lining up on her torso. Inside her environment suit's closed visor, her eyes widened in surprise and fear.

"Dammit, Doctor!" Taggart snapped the rifle's muzzle up toward the bay's overhead, away from her center-of-mass. "You ought to know better than to sneak up on a man like that."

"*Madre de Dios,*" Cortez lapsed into her native Spanish for the first time in the long weeks Taggart had known her. There was a distinct quaver in the whispered phrase. The blood had drained from her face, leaving it the color of old parchment, but only for a moment. Recovering quickly, she hid her shock behind a flat professional mien.

"I just thought you'd like to know. Michelli is stable. It looks like we got here in time, but only just. He has good nerve responses in his extremities; his eyes are equally reactive to light. I don't think there is brain damage, but until he wakes up, *if* he wakes up, we won't know for certain."

"Very well. Anything else?"

Cortez nodded. "I had a look at the bodies your men pulled from the ravine. Most of them look to have died of some kind of trauma. I don't have the facilities here to do an autopsy. That will have to wait until we get back home."

"You said 'most.' What did the rest die from?" Taggart asked.

"It looks like exposure to the atmosphere," Cortez replied with a suppressed shudder. "The air on this planet is mostly carbon dioxide and ammonia. The dioxide accounts for the cyanosis and the ammonia would cause the inflammation of the tissues around the eyes and mouth. They died of a combination of suffocation and ammonia poisoning."

"What a hellish way to die," Taggart said.

"Do you think there is any *good* way to die, Captain?"

Cortez snapped. Then her tone of voice softened. "Any luck in finding the missing men? Or their bodies?"

"No," Taggart said wearily. "Not a trace, and no sign of the flight data recorder, either."

He turned to look out into the swiftly falling darkness just in time to see the last four of his Marines returning to the ship. Gunny Frost shook her head. Taggart nodded and held up a finger, indicating that he wanted them to wait for a moment.

"Doctor," he said, turning his attention to the medical team leader, "we're going to spend one more day searching this area for survivors and for that missing recorder. You and your team will bunk in the ship tonight. Set up your bivouac in the crew quarters on the upper deck. I don't want any of your people wandering around the ship. Remember, I just about capped you when you came up on me unawares. I don't want to get one of your medics greased by accident."

"Very well," Cortez said in an oddly pleasant tone. It was almost as though she enjoyed agreeing with Taggart for once. "I was going to request another day before we returned to the shuttle anyway. Since we just got Michelli stable, I'd like to give him at least twenty-four hours to recover. Who knows? He may even regain consciousness by then."

"What are his chances?"

"Of surviving? Assuming no further complications, ninety percent," Cortez answered after a moment's thought. "Of making a full recovery? Fifty-fifty. The sooner we get him into the *Gallatin*'s sick bay, the better his chances are going to be. But what about your Marines, Captain? They've got to be exhausted."

Cortez's sudden and unwonted concern startled Taggart. He put it down to fatigue, and a genuine concern for the welfare of his men. As much as a pain in the neck as Cortez could be on more "political" subjects, Taggart realized that the doctor would exert every effort on the behalf of the men and women under her care.

"They probably are exhausted," he admitted. "We're gonna bivouac here in the cargo bay. We'll rotate sentries in and out through the night. That's why I want your people to stay on the upper deck. If they go wandering around the ship, they're liable to be mistaken for hostiles and get themselves shot."

"There's something else, isn't there?"

"Yes, Doctor, there is. The upper deck is going to be the most secure area of the ship. You and your people will be safest there, in case those critters decide to come back tonight."

"All right, Captain," Cortez agreed. "I'll pass your orders along to my people."

As soon as the doctor made her way forward, and out of the bay, Taggart turned to the Marines.

"Okay, Gunny, let's have it."

"Nothing, sir, not a goddamn thing. We went through the debris field as best we could with the daylight we had left. We found a lot of junk, and about half of it had that dried purple blood stuff on it. But no data recorder." Frost jerked a thumb at Corporal Henry. "Tim here took a couple of guys back along the valley about a klick or so, following the gouge *Cabot* made in the ground when she skidded in."

"That's right, boss. We found lots of junk, bits of hull plating, pieces of structural members, even a piece of what might have been a control jet." The tall, prematurely gray-haired Marine shrugged. "But no sign of the black box."

"How about you, Dade?" Taggart asked.

"Nothing, sir, just like Gunny said." The scout shrugged, with a note of bitterness in his voice. "If it had just been Krista and me moving down here, we might have been able to find something. But you've had twenty Marines and a dozen medics stomping all over the area. Every time we picked up a decent trail, it only ran a few meters before some clodhopping character wiped it out. We went out a ways farther, maybe two hundred, two hundred fifty meters. Picked up a couple of decent trails, but they lead in all different directions. It was getting too dark to follow any of them. We marked them. If you like, we can start tracking the bad guys in the morning."

"For all the good it's gonna do," Black put in.

"How's that, Private?"

"Captain, we can try to track those mutants, or aliens or boogeymen, or whatever you want to call them. But most of those trails are at least a couple of days old, near as we can tell on this damn screwy world," Black gave a rueful chuckle and continued. "The soil is so dry and dusty, it doesn't look like it's rained for a couple of months. Yet that blue-green stuff that passes for grass looks nice and fresh. Makes it hard to tell how old tracks are when they start caving in along the sides as soon as they're made. It's almost like tracking in soft sand."

"So give me the bottom line. You think it's worth trying to backtrack the bad guys? We still have a few crewmen unaccounted for. The Mashers may have taken them as prisoners."

"I think we might be able to pull it off, sir," Dade answered, waving Black to silence.

"Okay. You two go get some rest." Taggart motioned the scouts into the cargo bay's shadowy recesses. "We'll try it again as soon as it gets light. I'm gonna send Second Squad with you, just in case."

"Aye, aye, sir," Dade said with a grin. "Krista and I will be glad of the company . . . and the backup."

"Yeah," Black said with a touch of pensive hopelessness. "As long as they know to stay far enough back to keep from disturbing any more signs, and to be close enough to help if we run into hostiles."

Taggart let out a snorting laugh and said, "Go get some sleep."

"One more thing, sir," Dade said. "The tracks we've been seeing? The ones that look like some kind of mechanical walker? On the approach to the wreck, Krista and I saw signs of at least two of the blasted things. Out there?" He gestured toward the open bay door and the gathering darkness beyond. "We saw signs of what might have been three more. I say 'might have been,' 'cause the signs are so confused it's hard to tell. It might have been the same ones, but I can't say for certain."

"Oh, that's wonderful, Dade," Taggart said sarcastically. "Go get some sleep before you think of any more good news."

As the Marines headed into the cargo bay's interior, seeking a clear space in which they could bunk down, Taggart gestured to Gunnery Sergeant Frost, beckoning her to follow him. Stepping out of the bay, Taggart easily picked out the two Marines stationed near the bay's open door. He knew if he flicked on his suit's light-amplification system, he'd be able to see two more men, stationed at listening/observation posts near *Cabot*'s bow and shredded stern. The close-in sentries had constructed fighting positions by digging a meter or so into the dry rocky soil. To complete the positions, they had piled up white limestonelike rocks in a makeshift parapet around the shallow foxholes.

"Gunny, we're gonna be here at least overnight. Maybe

tomorrow night, too, I don't know. Dr. Cortez wants to wait until her patient is stable before we head back to the landing zone," he said quietly. "Even though we'll be rotating sentries all night, I'd like to have more advance warning if any hostiles decide to approach the ship. What have you got in the way of remotes?"

"Well, sir," Frost said, "if you mean ground sensors, we aren't in bad shape. We've got a dozen or so remote sensors, sentry-remotes. Nothing too big or fancy, mostly just trip-wire alarms, flares, that kind of thing. We have a few seismic and thermographic sensors. And I bet we could jury-rig a couple of *Cabot*'s survey probes into makeshift packages. All we'd have to do is tap into their telemetry and link it into our sensor monitoring systems.

"If you want combat systems, you're out of luck. We don't have anything like an Automated Defense Drone, and I doubt we'd be able to lash one up, at least not too easily."

Taggart listened as Frost spoke. He knew the platoon's remote sensor inventory as well as she did. This was merely his way of opening the discussion.

"Personally, sir," Frost continued, "I'd place our seismic and thermo sensors out toward the gully where we found the bodies, maybe one of *Cabot*'s probes, too. Put the trip-wire systems in closer. I'd also think of putting a couple of sensors and a probe on the far side of the ship. So far the aliens or whatever the hell they are haven't displayed much tactical sense, just low animal cunning. Still, I'd hate to rely on the notion that they couldn't learn from their mistakes, only to have them come at us from our blind side."

"Agreed," Taggart said with a nod. "How many men will you need for the job?"

"Six ought to do it sir," she answered after a moment's consideration. "And a couple more to see about the probes."

"All right, get to it. I want this area secured, before midnight if possible. I'm not really expecting an attack, but if one *is* headed our way, I'd like a little advance warning about it."

"Aye, aye, sir," Frost said.

"Onawa, this is for your ears only," Taggart said, leaning close to his top sergeant. "My primary concern here is for the safety of this team, Cortez's people as well as ours. However, I'm thinking we have another responsibility here. If we *have* encountered another alien race, like we think we have, I think we have a duty to bring back whatever intelligence we can gather on them.

"The things that attacked Dade and Black have got to have a different physiology. They were not wearing any kind of mask or environment suit. Yet they seemed to be unaffected by this planet's toxic atmosphere. I don't think the Sovs are sophisticated enough to come up with some kind of mutant that can breathe carbon dioxide and ammonia, and live, even thrive, in a low-pressure environment. At best, they've found another race that can survive under these conditions, enslaved them, and turned them into a new kind of mutant."

"Well, sir, whatever they are, if they cross us again, we'll do our best to blow 'em straight to hell. Still, begging the captain's pardon, figuring out what those things are isn't exactly in our department," Frost said reassuringly. "Our job is to kill people and break things. Leave the heavy headwork to the high-priced pantywaist brain trusts back home. We get a chance, we'll bag a couple of those ugly little bastards and take 'em home with us. Let the geniuses at UCLA and Caltech get the migraines on this one."

"Aaah, you're probably right, Gunny," Taggart said

with a laugh. "Get those sensors on-line as quick as you can, okay?"

Gunnery Sergeant Frost, working with a fire team from First Squad, planted the seismic and thermographic remote ground sensor units as Taggart had directed. These devices were set to ignore anything weighing less than thirty kilograms or having a heat signature smaller than that of a ten-year-old child. The trip-wire-activated devices would have to wait until the jury-rigged sensor platforms cobbled together from two of *Cabot*'s probes were put into service.

Three men in the already-divided platoon were found who knew enough about sensor packages to convert a scientific probe into a makeshift sentry drone. The work went remarkably fast, and the reprogrammed probes came on-line at 2130 hours.

All that remained was to wait the night out and hope that the enemy lurking out there in the darkness would leave them alone.

23

D r. Rebecca Cortez's eyes flicked open, sleepiness vanishing as her vision rapidly adapted to the darkness of *Cabot*'s crew quarters. She sat upright in the bunk. Straining her senses, she concentrated on her surroundings. Was the noise that had awakened her a figment of her own imagination, a dream-sound inspired by the tension of the past few days? Cortez rarely remembered her dreams after being awake a few minutes, but her nightmare of being trapped in a charnel house had stuck with her, making her reluctant to close her eyes.

If the sound hadn't been a dream, what was it? Was it the badly damaged ship settling? Had one of her colleagues rolled over in sleep, knocking aside some small object, causing the slight skittering noise? Or was it one of the Marines? She knew Taggart had detailed one of his jarheads to check *Cabot*'s upper decks at irregular intervals. Had a sentry accidentally caused the sound that had dragged her from her fitful sleep?

When the sound failed to repeat itself, Cortez put it down to a random noise. She lay back down on her bunk.

Perversely, the more she tried to sleep, the more obstinately sleep refused to come. With an angry snort, Cortez tossed the blankets aside. She clambered to her feet, making as little noise as possible, trying not to disturb her sleeping colleagues.

If I can't sleep, she told herself, *I might as well go check on Michelli.* The comatose ensign had been taken to the other berthing compartment, just forward of the one she and her teammates occupied, which her team had converted into a makeshift sick bay.

Picking up her bulky field jacket, she draped the garment over her shoulders. As she slipped into the companionway she glanced at her chrono. It was well past midnight, local time. The narrow corridor was dark, save for a few long-life, cold lightsticks the Marines had strung from the overhead. No doubt the sentry who made an occasional pass through this area of the ship relied upon the bioluminescent sticks to help him negotiate the twisted and buckled deck of the corridor.

Something clanged in the darkness. The sharp metallic sound came from the ship's forward section, near the bridge. Cortez fumbled in her jacket pocket for a small pencil flash she kept there. Not nearly as powerful as the Marines' bigger angle-headed flashlights, the miniature light was primarily useful in checking pupillary reactions to light. Still, it provided a tiny pool of illumination that was somewhat brighter than the unearthly green glow given off by the lightsticks.

Cortez pointed the small flashlight toward the bridge and thumbed the plunger switch. The weak beam did little to repel the darkness in the companionway. Instead, its pale light only served to destroy her night vision and to highlight the deep pools of shadow beyond its feeble reach. The doctor took three careful steps toward *Cabot*'s bridge, when a soft scrabbling noise sounded from the ship's command deck.

Nervously, Cortez transferred the light to her left hand and groped around her right hip, searching for the Pug auto-pistol she wore there. With a chill, Cortez realized she had left the weapon next to her bunk in the crew's quarters.

At that moment, the door to the forward berthing space–cum–sick bay slammed open, and medical technician Nancy Reed stepped into the corridor, colliding forcefully with her chief. As the women reeled, fighting for balance, Cortez more imagined than heard a louder scurrying noise, punctuated by what sounded like a yelp of pain and surprise.

"Dr. Cortez, I was just coming to get you," Reed said breathlessly. "He's awake. Ensign Michelli—he's regained consciousness."

"Good," Cortez said. "Go wake Dr. Grippo. Tell him. Then send someone to fetch Captain Taggart."

All thoughts of invisible boogeymen evaporated from Cortez's mind as she pushed aside the door to the makeshift sick bay.

Michelli lay on one of the crew bunks that had been converted into a jury-rigged pressure tent. She saw his eyes were open, but held a fuzzy, unfocused look, as though the ensign was having trouble knowing where he was. A nurse crouched on her knees next to the bunk, checking Michelli's vital signs by means of a small electronic monitor. The device's leads ran through the thick plastic of the pressure tent, and were attached to self-adhesive pads on Michelli's chest, temples, and arms.

The nurse, a thin, pale man originally from the American Midwest, looked up at Cortez's entry.

"He's awake and responsive, Doctor," the nurse said,

getting to his feet. "Vitals are all good, though he seems to be having trouble concentrating."

Stepping closer to Cortez, he continued. "Doctor, he's been asking about his ship and crew. I didn't know what to tell him."

"It's okay, Sam," Cortez said. "I'll handle it." She took a deep breath.

"Hello," she said, giving Michelli the benefit of her best bedside smile. "I'm Dr. Lieutenant Rebecca Cortez, Union Space Force. How are you feeling?"

"Ens . . ." Michelli tried to respond, but his words came out as a croaking whisper. He cleared his throat and tried again. "Ensign Walter Michelli, ma'am. Third officer USS *Cabot*. I feel like death on a bun, ma'am."

"Mmmm, that's to be expected." Cortez knelt and scanned the condition monitors. Michelli's blood pressure was slightly depressed, and his pulse rate a bit slow, but everything was within the range of acceptability. "You were in pretty bad shape when we found you. I wouldn't worry, though, we've got a whole team of doctors here. You're going to be fine."

Rapid footsteps sounded in the doorway behind her. Cortez turned just in time to see Captain Taggart and Gunnery Sergeant Frost enter the room. To his credit, the Marine officer hung back, waiting for Cortez to finish her examination of *Cabot*'s sole survivor before quizzing her on Michelli's condition. Even so, there was a certain anxiousness in his stance.

Cortez gave Michelli another smile, and said reassuringly, "You'll be fine, Ensign. As soon as you're fit, we'll get you out of this bag and into an environment suit. We've got a rescue cutter waiting to take us back to Earth. We'll leave as soon as you're able. How's that sound?"

Michelli nodded, though sadness drifted across his drawn features.

The doctor patted his arm through the thick plastic of the pressure tent. "Don't go anywhere for a minute, okay?"

She got to her feet and motioned the Marines to accompany her into the companionway.

"How is he, Doc?" Taggart asked.

"Physically? He's fine. I can say without reservation that he's going to make it. Emotionally?" She shrugged. "That's hard to say. Sole survivors tend to have a lot of guilt. It's stupid, but it's true. They feel guilty because they survived and all their buddies didn't. We're going to have to wait and see."

"Can he answer a few questions, do you think?"

Cortez considered the captain's request for a few moments before answering.

"A few," she said. "If he balks at answering something, don't press him. And when I say you're done, you're done, understand?"

"Understood, Doctor." Taggart nodded.

Cortez stepped back into the compartment.

"Ensign, this is Captain Maxwell Taggart, Union Ground Forces. He's in charge of the rescue team," Cortez said gently. "Do you feel up to answering a few questions for him?"

Michelli's face blanched. Cortez was afraid he was going to faint.

"Captain, I'm sorry, I . . ." she began, but Michelli cut her off.

"No, Doctor, it's all right. I'll answer the captain's questions."

"Walter, are you sure?"

"Yes, ma'am. I've got to answer these questions sooner

or later. I might as well do it while things are still fresh in my mind," Michelli said resolutely.

For a moment, she looked from Michelli to Taggart, then stepped aside to make a place for the Marine officer.

"Just remember," she said quietly to Taggart.

"I know, Doc. I'll be gentle." He turned to Michelli.

"Evening, Ensign. I'm Max Taggart. Dr. Cortez was right. I'm the CO of the rescue team. You feel like answering some questions for me?"

"Yessir."

"Good, good," Taggart said, smiling. "Ensign, you've got to know the first thing I've gotta ask you. What happened here? Why did *Cabot* crash?"

A cloud crossed Michelli's features. He took a deep breath, sighed wearily, and began.

"We were doing an in-atmosphere survey of the planet's surface, using our ground-scan radar and thermal imagers. Captain Hu wanted to use the visible light cameras, too, but there was too much cloud cover. I've never seen a world where so much of the planet was cloudy all the time. We got three orbits in clean. Good imagery, nice clean scans. On our fourth pass, coming in over the plains west of here, we started picking up some chop, really severe stuff. Funny thing was none of the detection gear gave us any indication of why we were getting the turbulence.

"As soon as we passed over these mountains, the turbulence kinda petered out. We figured it was a local phenomenon. God knows we've seen enough weird stuff since the Earth got sucked into the Maelstrom.

"On our next pass, it was like someone tossed us into a mixer. I was off duty, in my rack, that one right over there." Michelli pointed at an upper bunk opposite the one he occupied. "I got tossed out onto the deck. Landed on my back and got the breath knocked out of me. I was trying to get up when I heard the engines blow."

"Hang on a second, Ensign," Taggart interrupted. "The engines blew?"

"Well, the starboard engine anyway. It suffered a catastrophic failure in the reaction chamber. The engine blew itself all over the compartment. The portside plant got shredded in the blast. The explosion ripped a big gash in the hull and caused a big fire in the engineering spaces."

Michelli shuddered.

"If *Cabot* had been in space at the time, I don't think any of us would have survived long enough to know what was happening to us.

"I headed for my duty station, on the bridge. I could hear the pilot swearing at the ship, trying to keep her under control with nothing but auxiliary power. I still can't believe he managed to get us down without smacking us into one of the mountains."

"What about the crew?" Taggart asked.

"I don't know. I think most of the engine-room gang must have been killed when the engine blew. Those that survived were either killed by the fire, or lost to explosive decompression when the hull let go.

"The rest." He sighed. "All the rest were killed in the crash, everyone but me."

"How did you manage to survive?" Gunny Frost asked with no hint of accusation in her voice.

For a long while, Michelli did not answer. He lay back on his bunk, his face twisted. Tears leaked from the corners of his tightly shut eyes. His chest heaved as he gasped for breath. For a moment Cortez feared he was having a heart attack. When he spoke again, it was in a voice thick with grief and self-condemnation.

"The truth is, I panicked when the engines blew. I ran right for the escape pod and sealed myself in. I tried to launch the pod, but it wouldn't drop. The explosion must have warped part of the ship's superstructure."

"Everybody else was at their stations when we hit. The whole flight crew was on the bridge. They were all killed instantly. Captain Hu was almost cut in half. I had to take her out of there in two different body bags." Michelli's voice had become a tortured sob. "Lieutenant McBride didn't have a mark on him, but he was just as dead as the captain. Everybody else was either killed by the crash or badly injured. After the crash, I tried to help the survivors, but I'm not a doctor. All I could do was keep them doped up so they didn't suffer too bad.

"Hayes had lost both legs. Piper was pretty badly burned, third degree, over most of his body. I couldn't do anything for them, Captain. I gave them morphine, a lot of it. I couldn't let them suffer."

"It's okay, boy," Taggart said, laying a hand on Michelli's arm through the plastic of the pressure tent. He looked at Cortez, who shook her head.

"No, let him talk it out," she said. She could feel the anguish the young ensign must have lived with every day since the crash. "The sooner he gets all this out of his system, the better."

Taggart nodded grimly and, after giving Michelli a moment to compose himself, asked him to continue.

"Well, sir," Michelli said, sniffing and wiping his eyes with his fingers, "the central section of the ship was pretty much intact, or at least it was holding pressure. I did what I could with what I knew, and what I could scrounge out of the hard-copy manuals. I rigged up the ship's auxiliary power cells to run the emergency communication system in the life pod. I was almost finished when those things came.

"I managed to drag Krinock and Bogi inside the pod before the monsters found us. I had to seal up the pod or they'd have gotten us too. They slaughtered everybody left outside. For hours, those creatures crawled all over the ship, looting her. They gutted her, sir. They smashed up systems, ripped out components, and stole everything they could carry away. When they finally left, it took me a couple of hours to get up the nerve to open the hatch again. I went outside to see if anyone was left alive. There wasn't. The creatures had killed them all and dumped them in a ravine out there." Michelli gestured vaguely toward the ship's hull and the rift valley beyond.

"We know Walter," Cortez said gently. "We found them. We'll take them home for proper burial."

"Yes, ma'am." Michelli's voice was a bit stronger, the emotion having spent itself in a cathartic rush.

"So what happened to the other two, Krinock and Bogi?" Taggart asked.

"Phil Bogi died the next day, and Tom Krinock a few days later. They were just hurt too bad. I couldn't help them," Michelli said in a hollow tone. "I carried them outside the ship. I wanted to bury them, so that the monsters would leave them alone, but I couldn't. I was so afraid those things were coming back. All I could do was leave them in the ravine with the rest of the crew. Then I came back here. I dragged in all the supplies I could find and sent off that call for help. There was barely enough power in the batteries for that one shot. Then I sealed myself in and sat down to wait. It wasn't an hour later that they came back. And they kept coming back, every day, just about nightfall. They tried a couple of times to break into the pod, but I guess the lock stumped them. Honestly, I didn't think I was going to make it."

Michelli stopped and leaned back against the bunk. For several seconds he looked steadily from Taggart to Frost to Cortez. His face and eyes were as empty as a doll's. Then a sudden look of realization flashed across his face.

"Captain, there were a couple people outside the ship when those things came," Michelli said, pushing himself into a sitting position. "I couldn't find their bodies. I think the creatures might have taken them prisoner."

24

Word that Michelli had regained consciousness spread quickly among the men and women of the rescue team. The shipwrecked ensign's fears concerning his possibly abducted crewmates spread with equal rapidity. Marine and medic alike expressed the same thought: "We've got to go find them, dead or alive. We don't leave our people behind."

But there were a few Marines for whom the possibility of a rescue mission within the larger rescue mission held a distant second to the task immediately to hand. Those men were the sentries Taggart had deployed around the perimeter of the wreck site. As Taggart and Frost stood in the corridor outside the makeshift sick bay, Private deSilva scrambled up the ladder from *Cabot*'s lower deck.

"Captain, Corporal Henry sent me to fetch you and Gunny Frost, sir. Something's going on outside."

Taggart and Frost ran for the ladder. As he waited for his subordinates to descend the steel rungs, Taggart shouted to Cortez.

"Remember, Doctor, tell your people to keep to the

upper deck. If you need us, use the communicators and we'll come a-runnin'."

Not waiting for the doctor's reply, Taggart dropped swiftly out of sight, following his troops down the ladder.

"What's going on, Corporal?" Taggart asked as he strode into the cargo bay.

"Don't rightly know, boss," came the reply. "We've been hearing kinda funny noises off and on all night. At first I thought it was loose rock sliding off those big white piles all over the valley. It doesn't really sound right, though. I can't explain it any better than that."

"Did you send out a patrol?"

"Well, sort of, sir," Henry said. "I took one out myself. We poked around for an hour or so and didn't find anything. It's as black as hell's heart out there, sir. If I had to make a guess, Captain, I'd say it was just what we thought it was, rock sliding down a hillside."

"But we can't assume that," Frost said in a level voice. "It could be the Mashers, trying to draw us away from the ship."

"Hmm." Taggart pursed his lips and thought a bit. "I think you may be right, Gunny. All right, I'd rather not risk any men in the dark. Double the guard. I don't want to go chasing sounds in the night. We know there are hostiles out there; we just don't know anything about them. Could be this is the aliens' way of trying to draw some of us away from the ship."

Taggart turned away from the chorus of "aye, ayes" and headed toward the corner of the cargo bay he had staked out for his own bunk roll. As he wearily lowered himself to the steel decking, his mind was full of the concerns of the past and coming days. Thus far the operation had been relatively easy. Losing PFC Kowalski and Dr. Ake weighed heavily on his mind. Never mind the Union's policy of making every effort to recover the bodies of men lost in action, his inability to locate either the men or their remains was a mark of personal failure, at least to his way of thinking.

At least, with Michelli's recovery, Dr. Cortez had finally broken her stony silence toward him. And yet the underlying hostility remained. Try as he might Taggart could not quite wrap his mind around the woman's reasons for disliking him. She claimed she bore him no personal animosity, yet her attitude showed a fierce antipathy. Perhaps Frost's assessment had been correct. It was a sort of case of reverse discrimination. Many members of the Mexican Contribution Force *were* discriminated against—there was no denying that. Taggart wondered if Cortez had made up her mind that he was going to be a prejudiced bigot before she learned the truth of his character and had erected a wall of barely concealed hostility as a means of defense.

Taggart snorted at the idea. He thought briefly over the short time he had known Rebecca Cortez. In that brief period, he *had* treated her with a certain lack of courtesy. But his attitude had not been birthed out of racism. Pride and tradition ran deep in what had once been the United States Marine Corps, as illustrated by many Marines' refusal to accept the all-encompassing label of Ground Corps. As a professional soldier, Taggart had a low opinion of officers who were *given* their rank based solely upon their career choice. In all likelihood, it had been that prideful disdain that Cortez had mistaken for bigotry.

With a sigh, he pushed the thoughts and emotions out of his mind. He consulted the life-support display on his combat environment suit's monitoring system. The unit was functioning properly. The current charge had over 150 hours left on it. A well-maintained suit could keep a man alive for nearly two weeks in the field, depending upon his level of activity.

He lay back on his thin sleeping pad. He could feel the cold of the cargo bay's steel deck through the foam-rubber pad and sleeping bag. That would not prevent him from catching a few hours' sleep. His consciousness was drifting away even as he shrugged his body into a more comfortable position.

"Boss, we got trouble."

Taggart snapped awake at Gunny Frost's first shake of his shoulder.

"What is it?"

"Three of the sensor packages have gone off-line, including one we cobbled together out of a probe," Frost replied. "They went black within a few seconds of each other. The operator woke me as soon as it happened. I've got all of the boys up and alert. We're scanning the area with starlight gear, but so far nothin'."

"All right. Show me." Taggart stood up and threw off the dopey feeling that being yanked out of a sound sleep sometimes caused.

Frost led him across the gloomy cargo bay toward the spot where they had installed the monitoring system for the platoon's remote ground sensors. As they went, Taggart could see the shadowy forms of his men. Some crouched behind the low barricade of rocks and dirt they had erected as an improvised fighting position before the open bay door. Others were "pinched up" just inside the bay itself, waiting for the enemy to make his presence felt before they swung into action.

"Here it is, Captain," the sensor operator, a private first class from Second Squad, said, tapping the liquid crystal display of the monitoring unit. "First to go was a seismic right here. Then we lost a thermal, and then the survey pod. They all blanked out within a minute or so of each other. I tried reestablishing the link, and even rebooting the system, but no dice. They're out of commission. My guess is somebody knocked them out."

"Concur," Frost said in reply to her captain's questioning look.

"Very well." Taggart made his decision quickly. "Gunny, send a fire team out to check on those sensors. The rest of us will stand ready to jump in if this is anything more than a coincidence, and I think it is."

"Right, sir," Frost said. "I'll take a fire team from Second Squad, if that's okay with you, sir."

Taggart looked sharply at his senior noncom. While there were no specific regulations barring it, dividing a squad into two smaller fire teams in the face of an enemy was generally looked down upon by both the brass and the soldiers on the line. Assigning the platoon's senior noncommissioned officer to handle a detached fire team was usually treated with similar disdain. Breaking a squad down into four- or five-man teams diminished the amount of firepower that might be brought to bear on a target, while detaching an officer or senior noncom usually took that leader out of a position from which to more effectively control the actions of the entire squad.

Still, he had little choice. With only two squads at his disposal, Taggart needed to keep most of his force in position to defend the ship and the noncombatants inside. Gunny Frost would have to take out a five-man fire team.

As Frost called out the men she wanted, Taggart slipped through the open bay door, settling down behind the stone and earth barricade. From there he would have better control over the situation, if things degenerated into a shooting match.

It took Onawa Frost only a few seconds to assemble the men she wanted. All were experienced fighters, and all were good levelheaded Marines. As she moved her men out of the bay, she caught Captain Taggart's eye. The captain lifted his hand in a farewell gesture, which Frost returned, feeling none of the good cheer that such a gesture sometimes implied.

"All right, move out," she whispered.

One by one, like faceless ghosts, the men slipped over the breastwork and into the darkness beyond. Frost was the last to go. When her feet touched the soil on the far side of the makeshift parapet, she keyed in her low-light viewing system. The valley floor leapt into a clear, eerie vista of black, gray, and green. Her troopers were spread out ahead of her with three meters between each man. They moved cautiously, taking their time. Occasionally, one would pause and look around, his weapons following his eyes. They listened intently for sounds that might betray the presence of an aggressor. As she watched the slow, careful progress of her fire team, Gunny Frost felt a sense of pride. These men were *Marines*, no matter what the politicians back on Earth called them.

Suddenly one of the men stopped. He pointed at the ground a few feet in front of him. The extended index finger, told Frost that he had not seen the enemy, as a fully splayed hand would have indicated, but rather had located one of the crippled sensor packages.

"Halt," she whispered into her communicator. She knew there was little chance of the enemy overhearing the hissed command, but old habits die hard, and when they do, they usually kill the one who ignores them. "Hold position."

Hefting her shotgun, Frost moved quickly and quietly to join the man who had found the disabled remote. The ground sensor was a dark green metal box, a bit larger than a family-size soup can. Once it had housed delicate seismographic sensors capable of detecting something weighing as little as twenty-five kilos, along with telemetry units that allowed remote monitoring of the device. Given its condition, an old model tracked tank could have rumbled over the sensor's location and it wouldn't detect a thing. The unit's metal housing seemed to have been ripped open with a hacksaw, and the internal components looked like they had been smashed with a hammer.

Frost clicked her tongue against the roof of her mouth, breaking static to attract the attention of her men. Using hand gestures she instructed her men to move off on a right oblique heading northward, toward the next out-of-service sensor package. When they found the next device, the thermograph's casing had been pried open, and the heat-sensing unit torn away.

Thirty meters further north, the survey probe-cum–ground sensor had also been trashed. The thick steel outer shell had been hacked open and all of the internal electronics ripped from their mountings. After warning her troops to shield their night-vision-equipped eyes, Frost pulled her flashlight out and began to quarter and search the area, hooding the light's beam with her hand.

A few meters southeast of the ruined probe, she found a small pool of dark reddish purple fluid. The sticky liquid was beginning to seep into the dusty ground. On the edges of the puddle, a dark purple black flaky material had already begun to form.

Dammit, she swore under her breath. Then keying open her communicator, she contacted Captain Taggart.

"Lion Six, this is Lion Three. We found the sensor packages, boss. One is smashed. The others have been ripped open and gutted. I think our ugly little friends have been looting again."

Taggart's reply was lost as a shower of metal spikes tore into the Marines' position.

"Cover!" Frost screamed, diving behind the probe. Only three of her men responded. One slumped forward with his belly against a rock outcropping. His head lay at an odd angle to his shoulders. A thick rod of metal jutted out of his neck, just below the right ear. The man had died instantly. A second man lay writhing on the ground, his hands locked around a spike protruding from his left thigh.

"Corpsman!" a Marine yelled, and scrabbled on his belly to reach his wounded comrade.

"Ortega, will you get the hell down!" Frost shouted.

The man gave no indication of having heard her. Instead he grabbed his buddy by the shoulder straps of his load-bearing gear and, crawling, dragged him toward the shelter of an outcropping. Three spikes dug into the soft earth not far from Ortega's struggling body, but none touched either the Marine or the man he was risking his life to save.

Frost snapped her shotgun up to her shoulder and pulled the trigger. A hollow boom roared out, almost blanketing the lighter cracks of the Pitbull rifles. The fire team's heaviest weapon, a Bulldog support rifle, lay in the open, where the dead man had dropped it.

Ortega was still screaming for a corpsman and trying to staunch the flow of blood from his injured comrade's leg by clamping his hands over the wound. The protruding spike made that difficult, but to pull it from the man's leg might do more harm than good, and Ortega knew it.

Frost let go another blast of buckshot from her Jackal. Without a clear target, she knew her chances of hitting anything other than the landscape were thin. But the deafening report and huge muzzle flare of the big eighteen-millimeter weapon would have as much psychological effect as a full-auto burst from a Pitbull.

As she racked the slide, chambering another round, a second volley of spikes fell on the Marines' position. Two sharpened steel projectiles struck the probe's casing. One glanced away in a shower of pale sparks; the other embedded itself in the device's metal skin. A third slammed into the dead Marine's chest and pitched him over on his back, arms and legs splayed obscenely. None of the projectiles found a living target.

With a yell of anger Frost loosed two more blasts of shotgun fire into the night and ducked back into the cover of the probe to reload. As she slammed shells into the loading port in the weapon's lower receiver, she heard a low, guttural snarl.

A dozen or so short, brutish figures came bounding out of the darkness toward the Marines. Frost had time for only one shot before the creatures were upon her, but the wide-spreading blast of heavy lead pellets ripped into two of the ugly monsters. They dropped to the ground. She reversed her weapon and smashed its stock into an onrushing creature's face.

A fourth monster rose up in that one's place and slashed at her belly with a weapon that looked like a combination buzz saw and entrenching tool. Frost twisted out of the way. The weapon caught some part of her combat harness, jerking her in a quarter circle before coming free. For one horrible second, she wondered if the attack had torn her suit.

The creature stepped in toward her, swinging the strange melee weapon as it came. With its free hand it grabbed for the Jackal, trying to tear it from her grasp. Frost could either dodge the blow, or hang on to her shotgun. She released the stubby weapon and stepped back. Scrabbling for her sidearm, she found only an empty and torn nylon holster. That must have been what the creature's weapon had snagged on.

Vaguely, on the edges of her senses, she heard a high-pitched wail of horror and pain, but had no time to wonder if it was a friend or a foe.

Frost yanked the heavy Ka-Bar combat knife from its upside-down sheath on her left shoulder and lunged at her attacker. The monster came up short. It dropped the Jackal and met her charge hand to hand. Frost grabbed the thing's weapon hand with her left hand in what would have been a bone-crushing grip had the creature been human. She felt the cords of steely muscle beneath the being's filthy hide. She attempted to stab it in the guts, but the creature writhed its belly out of the way of the knife and grabbed her knife wrist in a powerful hand the size of a shovel.

The thing's appearance was even more hideous at close range. Dust and dried mud seemed to be caked in its hair. Scars of every size and description covered its body. Where there were no scars, the thing seemed to have had metal bolt heads implanted in a sinuous pattern along its arms and legs. The creature snapped at Frost's visored face with large, powerful, but rotted teeth. She was glad of the combat environment suit's filter mask. She was certain the Masher had a reek more foul than a week-dead skunk.

Chest to chest they struggled. Frost, with her years of

training, against the creature's brute strength and cunning. The thing lashed out with a foot, trying to smash Frost's knee from beneath her. The gunnery sergeant anticipated the attack and avoided the blow. Twisting her upper body, she tried to lever the monster off its feet in a sort of hip toss. The creature was too heavy for her to do more than drag in a quarter circle.

But that proved to be enough. The creature tumbled to the ground, its thick fingers still locked around her wrist. The thing's weight dragged her down with it. Fearing an on-the-ground grapple with the powerful monster, Frost tore her hand free. She pulled back and, with both hands, plunged the Ka-Bar into the thing's throat. She jerked the knife from the wound and drove it in again, and again, and again.

Struggling to her feet, Frost looked about wildly, the gore-dripping combat knife held aggressively in front of her.

"Gunny, you okay?" Ortega asked, stepping in close to her, carefully avoiding the purple-stained blade.

"Ortega? What?"

"It's okay, Gunny. We're clear. The bad guys are either dead or bugged out."

Frost stared at him, fighting to get her breathing and her killing rage under control.

"Casualties?" she said at last.

"Rice is dead. So is McBride," Ortega replied. "Panchard is pretty badly ripped up. The docs are with him now. They don't know if he's gonna make it."

"What happened?"

"The captain sent out the rest of Second Squad to bail us out," Ortega explained. "They smoked at least five of the ugly fraggers, and the rest bugged out. The boss wants everyone back at the ship ASAP."

"Right," Frost said with a sigh of exhaustion. Her hip ached where the creature's weapon had smashed into her body. She was dreadfully thirsty.

"Where's my Jackal? And my Pug? Thank God I had that pistol. Otherwise, that thing's ax, sword, or whatever the hell it is would have ripped my suit."

Ortega looked around and found both her weapons. The Jackal was intact, but the heavy M-43 automatic pistol had been badly damaged by the attack that had almost cost her both her leg and her life. She stuffed the weapon into a pouch on her combat harness. Ruined or not, she would not leave the Pug behind for the enemy.

Frost turned her attention to the monster that had nearly taken her life. It was only about five feet tall, but its frame was layered with dense slabs of muscle. The thing's head seemed too large for its body. The facial bones were coarse and large, as were all its features except the eyes. Those were small and beady, under massive, prognathous ridges. Its hair and skin were filthy and caked with the dusty loam that characterized the soil of the rift valley's floor. Its mouth, full of snaggled, rotting teeth, was locked open in a surprised snarl.

Something odd about the admittedly strange corpse caught Frost's attention. Like those of the creatures in Dade's recording of the attack on the scouts, this creature's body was studded with small knobs and bosses of metal which seemed to be implanted in its flesh. In studying these implants, Frost saw yet another anomaly.

Embedded in the thick muscle of the thing's left shoulder was a drab green box with a metallic gray face. It was one of the infrared sensor packages from the converted probe. Wires trailing from the device seemed to run straight into the thing's flesh, all clustered near the nerve plexus under the collarbone. The flesh surrounding the metal box appeared to be raw, and a dark reddish purple fluid oozed from it.

"All right," Frost muttered. "Let's head back, like the boss said."

As the surviving members of her fire team and the Marines who had been sent out to rescue them filed past her on their way back to the wrecked survey ship, she looked down at the dead alien and sighed again.

Fighting her sense of revulsion, Frost hoisted the creature onto her shoulders. Whatever happened, she was going to make sure that the brain-boys in the Technical and Intelligence Corps had at least one of the dead monsters to examine.

Staggering under the unexpectedly heavy load, Frost headed back toward the ship.

25

D r. Cortez leaned against the bulkhead outside the makeshift sick bay. The night had grown cool, and the clamminess in the air carried the cold straight through to her bones. Not five minutes ago, Captain Taggart had sent a runner asking for three of her medics to stand by in the cargo bay, should a patrol he had sent out run into trouble. Since then, the wrecked survey ship had taken on a menacing quality that seemed to come from her nightmares. Broken conduits and dangling wires resembled snakes and tentacles. The creak and pop of settling metal took on the menacing tone of a deranged killer's footsteps as he slipped through the companionways and berthing spaces seeking his next victim. The odd green glow of the cold lightsticks only added to the otherworldliness of the scene.

As she ducked under the ragged, pendulous tentacles of broken wires, her holstered sidearm jabbed into her short ribs. As a naval doctor, she was unused to carrying a pistol, usually finding herself aboard a hospital ship, where such a weapon would be of little use. Here, in the ghastly setting of a wrecked survey ship, cast away on an alien world, the Pug's two-kilo bulk was a comforting presence on her hip.

A sharp metallic clang echoed up the corridor, muted by distance. It seemed to her that the noise had come from the twisted bulkhead separating the ruin that had once been *Cabot*'s engine room from the rest of the ship. Cortez tried to melt into the shadows, pressing her back against the cold steel of the corridor wall. She breathed as shallowly and as slowly as she could, straining her ears to catch any sound drifting up from the engineering spaces. A faint scuffing sound reached her ears, followed by a sharp metallic clatter. A cold sweat prickled across her forehead and along the skin of her arms. She knew Taggart had not stationed any of his men inside the engine room.

A patch of shadow of a darker shade than the surrounding murkiness seemed to flow from near the engine-room hatchway. A faint shuffling noise, like a leather bag being dragged along the deck, reached her ears. The half-seen specter stopped with a jerk. The sibilant patter was replaced by a deep, questioning shuffle, like some huge dog casting around for a scent.

Cortez's nostrils were invaded by a sour odor, the stink of her own fear.

The doctor's combat environment suit had been equipped with the same low-light vision system as those worn by the Marines. As she huddled in that pool of shadow, she desperately searched her mind, trying to remember how to switch on the night viewing unit.

Cortez heard a rapid, stuttering series of sharp, flat cracks coming from outside the ship. The reports sounded like a burst of loud firecrackers, but she knew it was automatic rifle fire. Then a deeper boom rang out. Footsteps sounded on the deck below. The shadow let out a guttural bark and lunged into the center of the corridor. A hollow thump, and the rattle of small metal objects spilled across the steel decking reached her ears. The sound of bare feet against the metal decking slapped off the hard walls of the companionway as the thing ran toward her.

The doctor let out a sharp cry of surprise, and the thing skidded to a stop only a meter or two from her shadowed niche. For a long moment, neither moved. The black hulking thing stood frozen in the middle of the corridor, snuffling and wheezing. Cortez tried to shrink back even farther, almost willing her all-too-solid physical body to melt through the steel bulkhead and into the room beyond. Slowly, carefully, she slid her hand along her body, trying to reach the penlight tucked securely in the environment suit's left breast pocket. It seemed almost as though her consciousness was detached from her body. She knew she was controlling the movement of her hands, but it was as though she was doing so from outside via some sort of remote control. Curiously, the fear which had been building up inside her was almost gone, banished to some small corner of her mind where it slavered and snarled like a chained, rabid dog, wanting to get loose and run ravening through the streets of her mind, but impotent against the thick steel bonds.

The thing in front of her seemed to sense the movement. It let out a terrific yell and surged toward her. The penlight came free. At the same time her right hand, almost of its own accord, flew to the nylon holster strapped against the point of her right hip.

The light clicked on, illuminating the dirt-streaked face, matted black hair, and crooked decaying teeth of a Masher. The thing's tiny, piggish eyes screwed shut, and it brought its broad hands up to shield its face against the sudden glare of the penlight. A fresh wave of horror and revulsion rose in her gorge. In that fleeting moment, which seemed to stretch into hours, the image of a creature that should not be allowed to exist outside of nightmares was burned indelibly into her brain. It was almost as though she had come face-to-face with a *chupacabra*, the hideous goat-killing vampire of old Mexican legends. Incongruously, the doctor in her noticed an angry purple weal running across the alien's face and down its right cheek. She took the disfigurement to be a half-healed scar. Cortez saw a large object drop from the creature's hands and heard the flat metallic clatter as it bounced across the steel deck.

The Masher recovered quickly. It barked out a short, staccato series of guttural sounds. Cortez got the distinct impression that the thing was cursing at her. A macelike weapon seemed to blossom from its right fist, which the creature drew back over its head.

In desperation, still feeling no panic, the doctor yanked the Pug free of its flapped holster. She rammed the weapon's muzzle into the alien's belly and jerked the trigger. The normally reliable pistol failed to fire.

The creature doubled up from the force of the blow. Its spiked club hammered into the bulkhead, gouging furrows in the steel only a handspan from the doctor's head.

Cortez dodged to her right. The partially winded thing tried to follow her. The sidestep had been a feint. Cortez arrested her movement and ducked away from the creature, putting a handful of meters between them before the monster realized she had outfoxed it. With a bellow, the thing turned on her again. It had not fully recovered from Cortez's frantic blow to its midsection, and what would have normally been a swift rush turned into a shambling lunge.

With remarkable clarity of mind and calmness of spirit, the doctor ran through the standard "failure drill" for the M-

43 Pug autopistol. She slapped the bottom of the protruding magazine to ensure that it was properly seated, yanked the charging handle back, and released it, allowing the bolt to slam forward into battery once again. Extending the weapon in both hands, she squeezed the trigger.

The big pistol went off with a flat whipcrack report. In the expanded consciousness that sometimes accompanies combat, Cortez noted a wave of reddish purple splattering from the creature's forehead. She hauled the weapon back down and fired a second shot, then a third. The alien gave a gurgling sigh and collapsed to the deck. For several seconds it lay there twitching, as though its nerves were still sending messages to its muscles from a brain that was no longer functioning. Then it was still.

Cortez let out a deep breath she hadn't realized she'd been holding and slumped against the bulkhead. The Pug, which suddenly seemed to weigh a hundred kilos in her nearly nerveless fingers, dropped to her side.

Footsteps thudded in the corridor. The doctor snapped erect, bringing her weapon back up into firing position. Two Marines, their rifles held at the ready, advanced down the companionway toward her. Behind them came George Grippo, holding his autopistol in a loose, nervous grip, as though he were afraid the weapon was about to turn and bite him.

"Dr. Cortez, are you all right, ma'am?" one of the Marines, a young blond woman asked, laying a hand on Cortez's wrists, gently forcing the medic to lower her pistol.

"Yes, I'm all right, Private." Her voice was so even it surprised her.

"We heard the shots, and the captain sent us to check it out," the female Marine continued. "What happened? Did you see any more of these things?"

Before Cortez could answer, the second trooper straightened from his crouch next to the alien body.

"It's dead."

Cortez caught sight of a big, pistol-shaped weapon dangling from the Marine's right hand. A long steel spike jutted from the gun's muzzle. A black insulated cable about as thick as two of Cortez's fingers ran from the weapon's grip to the dead alien's torso. There, the heavy wire seemed to meld with the creature's right side, just under its short ribs. In a strange, detached way, she noticed that this alien was somewhat taller than the one that had attacked the Marine scouts.

"Doc?" his partner prompted.

"I don't know, really." Cortez tore her eyes away from the corpse she had just created. "I was just standing out here in the corridor when I saw something move back by the engine room."

As the doctor began to relate her experiences to the Marines, the female Marine reached out and gently took the big autopistol from Cortez's hand. She removed the box magazine and pulled the charging handle, ejecting the live round from the chamber. The M-43 was considered a supremely reliable weapon. If one malfunctioned in the field there was usually some serious problem in the pistol's mechanism.

The trooper worked the pistol's action several times, testing its operation.

"How many shots did you fire, Doc?"

Cortez thought a moment. "Three, I think."

The Marine looked around the deck and finally located a trio of spent shell casings. With a low chuckle, she thumbed the loose round back into the magazine before slipping the steel box into the well just ahead of the Pug's trigger guard. Again, she racked the charging handle, feeding a live cartridge into the pistol's firing chamber. Safing the weapon, she passed it back to Cortez.

"That's why you had a misfire, Doc. There was no round in the chamber. I suggest you keep it cocked-and-locked until we get off this mud-ball."

"What?" Cortez said, feeling a subtle tremor seize her right hand.

"I wouldn't worry about it too much, Lieutenant," the blond Marine said with a reassuring smile. "It happens. The trick is to learn from the mistake."

Rapidly, the uncontrollable shaking ran up Cortez's arm and spread to her whole body. Grippo dropped his pistol and darted forward to catch his chief before she fell to the deck.

"Is she all right? What is it?" the Marine asked anxiously.

"Adrenaline reaction," Cortez answered through chattering teeth.

"It happens sometimes," Grippo said. "Sometimes you get so charged up by adrenaline that you get the shakes when things are all over. It's a natural reaction. Now, why don't you two heroes check this place out and make sure there aren't any more of those damn things lurking around in here?"

26

S ay what?" Gunny Frost snapped as Dr. Cortez concluded the account of her encounter with the alien on *Cabot*'s upper deck. The doctor had met the Marine platoon leaders at the entrance to the cargo bay, just as Frost and her companions were returning from their disastrous foray to check on the disabled sensor packages. "How the hell did *that* happen?"

Fuming, she turned on her heel and stalked out of the cargo bay, stepping over the body of the dead Masher she had carried back to the ship.

Captain Taggart watched her go, feeling a pang of sympathy for those Marines who had been on sentry duty when the attack occurred. Gunnery Sergeant Onawa Frost in full hue and cry was an awesome sight, fit to unnerve even the toughest combat veteran.

With a short, choppy gesture, Taggart summoned Corporal Henry.

"Tim, we may have a security breach."

"Yeah, I heard," the tall gray-haired corporal replied. "Somebody let a Masher sneak aboard the ship."

"I don't know if it sneaked aboard or if it *remained* aboard, and we just never found it," Taggart said with a tightness in his voice that spoke of self-reproach. He and Gunny Frost had made an inspection tour of the ruined ship themselves, and hadn't spotted the hidden alien. "How it got aboard doesn't matter. What *does* matter is finding out if any of those damn things are *still* aboard. Corporal, I want you to organize a search party. Go over every square centimeter of this ship. Check every compartment, every companion-way, and every ventilation duct. If you see one of those things, grease it."

"Aye, aye, sir."

"And, Corporal, if you miss one of those things this time," Taggart said, with a grim smile, "I'll bust you so low, you'll think a transfer to a Neo-Sov Rad Squad is a promotion."

"Aye, aye, sir," Henry repeated. He turned smartly on his heel and headed into the cargo bay, calling his squad-mates together.

Taggart watched him go. Ignoring Dr. Cortez for the moment, the Marine officer leaned wearily against the edge of the sprung cargo bay door and stared off into the darkness. His mind was already in motion. If the Mashers had left one ambusher behind, they could have left two or more. The aliens had adequately demonstrated that they had no fear of the more heavily armed Marines, at least not when the Mashers outnumbered the humans. The attack on Gunny Frost's party proved that.

Taggart momentarily considered pulling out, taking with him only those casualties he had already discovered. He pushed that notion aside. The terrain of the rift valley would be easy enough to negotiate if the Marines and med-ical team were unburdened. But carrying the dead and wounded along would make the passage too difficult to attempt at night, even with night vision gear.

Besides, Marine traditions, not to mention those of the Union Armed Forces, dictated that every reasonable effort had to be made to rescue prisoners and to recover the bodies of the slain. With that in mind, he needed to take out a search party to rescue or recover those of *Cabot*'s crew the Mashers had carried off as prisoners.

Recent events demonstrated that he was not facing a tribe of primitives, but a savage race of cunning, if not necessarily intelligent, beings. Though the Mashers' weapons were crude, they were undeniably effective. They had exhibited little in the way of tactical ability, yet they were capable of executing an ambush against experienced combat troops.

There were far too many unknown factors. How many aliens were there on Sierra Seven-Five? He had no way of knowing. Taggart had sixteen effectives of his original twenty Marines. When he launched his search and rescue operation, he'd have to leave at least two, or more likely four, of those behind to protect the medical team.

My God, can that be right? Have I really taken twenty-percent casualties?

The realization jarred him. Such casualty rates in larger, mainline units often brought disciplinary actions. Special Operations units like his Marines were expected to take slightly higher casualties because of the nature of their missions, but no commander liked to think that he had cost almost a quarter of his men their lives.

Thus far, all the Marines had seen were the spike guns and those wicked saw-edged clubs, which his men had taken to calling Thumpers. Did the Mashers have heavier weapons? His two depleted squads had four Bulldog support rifles and two Rottweiler machine guns available to them, but lacked anything more powerful. And then, there were the spider-walkers, the tracks of which Dade and Black had seen on the approach to the crash site and in several places surrounding the wreck. The Marines had yet to see the devices. They were another unknown factor. Were the mechanical walkers simply cargo haulers? Or might they be weapons platforms, troop carriers, or some sort of armored fighting vehicle?

He briefly considered contacting the landing zone and calling in the intact squad he had left to guard the landing craft, or even using the Type 60 Antipersonnel Enforcer chainguns in a ground-support role. He discarded both ideas in short order. Even though his troops had received basic Pathfinder training, none of them was experienced enough to lay out a safe landing zone for the assault boats, especially given the unpredictable winds that continued to whistle through the rift valley at random intervals. Those same winds would make it suicidal to attempt an abseil or parajump from a hovering assault boat. That was why he and his men had had to hike over the rocky hills in the first place.

As for using the assault boats in a close ground-support role, there was still the unknown quantity of the state of the Mashers' heavy weapons. If the ugly little aliens had the capability of shooting the assault boat down, the Marines on Sierra Seven-Five would be stranded.

Nope, we've got to do this, Taggart told himself. *We'll just have to do it ourselves.*

At that moment, Gunny Frost reappeared out of the darkness. She caught sight of her commanding officer, who beckoned her to him. With a posture that fairly screamed of frustrated disgust, Frost squatted on her heels next to Captain Taggart.

"Well?" he prodded.

"Well, nothin', sir," she growled. "Nobody saw nothin'. Nobody heard nothin'. Either those ugly little buggers are the sneakiest thing since my Aunt May's housecat, or we had a couple of Marines asleep on the job. Or else the Mashers aren't as stupid as we thought they were, and they left a couple of stay-behinds in the ship when they pulled out."

"That's what I was thinking, Gunny," Taggart said. "I've got Corporal Henry conducting another search. I don't think he'll turn anything up, but we gotta check."

"Yeah," Frost echoed. "We gotta check. So what are you gonna do about Michelli's story? You really think the Mashers took any prisoners?"

Frost's sudden change of topic failed to take Taggart by surprise. He had been teamed with Onawa Frost long enough to become accustomed to the Mohawk sergeant's abrupt nature.

"I don't know, Onawa. I guess we can't afford not to." Taggart sighed wearily.

"I guess not."

"We'll have to wait until morning to get started," Taggart said. "I'll get the scouts out looking for a trail as soon as there is enough light to track by."

He tapped the visor of his environment suit's helmet. "Light-amplification gear is wonderful stuff. But Dade tells me it doesn't render the depth of field necessary to allow easy tracking, especially in this kind of soil. Since the Mashers all seem to go barefoot, he says it would be almost impossible to follow a trail in the dark."

"Wonderful," Frost said disgustedly. "So instead of hitting the bad guys in the middle of the night, we're gonna hit them in broad daylight."

"Gunny, I know doctrine says this kind of operation

should go off between oh-three-hundred and oh-four-hundred, when the enemy is at his lowest physical and mental ebb." Taggart's manner suggested that he was reciting from the G-Force manual. "But we haven't got much choice."

Dr. Cortez got to her feet, brushing the dust from her knees. She had not wasted the time Taggart had spent in silent contemplation of his future actions. She had used that long period of quiet to examine the Masher corpse lying outside the cargo bay.

"What about letting your scouts track the Mashers back to their base, or village or whatever, during the day tomorrow, then hitting them tomorrow night?" she offered.

"No good, Doc." Frost shook her head with a snort. "That would mean sitting here another day, bottled up in the ship. One-on-one, we outgun the bad guys. But if they try to storm the ship, come at us in a rush with any kind of numbers . . . well, I've faced Neo-Sov mass charges, and that was with a full platoon. Believe me, you don't want to be on the receiving end of a human-wave attack, especially if you're short-handed."

"We don't know if the Mashers even use human wave . . ."

"Begging the lieutenant's pardon, but yes, we do, ma'am," Frost cut her off. "Every time we've run across them, those little buggers have given us a couple volleys of spikes, then come up close with their Thumpers. Now, that may not qualify as a human wave, but that's only because the Mashers seem to be driven a little more by individual heroism and personal greed than by a group goal.

"We've got a lot of firepower here. Those Rottweilers and Bulldogs can lay down a real spit-storm, but I wouldn't want to rely on them to break up an attack. And, if the Mashers do get in among us, then machine guns and grenades aren't gonna be worth spit. Then it'll be down to knives, gun-butts, and dirty fighting. There just ain't enough of us to stand off that kind of attack."

"Oh," Cortez said, and subsided into silence.

"Yeah," Frost continued in an acid tone born more of weariness than a dislike for Dr. Cortez. "And it doesn't end there. Like the captain said, starlight gear is wonderful stuff for making your way in the dark, if you know exactly who and what your enemy is. It isn't so great for distinguishing fine details, especially at a distance. We go in at night, and we're gonna have a helluva time distinguishing the prisoners from the enemy, at least until we close up with 'em. And that's gonna eliminate any range advantage our weapons might afford us."

Cortez bowed her head in silence, partly in acquiescence to the Marines' superior knowledge and skill in this sort of operation, partly to conceal her embarrassment. Recovering her composure, she changed the subject.

"What I wanted to speak with you about, Captain, is the dead Masher Sergeant Frost brought in. Of course I haven't had the time to do a full autopsy. We don't even have the facilities here to do a proper job. All I could do is a cursory external examination."

"And?"

"Well, Captain," Cortez said in a detached, professional tone, "if I had to make a determination, I'd have to say that the Mashers are not Neo-Soviet mutants, but a new alien race. Of course, I can't make that determination for sure until we *do* complete a full autopsy, complete with a genetic analysis. No matter how twisted Neo-Sov mutants are, they still possess basic human DNA. But that's not what I'm basing my assessment on. It's this."

Cortez returned to the dead Masher's side, knelt beside

it, and tapped on the infrared sensor package implanted in the creature's shoulder with the blade of a pocketknife she took from a pouch on her web gear.

"Now, understand, please, I'm not an expert in bionics or cybernetics. Everything I know about those subjects comes from med school and the occasional journal article. Still, I've got some understanding of the matter. If this sensor package really came from one of the platforms we set up, it would be my opinion that there is no way the Neo-Sovs, or anyone else for that matter, could have stolen it and implanted it in this creature's body in so short a time, let alone have him up and in shape to start brawling with enemy troops. I suppose it's possible that the Neo-Sovs could have developed a mutant that heals at a vastly accelerated rate. That might explain it."

"Doc," Frost cut in, "my guys shot, stabbed, or clubbed the heck out of these little bastards. None of them showed any signs of instantaneous healing ability."

"I suppose the Neo-Sovs may have come up with a new kind of Mental, one that can perform a sort of 'psychic surgery' on these creatures, one who could help speed up healing. If that's the case, we should make capturing him a high priority."

"Well, Doctor, perhaps you could answer a question that's been bothering me," Taggart said, ending that course of speculation. "Ever since Gunny Frost brought this bugger in here, I've been wondering about that IR package. Do you think he can access it? Or is he just wearing it as a sort of decoration, like all those screws and bolts in his legs and arms?"

"I don't know, Captain. Without a full autopsy, it would be impossible to say for certain. If I had to hazard a guess, I'd have to say yes, it can access the sensor. Remember, they seem to be powering or controlling their spike guns through cables attached to their bodies." Cortez tapped a thick cable connecting the dead Masher's weapon to its torso. "On the basis of that evidence at least, and pending a full investigation, we'd have to assume that these creatures can access and operate any device grafted into their bodies."

"Hmmm," Taggart grunted. "Whether they can use any implanted devices or not, Doctor, I'd have to agree with your assessment that these things aren't any kind of Neo-Sov mutant, though I'm basing my assumption on different points of evidence. The Neo-Sovs aren't particularly tolerant of self-expression among their troops, not officially at least. They most especially are not given to assent to requests for decoration or embellishment from their mutants or slaves. We've seen at least three examples of that kind of implant among these creatures. The one that attacked Dade had a Union Space Force buckle implanted in its shoulder. Then there were the Star of David and the coffeemaker. Both were covered in what seems to be blood from these aliens." Taggart nudged the corpse with his toe.

"Now the Star would be considered a form of decoration, and a Neo-Sov officer might let it slide. But the coffeemaker? That strikes me as a little too weird. If I was to guess, I'd say these critters can't tell the difference between a practical item like that sensor package, and something completely useless like a coffee machine. They have to learn by trial and error."

"You may be right, Captain," Cortez nodded. "That could explain some of the scars, if the creatures had a useless item implanted and then removed."

"Doc, I mentioned this to Gunny Frost a little earlier, but I didn't want to say too much, because it sounds so crazy." Taggart paused, and took a deep breath. "I'm wondering if these creatures, be they aliens or mutants, can control their bodies to the point that they can sort of absorb a foreign object into their own flesh."

"It's possible," Cortez allowed. "We've had contact with a number of alien races since Earth was 'inducted' into the Maelstrom. Each one has had its own set of paranormal abilities.

"I think you may be right, Captain. I think we're in a first-contact situation."

27

Private First Class Saul Decker poked his head over the rim of the foxhole and peered out into the darkness shrouding the rift valley. Here and there, the odd blue-black bushes that dotted the valley floor showed up as dark patches in his helmet's starlight viewer. If he switched to his thermal-imaging system, he knew those bushes, unlike terrestrial plants, would glow faintly. Almost everything about the planetoid designated Sierra Seven-Five was unnatural. The vegetation grew seemingly without the benefit of water and had much stronger heat signatures than an earth plant would. The wind, which was not silent, could rise and fall without so much as a second's notice. Those unpredictable breezes would set the bushes to stirring, adding a layer of random movement to the scene. The low-light viewer tended by nature to restrict one's field of view, and the fluttering bushes always seemed to be on the edge of Decker's peripheral vision.

Worst of all were the unnatural creatures lurking in the darkness. Disturbingly human in their appearance, they seemed to thrive in an atmosphere that would suffocate a normal Terran in short order. To make matters worse, the gruesome monsters seemed to be growing increasingly hostile and aggressive with every hour the rescue party hung around the wreck site. It was almost as though the creatures had been afraid of the humans when they first arrived on Sierra Seven-Five, but over time they had become acclimated to and then contemptuous of the Terrans.

Decker shivered, the involuntary tremor born of a deep-rooted, morbid fear of the alien beings hiding behind the curtain of darkness. Something moved on the edge of his restricted field of vision. Hitching his eyes another centimeter over the lip of the earth-and-stone parapet, Decker scanned the area carefully. For long seconds he peered into the weird green-and-gray landscape, straining his eyes against the flattening effect of the starlight viewer

There, about seventy-five meters out. What's that?

The young Marine studied the odd-looking dark gray mass, flicking between his helmet visor's light-amplification and thermal-imaging systems. Automatically, he brought his rifle to his shoulder, ready to engage the anomalous target should it turn out to be hostile.

A gust of wind swept over his position, blowing loose grit against the back of his neck. The coarse sand hissed against his helmet and momentarily clouded his vision. When it cleared, he saw the shadowy form toss and sway as the stiff breeze whipped across it.

Another lousy bush.

Decker let a half laugh escape his lips as he relaxed back into the foxhole. The tension of the moment had left his mouth so dry that his tongue was sticking to his palate. With a self-disparaging snort, he lowered his weapon, cradling it in the crook of his left arm. Reaching behind him, he pulled his canteen from its nylon carrier on the back of his belt. Like most of his comrades, Decker had packed in as much water as he could carry along with his regular combat load. They had been told that the likelihood of finding a source of fresh, drinkable water on Sierra Seven-Five was virtually nil. A good portion of *Cabot*'s store of fresh water had been lost in the wreck, but enough had remained in her storage tanks for the rescue team to top off their somewhat depleted canteens.

Decker did not unscrew the canteen's large knurled cap. Instead, he flipped aside a small friction-fitted cap, exposing a thick rubber O-ring. From a small pocket on the front of the canteen carrier, he extracted a heavy rubber tube with a hard plastic nozzle on each end. Decker inserted one of the nozzles into the canteen's O-ring and tried attaching the other to a special fitting on his helmet's jaw-guard. The lightweight, bulky Pitbull rifle resting in the crook of his left arm made the job almost impossible. With a growl of mild frustration, Decker let the rifle slide through his grip until he held it by its stubby flash-hider, and lowered the weapon to the ground, resting it carefully against the side of the fox-hole.

Freed of the impediment of his rifle, Decker easily locked the plastic nozzle into the helmet fitting that was connected to a "bite valve" on the inside of the reinforced kevlon band protecting the lower half of the trooper's face. Upending the canteen, he took the bite valve in his teeth and sucked in a mouthful of the flat, tepid water. Decker closed his eyes, relishing the water's soothing effect on his dry mouth, despite its stale flavor.

He took two more swallows before disconnecting the canteen and returning it, along with the drinking tube, to their respective places in the canteen carrier.

With a satisfied sigh, Decker reached down to retrieve his Pitbull. The weapon was gone.

He knelt, searching the dusty bottom of the shallow foxhole with his starlight viewer. The assault rifle was nowhere to be found.

A strange sensation prickled along the back of Decker's neck. Fear gripped his belly. Slowly he turned his head, rotating his shoulders as the helmet reached its limit of motion. There, perched on the rim of the foxhole, was a Masher. The thing squatting above him wasn't as big as the dead one Gunny Frost had carried back after the attack on her party, nor was it so tall as the one that had attacked Dr. Cortez on *Cabot*'s upper deck. But its filthy hide bore more scars than either of the other two. An arching row of bolt heads followed the line of the creature's ridged eyebrows, looking like a rounded *M* of metallic war paint across the thing's forehead. Even more horrible than the monster's disfigurement was the fact that it held Decker's Pitbull in its massive hands.

The weapon was not aimed at the young Marine. The Masher had it resting across its knees. The thing seemed to be ignoring Decker and gazing at the black rifle. Then, a light of comprehension dawned into the creature's small, black eyes. It laid its right forearm along the rifle's lower receiver. An expression of concentration, more intense than Decker would have believed possible for the savage alien, crossed the Masher's face. The flesh of its forearm rippled and parted, flowing over the weapon's firing grip and collapsible shoulder stock. The Masher tipped its head back and let out an eerie high-pitched gasp of pain. Thick purple fluid seeped from the juncture between the weapon and the thing's crawling flesh as the Pitbull continued to sink into the monster's arm.

Decker was frozen in sick fascination by the spectacle. He tried to will his hand to move, to reach for the Pug holstered on his right hip, or the Ka-Bar hanging from his combat harness, but his flesh was as unresponsive as the dirt beneath his feet.

The Masher's long moan continued, even after its flesh had sealed itself up around the Pitbull. Small writhings in the alien's forearm told of some internal process at work. In a remote corner of his horror-stricken mind, Decker guessed that those little jumps and twists in the thick muscle behind the thing's wrist meant that the creature would soon be able to use the rifle.

That thought sent a galvanic shock through the young Marine, and he found his muscles were his to command once again. Moving as slowly as he could, so as to avoid the Masher's attention, Decker reached carefully for his Pug. A flip of his fingers undid the catch on the holster flap.

He glanced up at his enemy. The creature was rocking back and forth, cradling its right arm, whimpering. The thing's cries reminded the Marine of the sounds a wounded dog might make just before expiring. Decker hardened himself to the piteous mewling and slipped the big autopistol from its holster. Slowly, cautiously, he turned, bringing his weapon up in both hands. The laser sight affixed to the pistol's frame superimposed a small red dot over the Masher's torso. The thing was still sitting on its haunches sniffling.

Decker thumbed off the Pug's safety, took a deep breath, and began to squeeze the trigger.

The soft, flat click of the safety catch being removed might as well have been an alarm Klaxon. In an eyeblink, the Masher surged to its feet and leapt into the foxhole with the startled Marine. It swung its beweaponed forearm at Decker's head. The Marine ducked, trying to parry the creature's follow-up attack. A fist the size of a child's head smashed into Decker's right elbow. Pain shot up his arm as the joint was dislocated. His Pug went spinning off into the darkness. The Masher swung again, battering Decker's helmeted head with the stolen rifle's fore end.

Fear gripped the young Marine again; this time, it was tinged with the red stain of panic.

Decker lashed out with his right foot. The blow landed exactly where he intended and produced the results he had hoped for. The Masher let out a sharp yelp of pain and doubled over, clutching itself.

Wasting no time, Decker scrambled out of the foxhole. Even through the curtain of pain that had accompanied the injury to his elbow, he had seen the direction his Pug had flown when it was knocked from his grasp. In desperation he loped off into the darkness after the big pistol.

A howl of rage split the darkness, followed by the sound of a burst of automatic fire from a Pitbull rifle. Small black geysers of dirt erupted from the ground over a meter to his left. The Masher might have learned how to fire the Pitbull, but its accuracy left a lot to be desired. A second burst laced the ground almost beneath Decker's heels, telling the Marine that the creature was learning quickly. He hoped that the sound of gunfire had attracted the attention of his comrades. Soon, surely, there would be a half dozen Marines coming to his rescue.

Something gleamed faintly in the darkness ahead of him. Decker raced forward, praying that the softly shining object was his Pug. Even if his buddies were coming, he didn't want to be caught alone and unarmed in the darkness. Another burst of fire lanced through the night, missing him by centimeters.

He dived for the shining metal. His injured right arm hit

the turf, sending a fresh wave of agony through his body, clouding his vision, but his healthy left hand closed around the cold, comforting bulk of his Pug. Gritting his teeth against the pain, Decker rolled onto his back, pointing the M-43 back the way he had come.

Movement to his left signaled a new threat.

Crabbing around on his back, Decker lined the pistol's sights up on the breast of an alien that approached him out of the darkness, its ungainly spike gun at the ready. The young Marine squeezed the trigger twice in rapid succession, and the Masher tumbled to the ground.

Training and instinct began to override the fear in Decker's guts. No sooner did the alien fall under the slamming effect of the pistol's heavy slugs than the Marine was on his feet. Running a few steps, he took cover behind an outcropping. Exertion, injury, and terror all combined to set his heart pounding in his chest.

Two more Mashers appeared out of the night. Decker killed one with a single round to the creature's massive chest. He was swinging the Pug toward the second when a fifteen-centimeter spike punched into his belly.

Decker collapsed.

There wasn't any pain, not yet. He groped around weakly, searching for the pistol that had fallen from his shocked and nerveless fingers. It was no good. He couldn't see the Pug, and he couldn't make his legs work enough to carry him to safety.

Looking up, he saw the Masher ramming another sharpened steel projectile into the muzzle of its weapon. Decker stared at the blunt, asymmetrical point of the crude killing tool. The Masher seemed to be in no hurry. It looked at him, a cruel gleam in its small piggish eyes. The thing's face split in a hideous grin full of broken and crooked teeth.

Decker tried to curse the Masher, but all that came out was a harsh rattle.

With an odd, almost apologetic cock of its head, the alien leveled the big pistol-like spike gun at the crippled Marine.

Father, Decker prayed, *into Your hands I commit my spirit.*

His ears did not have time to register the spike gun's pneumatic report before the long steel projectile tore his life away.

28

Gunnery Sergeant Frost crouched in the shelter of *Cabot*'s ruined starboard tailplane, her Jackal combat shotgun held at the ready. Behind her Corporal Henry and five Marines waited for her signal. It had taken only thirty seconds for the troopers to converge upon the spot that had so recently echoed with gunfire. The explosion-shredded combination stabilizer and elevator gave little in the way of hard protection, but afforded the Marines excellent cover under its black shadow.

"Post Five, Arrow?" she called out, waiting for the countersign, "Longbow", but it never came.

"Post Five, Arrow!" Frost said again urgently.

Again silence.

"Post Five, Arrow! Respond!" Frost shook her head. "That's it. Something's wrong. Tim, you and Martinez swing out to the left. Scarpetti, you're with me. Koll, you're backup. Just watch where you fire that bloody thing. I don't want you dropping any grenades in our laps, got it?"

"Yes, Gunny," Kevin Koll said with a grin, hefting the six-kilo bulk of his Bulldog support rifle.

Frost gave the cheerful private a cold look and peered around the edge of the stabilator. The darkness that was so often a Special Forces trooper's best friend had turned against the Marines, becoming a somber, threatening curtain. Frost hesitated a moment, straining to pick out the details of the area surrounding the sentry post.

In her starlight viewer, she could make out a broad band of disturbed soil around the foxhole's rim. By itself, that meant nothing. Marines had been entering and leaving that hole all night, as their turns at guard duty came and went. What was significant was the breach in the low parapet of earth and stone that had been raised around the foxhole's rim. The scattered rocks looked as though someone or something had clambered across them in a tearing hurry. The appearance of the crude fighting position, combined with the gunshots and a sentry who did not respond to calls or passwords, spelled trouble.

"All right, Tim . . . go!" Frost rapped out.

Corporal Henry and Private Martinez dashed from the shadow of *Cabot*'s destroyed tail section, running a dozen steps before suddenly hooking to the right. At the moment they turned, Frost slapped Private Mark Scarpetti on the shoulder, sending the stocky Canadian loping forward, with his gunnery sergeant right on his heels. Frost sensed rather than saw Koll step up into a covering position. Her words of caution to the Bulldog gunner had not been entirely a jest. The big rifle was capable of spitting out six variably fused high-explosive dual-purpose rounds in rapid, semi-automatic fire. With an airburst radius of six meters each, the grenades could devastate a significant section of real estate, and Gunny Frost had no desire to be caught on that deadly ground.

Frost and Scarpetti made straight for the foxhole, covering the ten meters in a half dozen long strides. A few meters short of their goal, both Marines went to ground and scrambled into what cover they could find.

A final time Gunny Frost called out the password.

"Post Five, Arrow!"

When the stubborn silence held, she looked toward Corporal Henry where he and Martinez had taken up a flanking position from which they could cover their partners and the guard post. The tall corporal shook his head.

Frost lifted her left hand, three fingers extended. Beside her, Mark Scarpetti nodded. She folded in her ring finger, then the middle. At last she jabbed her index finger toward the hole. Frost and Scarpetti surged to their feet and lunged toward the sentry post, their weapons held at low ready. Neither was surprised to see that the position was empty.

The Marines immediately knelt to reduce the size of the target they would present to a potential enemy. As she did so, Gunny Frost caught sight of several gleaming metallic cylinders scattered around the rim and the floor of the foxhole. She plucked one from the soft, dusty ground, realizing that the objects were spent 5.56 mm shell casings.

A more careful inspection of the area revealed a now-familiar dark stain spreading across the lip of the foxhole. Gunny Frost did not move from her spot, having taken Lance Corporal Dade's lecture on spoiled signs to heart, but rather scanned the stretch of ground adjoining the foxhole. One large depression in the rim of the hole just behind the dark splotch gave a clear impression of a large, flat, bare foot, such as the rescue party had come to associate with the Mashers. Other scuff marks and the partially destroyed parapet on the side of the hole away from the wrecked survey ship suggested that someone, most likely Private Decker, had left the fighting position in a big hurry.

Though not the expert Rick Dade and Krista Black were, Gunny Frost had little trouble interpreting the signs.

"Lion Six, this is Three," she said, contacting Captain Taggart. "Sir, it looks like we've got a missing man. Private Decker is not at his post, and from the looks of this place, I'd say the Mashers got him."

The first three words of Taggart's reply were the vilest of oaths.

"All right, Gunny," he said, mastering himself. "Hold position there for a bit. I'm sending Dade and Black over. Maybe they can make some sense of things. Assign two of your men to that position. Those bloody damn monsters are getting more aggressive. I'm going to double the guard for the rest of the night."

"Yessir," Frost said laconically.

A few moments later the scouts approached their gunnery sergeant. Frost knew that the strain of this mission had fallen heavily on the recon team. It was beginning to show. Both looked weary.

Frost pointed out the signs and then stepped away, giving the skilled trackers room to work. Rick Dade squatted at the edge of the hole, his rifle braced across his knees, studying the churned-up ground. His partner stood over him, keeping a watchful eye on their surroundings. Before long he straightened and stepped up to Gunny Frost.

"Looks like you're right, Gunny. The Mashers got him."

"Are you sure, Rick?"

"Sure as I *can* be, Gunny," Dade said with a shrug. "It's kinda hard to tell. It looks like he might have seen something and either engaged it or started to crawl out of his hole to investigate it. Either way, the signs suggest that a Masher snuck up on him. He turned around and blasted the thing, but didn't hurt it very bad. There's what looks like blood on the ground beside the hole, on one wall, and on the parapet where the tracks go across it. I think the thing jumped into the pit with him and took after him with a Thumper. I'd guess that Decker jumped out of the hole, trying to get some distance to use his weapon. After that, I can't say, unless you want us to go out a little way and look for him."

Frost sighed, shaking her head. She knew she would have to order the scouts to search for the missing man. Yet she feared for their safety.

"Okay, Dade. I hate to ask you this, but do you think you can track him in the dark?"

"He's wearing issue boots, Gunny," Dade replied, a faint thread of humor weaving itself into his tired voice. "As long as he doesn't take his shoes off, we should be able to track him."

"All right, but I'm coming with you for backup," Frost said. "Hang on a second while I call this in."

Dade had been correct. It had been painfully easy to track Decker's movements after he left the foxhole. The signs were so clear that Frost, with her limited training in reconnaissance and tracking, could have followed the trail.

As the scouts moved from footprint to footprint, Dade confirmed his guess that Decker had intentionally abandoned his post, probably out of a sense of panic. The tracks were heavily indented toward the toe, with considerably lighter heel marks, indicating that the man had been running. Only a few meters out, Krista Black spotted a large puddle of drying purple-black blood. Not far away, in the middle of many large, deep scuff marks, was another viscid stain. This one, in the glare from Gunny Frost's hooded flashlight, was the tacky brownish red of partially dried human blood. A nine-millimeter pistol casing lay in the center of the sticky puddle.

"I'm sorry, Gunny," the recon team leader said sadly. "I'd have to say Saul's dead. That's an awful lot of blood there, and there are no human footprints leading away from here, at least none we can find in the dark. We've got a lot of Masher blood, too, but no dead Mashers. My read here is that the monsters got him and carried him away, probably to loot his corpse in private somewhere." Dade's last words were an angry snarl. "You want us to try to track them?"

"No, Rick." Frost sighed. "I hate to admit it, but there's nothing we can do about this tonight. You said yourself it's too hard to track the Mashers by starlight. Even if we could follow them, what could the three of us do? No," she repeated. "We're gonna have to wait until sunup to look for him."

Four hours later, with the shadows of night barely faded from the deep rift valley, Dade, Black, and the Marines of First Squad stood on the rim of the ravine, just east of the spot where *Cabot* had come to rest. Naked, save for blood-stained brown-and-green-splotched uniform trousers, Saul Decker's body had been tossed into the same shallow defile where the rescue party had found the survey ship's crew. Like them, Decker had been stripped of every bit of metal he had been carrying. Unlike *Cabot*'s crew, the dead Marine had a hole through his belly, just below the waistband of his fatigues, and a second, similar hole in the center of his chest.

"Dammit!" Frost spat. "God *dammit!*"

"All right, get him out of there," she said, visibly mastering her anger. "Bag him up, and be quick about it. We still have a job to do."

29

Rick Dade dropped to his left knee as he examined the shallow, soft-sided impression of a large, flat, bare foot. The tracks left by the Mashers as they retreated from their ambush on Gunny Frost's party were easy to follow. The creatures seemed to be ignorant of the basic techniques of moving unseen; or, they just didn't care if the Marines followed them.

The deep shadows of night faded from the rift valley as the Marines zipped Saul Decker's corpse into a thick rubberized body bag and placed it next to those holding the bodies of the men who had died the night before. Dade viewed the dim light of morning as a mixed blessing. It provided him with enough visibility to discern, interpret, and follow the Mashers' tracks where they led away from the ruined sensor platforms that had been the focal point of the ambush on Gunny Frost's search party. On the downside, it would be full daylight before he and Krista Black would be able to locate the enemy's base. Even that had its good and bad points. The Marines' advantage of night-vision gear had already evaporated in the growing light of day. But, as Captain Taggart pointed out, daylight would make it easier to distinguish between the enemy and potential hostages.

"Lion, this is Falcon," he said, keying his communicator. "We've got their tracks, boss, right where I said they'd be. Based on the number of tracks, I'd guess there were ten, maybe twelve Mashers besides the ones that got greased last night. Looks to me like they were all infantry grunts. I don't see any signs of their walkers."

"Got it," Taggart acknowledged. "Anything else?"

"Yeah, there is, boss," Black put in. "This is a guess, mind you. There are signs that at least one of the buggers was badly hurt when they pulled out. We've got a significant blood trail here. If these things aren't some kind of Neo-Sov mutant, I'd say that shows at least a basic culture, if not a low-grade civilization."

"How's that?"

"They're carrying off their wounded, sir," Black replied. "We already know they appear to carry off their dead."

"She's right," said Dr. Cortez, who, with Taggart's grudging permission, had been listening in on the scout team's report. "Caring for wounded individuals and respect for the dead are two signs of a basic culture. Remember, Captain, we make every effort to recover our own casualties. Does it surprise you that the Mashers do likewise?"

"Oh, c'mon, Doctor. For all you know, their so-called respect for the dead may be cannibalism."

"Maybe," Cortez allowed. "But we shouldn't jump to conclusions."

"Doctor, at this point, any conclusions we draw are going to be assumption and speculation at best." Taggart's voice sharpened. "I'm not going to consider the Mashers civilized just because they carry away their dead and wounded."

"Besides, Doc, there's a bigger issue at stake here," Onawa Frost said.

"Oh? And just what is that, Sergeant?"

"A dozen or so of the little buggers escaped last night. They came back and hit one of our sentry posts," Frost said with no trace of impatience in her level tone. "I'd say they were probably testing our defenses and our resolve. It's entirely possible when we get to their base, or village, or whatever, that we'll be facing a forewarned enemy. They've displayed a helluva lot more creativity so far than I'd have given them credit for."

"Right," Taggart agreed. "I hate to keep saying we can't be certain, but it's true. We can't be certain that the Mashers didn't disable those sensor pods as a way to lure us into an ambush. If it was, they did it slicker than grease on a wet rock. Since we can't be certain, we've gotta give them credit for at least low cunning, if not intelligence."

"That's what I was saying!" Cortez's tone was one of exasperation.

"No, Doctor, you were ascribing a culture and civilization to the Mashers that we don't know they possess. I'm saying they're clever the way a wolf pack is clever. There's a big difference."

"Captain, I hate to interrupt this cultural debate," Frost said, laying a hand on the reinforced shoulder of Taggart's combat environment suit. "But this isn't our department. Let the brain-boys in T- and I-Corps figure out if the Mashers have a civilization or not. Our job is to go in and rescue the prisoners, assuming the little bastards haven't eaten them yet."

The Mohawk gunnery sergeant's tone was one of by-the-book propriety, though Taggart knew the last half of her quiet reminder was a barb aimed at Dr. Cortez. From the look on what he could see of the medic's visor-shrouded face, Cortez took it as such.

"Right, Gunny," Taggart said. Keying his communicator, he passed his orders on to the scout team.

"Falcon, proceed with your recon. Maintain communications. If you make contact with the enemy, let us know, then pull back and let him pass. We may be going in against an alerted enemy, I'd rather not kick his alert status up any higher."

"Roger, Lion, Falcon will comply."

Dade switched his communicator to standby and looked at his partner.

"Okay, Krista, it's showtime. Take the point, and don't let them spot you."

"Semper fi," Black replied with a touch of sarcasm. Though junior in both rank and time in service to Dade, Black had exhibited an uncanny ability to locate and follow signs that Dade had missed on more than one occasion.

Black looked down at the trail the aliens had left when they withdrew from the ambush site and chuckled to herself. Her extraordinary talent wouldn't be necessary to follow this particular set of signs, at least not yet. In their helter-skelter flight, the Mashers' heavy, running feet left deep impressions in the soft, dusty soil. The tracks were more deeply imprinted at the toe and ball of the foot, indicating that the creatures had been running when they passed over this stretch of ground. A few were deeper than the rest, and closer together. Some were nearly obscured by long, shallow furrows scraped out of the earth. Black interpreted these as being made by aliens carrying or dragging their dead or wounded comrades. This analysis was confirmed by the dark purple-black bloodstains she found in and around those tracks.

With a quiet hum of satisfaction, Black started off, following the trail as it stretched away to the east. She moved easily through the low brushy weeds that dotted the rift valley. Her eyes flickered constantly between the trail and the surrounding terrain. Every few dozen meters, she would turn around to ensure that Rick Dade was still behind her. Too many scout teams had lost their lives because the point scout had failed to notice that an enemy had silently picked off the trailing man. Occasionally she stopped, dropping to one knee. For several moments, she remained still, listening, moving only her eyes as she searched her environs for any sign of a threat.

The scouts had gone less than a kilometer when Black came to a sudden halt. She brought her Pitbull's buttstock to her shoulder, its muzzle held at chest level, in a low ready position. Without looking back, she knew that Rick Dade had moved to her right, taking up a covering position.

A few meters in front of her, Black could see what looked like a huddled corpse. The body was partially concealed by what, on Earth, would have been a mountain laurel bush, except for its dark blue leaves. Slowly, she released the Pitbull's forestock and laid the flat of her left hand on the crown of her head, silently signaling Dade to cover her. Cautiously, Black sidled up to the body.

It was a dead Masher. The creature lay on its back, its cloudy, sightless eyes staring accusingly at the Marine bending over it. The Masher's legs were covered with gashes, probably shrapnel wounds from a Bulldog's twenty-millimeter grenades. A single bullet hole puckered the alien's left breast. It clutched a loaded spike gun in both hands. A Thumper, fitted with a saw blade, obviously taken from *Cabot*'s engineering section, hung from its crude belt of poorly tanned leather.

From signs, Black figured the thing must have been wounded in the firefight with Gunny Frost's team and the party sent out to rescue them. The Masher probably tried to make it back on its own, but, due to its injuries, fell farther and farther behind its comrades. Feeling death overtaking it, the creature had apparently crawled under this bush and died.

With a qualm of revulsion, Black prized the spike gun from the alien's rigid grasp. As she straightened, the thick "power cable" attaching the weapon to the Masher's body came free. The line's end was surprisingly free of blood. Instead it was coated with fine black threads, which Krista thought were sections of the creature's nervous system. Suppressing a need to gag, she tossed the weapon away into the underbrush.

Black took a few steps past the dead Masher and stopped once again. Taking several deep breaths, she made an effort to clear her mind of the image of the alien corpse, consciously willing her roiling stomach to settle down. She shook herself, hefted her rifle, and headed off down the trail.

Not far from the lone body, the thin, weedy brush gave way to short thorny trees, most of which seemed to be slowly dying of some kind of alien blight. Their broad, blue arrowhead-shaped leaves were mottled with unhealthy-looking yellow-orange rings. Many of the scrubby plants had no leaves at all on their twisted black branches.

It was in this dying wood that the scouts finally located the object of their search.

"Lion, this is Falcon," Dade whispered into his helmet's boom microphone. There was no need for the *sotto voce*. The aliens could not have heard the Marine Scout's words unless he took off his helmet and shouted. "We have reached the objective. Objective is two kilometers east-northeast of the crash site. We are one-zero-zero meters west of what appears to be the enemy's main base. It doesn't look like a permanent installation, more like a long-term encampment. They have lean-tos and small huts erected, but nothing very solid-looking.

"We count eight aliens moving around. I see three sentries, stationed at intervals, about two-five meters from the center of the camp. Five creatures appear to be working around the camp. One laborer appears to be female. I guess the rest are still asleep. We see no vehicles or heavy weapons, and no sign of the spider-walkers. There are no hostages or prisoners in evidence, no signs of Neo-Sov troops.

"Falcon requests instructions," Dade continued. "Do you want us to move in for a closer look? It doesn't look like the bad guys have much of an alert status going. We might even be able to get right down into the camp and see if we can find the friendlies."

"Negative, Falcon," Taggart replied in a tone that left no doubt. "Do not approach the encampment. Find yourself a good hide, and hunker down. Maintain surveillance until the main body is up. Keep me posted if anything new develops."

"Roger, Lion," Dade said. "Maintain surveillance and report any changes. Falcon will comply. Falcon clear."

"So an approach is no-go, huh?" Black whispered.

"That's right." Dade seemed a little disappointed. "Hold position, hunker down, observe, and report."

"Hoo-rah."

30

Okay, Marine, report," Taggart said, as he crawled on elbows and knees into the scouts' hidden observation post. It had taken forty-five minutes for the main body to reach the outskirts of the Mashers' encampment. During that time only a few more of the ugly little humanoids had awakened and emerged from their rude huts.

"Not much to tell, boss," Dade answered. "We've got ten, maybe twelve aliens moving around down there, at least three of which are females. None of the females seem to be armed, and it looks like one of them is pregnant."

"Oh that's great!" Taggart growled. "Anything else? Any sign of heavy weapons or the walkers?"

"No, sir," Dade replied. "No sign of any wounded Mashers, either. I think they may be in that big hut off to the right there, sir. The one off by itself. We've seen a couple of the females going into that hut, carrying what might have been food. If that ain't a sick bay, then it's probably the chief's hut."

Taggart nodded and lifted his head another centimeter above the camouflaged screen the scouts had erected around their hide. Located at the bottom of a shallow bowl-like area, the encampment was large. Eight huts and a double handful of crude lean-tos clustered around a large central clearing. As Dade had indicated, one large shack stood off by itself on the south edge of the encampment.

Taking a pair of electronic binoculars from Dade, Taggart studied the camp. On the north side of this clear space three Mashers, all of them female, one of them with a massively swollen belly, worked at a low wooden table. Taggart surmised that they were preparing food for the rest of the aliens living in the rude shebangs. As he watched the creatures work, he was not surprised to notice that the females were just as ugly and unkempt as the male Mashers they had seen. All three of the creatures wore dirty saronglike garments.

As the pregnant one stooped over the table, a yellow metallic flash twinkled at her throat. Taggart turned up the magnification on the electronic binoculars as far as it would go. He could not be absolutely certain, but it appeared as though the females were all wearing necklaces made of small gold lumps and plates. It was then that it struck him that none of them had so much as a single screw or bolt head grafted into her body. Why such decorations were the sole province of the males, he couldn't say, nor did he especially care. That, as Gunny Frost might say, was not his department.

Taggart reduced the power on the binoculars and continued his scan of the compound. The guards were where Dade had said they were. All but one of the sentries seemed to be armed with spike guns. The remaining guard had a black Pitbull assault rifle grafted into its right forearm.

"All right, you two stay here. Keep an eye on things,"

he said, passing the binoculars back to Dade. "You'll get the word when we're ready to move in."

The Marine captain slithered out of the blind and crawled another ten meters before getting to his feet and returning to his troops.

"Okay, Gunny this is how we're gonna play it," he said. "Their camp is laid out like this—a small cluster of huts around a central area." As he spoke, he cleared a small patch of dirt and traced a crude map with the tip of his Ka-Bar.

"First Squad is in the best shape. Take them around this way and deploy them along the north edge of the camp. Sweep south through the camp. Your primary concern is to drive the Mashers out of the camp, so you can search for prisoners. I'll position Second Squad along the western edge of the camp to give you cover and fire support. I'll keep our scouts with me for a little added firepower.

"Gunny, I'd like this operation to go off with as little shooting as possible. We don't know where the friendlies are. This big hut here? That may be an infirmary, so try not to hose it down. And, just to make things more interesting, there are females down there, one of whom is probably pregnant. Tell your troops to be abso-frigging-lutely sure of their targets before they engage, but, under no circumstances are they to hold their fire if it puts their life or the lives of any friendlies at risk."

"Got it, boss," Frost said quietly.

"Dr. Cortez, you and your medical team will have to stay here. No arguments this time, Doctor. I don't want any of you getting greased." Taggart held up a hand to forestall the inevitable protest. "You may assign one medic to each squad, but *you* will stay here this time. I need you here to treat serious wounds. If you go in with the troops and get yourself killed, it might cost me some of my men, and I'm not willing to take that gamble, so *you stay here*. Understood?"

"Understood, Captain." Cortez's tone indicated that, though she would comply with Taggart's orders, she did not like them.

"That's it, then, Gunny," Taggart said with a weary sigh. "Move 'em out. When you're in position, give me a signal and we'll kick this thing off."

"A-ffirmative," Frost said. "I'll see you when it's over."

Gunnery Sergeant Onawa Frost froze in place. They were barely halfway along their circuit of the Masher camp when PFC Mark Scarpetti suddenly halted, his left hand clenched into a fist beside his head. The young Marine half-turned, catching her eye. He pointed toward the camp and held up two fingers, which he then turned downward, and wiggled in a walking motion.

Frost leaned first to her right, then her left, in an attempt to see the pair of aliens moving along the perimeter of the camp. She caught a brief flicker of movement. The dying, scrubby trees were too thick between her and the enemy to see anything else. She gave up trying to catch a glimpse of the enemy and fixed her attention on Scarpetti, who stood tensely, his rifle at low ready, watching the Mashers. After an agonizingly long interval, he relaxed, and with a jerk of his head, he signaled Frost to follow him.

Scarpetti had barely taken three steps, when a loud flat bang tore through the morning air.

Frost threw herself to the ground. A billow of white smoke marked the spot where PFC Scarpetti had been. The young Marine lay on his side at the base of a thorn tree. His left leg was missing below the hip.

"Dammit," Frost swore. "The bastards have the area booby-trapped."

A volley of spikes whistled through the air, landing closer than Frost liked to where she was lying. Beside her, Kevin Koll readied his big Bulldog support rifle. The weapon's twenty-millimeter grenade launcher barked three times in rapid succession. Before the echoes had faded, a trio of sharp flat bangs assaulted Frost's ears as the eighty-gram grenades burst in the air at preprogrammed spots, showering the area below with deadly steel splinters.

"That's torn it," she bellowed. "Everybody in! Let's go!"

Lurching to her feet, Frost started down the gentle slope in a twisting lope, hoping her zigzag course would throw off the aim of any Masher trying to draw a bead on her.

A Masher stuck its head out through the curtained door of the nearest hut, surprise and confusion on its prognathous features. Frost gave it no time to recover. A load of buckshot from her Jackal punched it backward into the hut and blasted splinters from the wrist-thick branches used to construct the walls of the hovel.

Off to the south, she heard a long chattering roar as Winslow Jones, eager to redeem himself for the loss of his Pitbull, unleashed the Rottweiler machine gun that had until recently belonged to Lucas Panchard. That blast of fire meant that Captain Taggart's Second Squad had gotten into the action.

Another creature, with a large flat piece of metal implanted in its chest like a crude breastplate, came at her wielding a big, two-handed version of the Thumper club. The weapon seemed to be constructed of a chain-saw blade mounted on a meter-long section of steel pipe. A section of thick insulated cable ran from the weapon's bulky cross-guard into the Masher's arm just above the wrist. As the Masher closed with her, its weapon let out a loud whining sound as the bladed chain started to move on its steel track.

The alien swung the long weapon at her head. Frost leapt backwards, careless of landing safely, seeking only to put space between herself and that monstrous weapon. More quickly than Frost would have believed possible, the Masher came on. Handling the weapon as easily as the Marine sergeant would have wielded a pugil stick, the alien thrust the wickedly screeching saw blade at her midsection. Frost twisted aside, getting her Jackal in front of her.

A jerk on the trigger, and the big shotgun roared and jumped in her hands. The buckshot sang off the Masher's breastplate, knocking him back a half-step. The thing let out a bellow of shock and pain. It rushed forward, swinging the two-handed Thumper. Frost pumped the Jackal's slide, feeding a fresh round into its chamber. She ducked below a stroke that would have ripped her head from her shoulders, rammed the shotgun into the alien's groin, and jerked the trigger.

The blast lifted the alien off its feet, dropping it into an untidy tangle of arms, legs, and weapon. The Masher's corpse twitched once and lay still. The whining chain-saw blade stopped. In some corner of her mind, Frost realized that the Mashers' weapons must be either powered by or controlled by the creatures' nervous systems. The anomaly of the idea that a race so primitive in appearance and culture should be able to perform such cybernetic implants was not lost on her.

Another of the hunched aliens lumbered toward her. She brought up the shotgun, pointing its stubby barrel at the center of the creature's body. The Masher let out a yelp, and, flailing its arms, came to a stumbling halt. For a split second, Masher and Marine eyed each other; then the alien screeched again and darted away into a hut. Only after the thing had retreated did Frost realize that it was the pregnant female.

"Lion Three, this is Six," Taggart's voice erupted from her headset. "We've got trouble here. The aliens have gotten organized and they are pressing us hard. Push your squad south as fast as you can."

"Roger, Six," Frost acknowledged. "First Squad, form up on me. The boss is in trouble and we're gonna go bail him out."

Private Cho Lim took one step before a Masher leaned around the corner of the same hut the pregnant female had taken refuge in. The alien's spike gun barked. Lim pitched over onto his back, his hands clutching his face. Corporal Henry tried to go to his aid, but was attacked by two more Mashers, one of which was armed with a stolen Pitbull rifle. The tall noncom was struck by two assault-rifle rounds before he could take cover.

"Henry, report!" Frost bellowed.

"I'm okay, Gunny," he answered breathlessly. "Damn, that hurts. They hit me center mass, but the armor stopped the slugs."

"Gunny, Lim's dying out there," Harris yelled, following up his angry shout with a long thundering burst from his Rottweiler. Splinters flew from the hut's wooden walls. Frost would have bet that nothing could survive the withering blast of gunfire. She was proven wrong, as a bleeding Masher leaned around the doorframe, taking a wild potshot at the machine gunner.

Harris was right. Lim was not dead. He was writhing on the ground, his hands pressed over his face. The wounded man's back arched violently. He kicked his feet.

"Koll, put a grenade in there."

"On the way, Sarge."

Koll's Bulldog thumped. Frost saw the shack's wooden wall splinter where the twenty-millimeter projectile struck and penetrated. Less than a second later, the package of steel and explosives detonated with a sharp bang. Koll had set his grenade for delayed point detonation, allowing it to pass through the hut's flimsy wall before bursting. Nothing inside the shack could have survived that deadly shower of high-velocity fragments.

"Mossier, deSilva, check on Lim." Without waiting for a reply, Frost darted toward the hut's open, smoke-shrouded doorway. Nothing moved inside. The Bulldog's grenade had done its work. There were five dead Mashers, including the pregnant female. For a moment Frost was sickened by the sight of the dead alien, her body torn by the deadly steel shards. But the veteran noncom quickly steeled herself and turned her back on the charnel house.

"Gunny, Lim's dead," Mossier called. "His faceplate was torn away by that spike, and he suffocated before we could get to him."

Captain Max Taggart flinched as a steel spike buried itself in the trunk of the diseased tree behind which he had been sheltering. He rolled right, came to his knees, and loosed a three-round burst of automatic rifle fire. A few dozen meters away, a Masher, scrawny by comparison to its fellows, clutched its left thigh and collapsed into a heap.

Off to his left, Taggart heard the loud, flat crack of a bursting twenty-millimeter grenade. Two more of the squat little monsters fell to the dusty soil, their bodies torn by shrapnel.

"Captain, they're coming in close!"

Taggart wasn't sure who raised the panic-tinged shout. A Masher, bounding through the dying trees swinging a Thumper, gave him no time to inquire. The creature was on him before Taggart could bring his Pitbull to bear.

The Masher let out a howl of rage and battle lust, and brought the metal-shafted club down in a vicious overhand arc, intended to smash the Marine officer's helmet and head alike. Taggart was able to save himself only by flinging himself recklessly to one side. At the same time, he brought his rifle up in a slashing counter-clockwise circle, hoping to deflect the Masher's primitive, but still deadly weapon.

Neither the blow nor the desperate parry connected. The Masher, impelled by the force of his missed stroke, lurched forward. Taggart stumbled, trying to get his feet back under him after his wild dodge. Both antagonists fell to the ground.

Taggart rolled away from the Masher. He felt his environment suit snag on some bit of debris and then pull free. He mouthed a silent prayer that his suit was not torn and surged to his feet. The Masher was gathering itself for another charge. The captain gave the creature no time to set itself. With all his strength, Taggart swung the butt of his Pitbull at the creature's head. The monster let out a snuffling yelp of shock and pain as the rifle's collapsible stock slashed into its jaw. A muted, wet snap reached Taggart's ears. The creature dropped twitching into the dusty soil. The Marine officer reversed his weapon and finished the creature off with a burst of gunfire.

Almost immediately, two more Mashers sprang up to take the first one's place. Taggart shot the one nearest him. As he was swinging the M-18's muzzle to engage the second, the Masher struck the weapon from his grasp with a fire ax, which had probably been looted from *Cabot*'s damage-control stores.

Taggart heard the weapon clatter across the ground as he fought to keep his balance. The force of the blow had twisted him half-around, leaving the Masher behind him and a bit to his left. Taggart took advantage of the writhing lunge he had to make to stay on his feet, and, continuing the turn, lashed out with the sole of his right foot.

The shooting back kick caught the Masher in the belly. Taggart heard the *whoop* as the breath rushed out of the creature's lungs. Completing the turn, he grabbed for the big Ka-Bar combat knife hanging upside down from the left suspender of his combat harness. At close quarters, the knife would serve him better than the heavy M-43 Pug autopistol holstered on his hip.

As Taggart yanked the heavy bowie-bladed knife from its kydex sheath, the Masher, still struggling to breathe after the devastating blow to its abdomen, lurched forward, its Thumper club lying forgotten in the dirt. One flailing hand snagged Taggart's harness while the other clipped the side of the Marine's head.

A star-shot red haze drifted across Taggart's vision.

God, this little bastard is strong.

Blindly, he lashed out with the Ka-Bar, feeling the weapon's blade strike flesh. For a split second, the blade hung up in the dense muscle sheathing the Masher's upper arm. Then the force of the slash dragged the weapon free. The Masher howled in pain, but never let go of Taggart's harness.

Summoning all his strength, which had been increased by rage and fear, Taggart thrust the combat knife into the Masher's body. Twisting the weapon's handle, he jerked it free and thrust again. He felt the viselike grip on his harness slacken, then release, as he rammed the Ka-Bar into the Masher's torso a third time.

A deep gurgle escaped the ugly alien's throat. It sagged backwards. The Ka-Bar embedded in the Masher's body was jerked from Taggart's hand by the fall. He thought that he had probably jammed the thick, broad blade against one of the creature's ribs. It would take more time and effort to free the weapon than Taggart had at the moment.

Taggart looked around for his Pitbull. He spotted the weapon lying against the base of a sickly, blighted tree. The M-18's barrel had been bent by the Masher's ax. A bright line gouged in the metal showed how close Taggart had come to losing his fingers to the alien's melee weapon.

Yanking his Pug from its flapped green nylon holster, the captain turned to survey the battlefield. The Mashers had pulled back. A few of his Marines were pursuing them. Dr. Fritz Mayer knelt over a camouflage-clad form, holding a pressure dressing in place with one hand while struggling to free a second bandage from its sterile package with the other.

Taggart dropped down beside the medic. He placed his hands over the thick bandage pressed against the wounded Marine's shoulder. Even through the dressing, Taggart felt the broken ends of Private First Class Lisa Parks's collarbone grate together. Mercifully, she was unconscious.

"It's through-and-through," Mayer said.

The captain half rolled the injured Marine toward him, allowing Mayer to apply the second bandage against the ragged exit wound in Parks's upper back. In a few moments, the medic had the dressings taped firmly in place.

"Is she gonna make it, Doc?"

"I think so, Captain," Mayer sighed, sitting back on his

heels. "She's lost a lot of blood, and her suit was compromised. I think we got to her in time, though."

The medic sighed again and jerked his head toward the Masher's encampment. "You go ahead, I'll look after her."

Taggart patted Mayer on the shoulder and got to his feet. A few meters away, Parks's Bulldog support rifle lay undamaged on the ground. The captain recovered the weapon in order to replace his destroyed Pitbull and headed through the grove of dying trees toward the rapidly fading sounds of battle.

"*Madre de Dios*," Private Jorge deSilva breathed.

Gunny Frost looked up at her trooper's awe-filled exclamation. There, striding between the huts, bearing down on her depleted squad, was the largest Masher they had seen yet. The creature would have been well over six feet tall, if it had been standing on the ground. As it was, the top of the alien's head towered almost three meters in the air. Grafted into the alien's waist were five articulated limbs, each ending in a sharp steel point. The Masher's own legs dangled limply a meter above the earth. Whereas most of its "normal" fellows had small bits of metal implanted their bodies, this monstrous specimen was almost completely encased in steel plates. Clutched in its hands was an elegant riflelike weapon, the likes of which Gunny Frost had never seen.

DeSilva recovered his composure and sent a three-round burst into the alien's chest. The alien replied by leveling the metallic green rifle at its assailant. A loud sizzling hum blanketed the sounds of gunfire, and deSilva dropped to the earth, screaming. His right leg had been severed at the knee, the stump cauterized by the eldritch energies projected by the huge alien's weapon.

His squadmates scattered, sheltering behind whatever

cover they could find, but not before the Masher cut down another Marine.

Gunny Frost dashed out of cover to grab deSilva by the back of his combat harness. A hissing burst of invisible energy scorched the earth only a meter away. She felt an indescribable wave of heat pass over her, causing her breath to catch in her lungs. She hefted the now-unconscious Marine across her shoulders and launched into a shambling run, barely reaching the cover of a rock outcropping before another blast of invisible heat energy tore through the air. The stone shattered beneath the energy weapon's beam, showering Frost and deSilva with shards of white shrapnel. A few rock splinters penetrated Frost's environment suit, stinging her legs and side like a swarm of enraged hornets.

Fighting panic, she took a deep breath of rubber-tasting, filtered air and held it. Digging in a pouch, she extracted a patch kit. Another blast of energy blew more stone to rubble, but Frost could hear the rapid, angry rattle of Pitbull and Rottweiler fire replying to the Masher's assault.

Working as quickly as she could, Frost slapped sealant patches over the gashes in her suit, hoping they would hold as well as the suit's designers claimed they would. When the last rent was sealed, Frost snatched up her Jackal and peeked cautiously around the base of the outcropping.

The big, enhanced Masher was still on its mechanical feet, though it was bleeding from a dozen wounds.

Tracer fire lanced in from behind the creature to spark off its mechanical legs. Through the smoke of battle, Frost could see a Marine lying prone in the shadow of a ruined hut, blazing away with a machine gun. Taking advantage of the distraction provided by that hail of fire, Gunny Frost yanked a hand grenade from its pouch on the side of a magazine carrier. She armed the fist-sized explosive package and lobbed it underhand beneath the big alien's dangling humanoid feet.

A roar of animal pain accompanied the bursting grenade. When she looked again, the Masher was down. Three of its five mechanical legs were twisted, splayed outward by the blast. The two intact limbs were twitching spastically. The creature's lower body had been shredded by the steel fragments, and yet it struggled to lift its arcane weapon. Gunny Frost lifted her shotgun, intending to put the creature out of its misery, when the Masher lifted its bloodied head, fixing her with small, beady eyes. A spasm of pain passed over the alien's apelike features. It let out a small mewling sigh and lowered its head as though it were settling in for a nap. The mechanical legs gave one final jerk and were still.

Almost immediately, the volume of fire echoing through the Masher camp slackened. It was as though the biomechanical monster's death had been a signal to the surviving aliens, for those able to do so took to their heels, dragging with them those of their dead and wounded comrades they were able to reach. As suddenly as it had begun, the battle was over.

31

Onawa Frost stood staring down at the dead body of the spider-legged Masher.

It must have been their chief, she thought. *When it was killed, the rest of the little bastards broke and ran.*

"Corporal Henry," she called aloud.

"Right here, Gunny." Though the 5.56 millimeter slugs from the stolen Pitbull did not penetrate the thick kevlon of his combat environment suit, the impacts had cracked two of the gray-haired noncom's ribs. His voice came out as a sharp-edged rasp.

"You okay, Tim?"

"Sure, Gunny. Nothing a little Earthside R & R wouldn't fix."

"Well, you ain't gonna get it until we get off this damn dustball," Frost snarled with the mock severity common to sergeants of every stripe and nation. "Get what's left of your squad organized. Check the dead Mashers and make sure they're really dead. And we still have hostages to find."

"Right away, Gunny," Henry replied.

As Henry turned to carry out Frost's orders, the Mohawk

gunnery sergeant saw Captain Taggart approaching. The front of his environment suit was slick with dark Masher blood. A Bulldog support rifle rested in the crook of his left arm.

"Looks like you had a time of it too, sir," Frost said.

"We did, Gunny. They came in close, and it ended up hand-to-hand." Taggart looked and sounded like he was exhausted. "I called Cortez and her people in as soon as the fighting stopped. They're taking care of our wounded. God, what a mess."

"Yessir," Frost said. "I've got Corporal Henry and what's left of First Squad looking for the hostages, but I doubt we'll find any, not alive at any rate."

"Yeah," Taggart sighed. "Then all this will have been for nothing."

"Yeah," Frost agreed. Out of the twenty Marines who had left the landing zone, eight were dead. Four more were wounded. The inverted wounded-to-killed ratio was hardly surprising. If a man's suit was breached, and he wasn't able to patch it, he'd suffocate in the poisonous atmosphere in short order, just as Cho Lim had.

"Take a look at this big bugger," she said shifting to a less painful subject. Frost nudged the dead Masher with her toe. "You think he was their chief, or boss, or whatever?"

"I can only guess, Gunny. Maybe he was the biggest. He had the best weapon. He even has the most metal grafted into his bod . . . Well, I'll be. Look here, Gunny."

Taggart knelt beside the dead bio-mechanical alien. He moved its left arm aside revealing a rectangular box of orange anodized steel. Black lettering on its surface proclaimed the device to be *Cabot*'s missing flight data recorder. He grasped the unit by an exposed mounting bracket and pulled. The device remained stubbornly in place.

Frost gently pushed her captain aside and, dropping to

her knees, drew her big Ka-Bar combat knife. The eighteen-centimeter blade was razor-sharp. Even so, it took considerable care and a fair amount of straight-out hacking at the creature's rapidly stiffening muscles to free the recorder. When at last the device came free, the thin silvery threads that Frost thought of as nerve fibers clung to the unit's input-output terminals like a clump of fine gray-black roots.

"You don't think these creatures had access to the data stored in this thing, do you?" Taggart said, taking the bulky device in his hands.

"I dunno, sir. Why?"

Corporal Henry, looking thoroughly dejected, approached. Taggart held up one hand to forestall any more questions or speculations from his gunnery sergeant.

"I'm sorry, boss," Henry said with a sad shake of his head. "There ain't no signs of any hostages, just lots of dead monsters and a couple big piles of junk. We didn't see any signs of Neo-Soviet involvement, either."

"Thank you, Corporal," Taggart said. "Round up the platoon. Check weapons and ammo. We're outta here in five minutes."

"Yessir."

"He's a good man," Frost observed, as the Corporal moved away to carry out Taggart's orders.

"Yeah," Taggart agreed. "He'll make a good sergeant someday."

"So what was that you were saying about the recorder?"

Taggart stared through Frost for a second, as though it was a subject he didn't want to go back to.

"If the aliens could access the data in the flight recorder, especially the course logs, where would that lead them?"

"Straight back to Earth," Frost said, a look of horrified realization creeping into her eyes.

"Yeah, straight back to Earth." Taggart sighed again. He jerked his thumb toward the edge of the encampment where the men had gathered. "All right, Gunny, let's get them organized and get the hell out of here. We'll bivouac one more night at the wreck. We'll recover whatever we can of *Cabot*'s survey records, take the voice and data recorders with us. The ship may be lost, but we can still take the data her crew died to gather back to Earth with us. And there's a lot about this cockeyed planet that the brain-boys back home will want to know about. That ruined city, the time distortion, not to mention the Mashers. We'll head back to the LZ in the morning."

Captain Taggart squatted on his hams, looking up at Onawa Frost. When he spoke again, there was a tone of weary reluctance in his voice.

"As much as I hate to admit it, I don't think we're ever going to find those missing crewmen. If I had to guess, I'd say they're dead. Michelli said the ship suffered explosive decompression. My guess is that they got blown out of the ship when she lost pressure. It's not only *Cabot*'s crewmen we're going to be leaving behind. Kowalski and Ake are still missing, too. If *any* of them are still alive, then, in all likelihood, the Mashers have them. If that's the case, they've taken the prisoners to another village. We haven't seen any indication of that. Gunny, I'm afraid they're all dead."

"So you're saying we don't continue the search?" Frost said. She was not questioning her captain's orders so much as confirming them.

"I'm saying we can't. According to our scouts, there are a lot more aliens on this rock than we've seen. We're *way* down in strength, and we've used up an awful lot of our ammunition. Under these circumstances, I'd rather not go into another major engagement. Even if we bring in Third Squad from the LZ, we aren't going to be in much better shape than we were when we first got here."

Taggart sighed and rubbed the back of his neck through his environment suit.

"I know it violates our most basic tradition, Onawa, but this time, we're gonna have to leave the lost behind."

Twenty-four hours later, the sadly depleted rescue party prepared for the long hike back to the landing zone. Ensign Michelli had recovered enough to walk under his own power. Two of Taggart's Marines were not so fortunate. They would have to be carried by their comrades.

"Boss," Gunny Frost said quietly, broaching a subject none of the rescuers wanted to deal with. "What are we gonna do about the dead?"

"I don't know, Gunny. Any suggestions? We've got twelve fit Marines and half a dozen medics. We can't have Dade or Black lugging body bags. We don't know if we've seen all the Mashers on-planet. We still need our scouts out on point."

"Yeah, and that leaves us sixteen able-bodies to carry two wounded and thirteen dead. The numbers just don't work out." Frost sighed deeply. "It's your decision, Captain, but, the bodies of *Cabot*'s crew have been out here a long time."

"Gunny, those people lost their lives in service to the Union, the same as my Marines."

"Yessir, I know that." Frost laid a hand on Taggart's shoulder. "Max, don't you think we should let their families remember them how they were? Those folks back on Earth don't need to see their loved ones in that condition. Let's bury them here, and allow their families to remember them as human beings, not as rotting corpses."

"All right, Onawa," Taggart nodded. "Thanks. I didn't

think about it that way. We'll bury them, and mark the spot. If someone wants to mount a recovery operation, at least they'll know where to dig.

"One other thing, Gunny. Round up whatever explosives we've got. I want to destroy the ship."

"Sir?"

"I think Cortez is right. The Mashers aren't—and never were—Neo-Sov mutants or slaves. Still, I don't want them looting the ship any more than they already have. Good people died aboard her. I don't want those filthy little bastards getting any use out of her, not after all this." Taggart swept his right hand in a broad arc, indicating the rift valley and the rescue team that had fought and died trying to save *Cabot*'s surviving crew. "Besides, we know that the Sovs are exploring the Maelstrom, same as we are. I don't want them stumbling onto the ship and salvaging anything useful out of her."

"All right, boss, I'll see it gets done."

The shadows of night had blanketed the floor of the rift valley by the time the rescue team, burdened with the dead and wounded, reached the broad shelf that had been its bivouac the night before they moved down to the crash site. Taggart glanced at his chrono. It was only sixty-odd hours since he had last stood on this rim of stone, looking into the bleak, narrow canyon.

He pulled his binoculars from their case and switched on their low-light systems. The shattered hulk of Union Survey Ship *Cabot* glowed a faint green-white in the starlight viewer. For all her hurts, there was still something elegant about her. But soon even that last vestige of beauty would be wiped out. Without lowering the binoculars, he gave a single jerky nod.

"Fire in the hole," Frost said, repeating the ancient demolitions warning twice more before throwing the protected toggle switch on the radio detonator unit she held in her hand.

Almost immediately, Taggart's starlight viewer was blanked out by a bright white flash. A few seconds later the sound of the explosion reached his ears, sounding like the rumble of an imminent thunderstorm. When the low-light imager cleared, there was nothing to be seen but a ruined pile of twisted steel smoldering sullenly in the night.

"That's it. Gunny, deploy your sentries. We'll bivouac here and start out again at first light."

Frost acknowledged the order and went to work.

Dr. Cortez approached, standing beside Taggart, gazing at the faint red-orange glow that had been the survey ship.

"Captain, I understand why you left *Cabot*'s crew down there. I'll support your decision." She hesitated, then, seeming to come to a decision, plunged ahead. "Captain Taggart, it's true I don't like you much. Maybe I never will. We just don't see eye to eye on so many things. But you've given me a few things to think about."

"Uh-huh," the Marine officer replied in a noncommittal tone.

"Well, one thing's for certain," Cortez said. "Whether the Neo-Soviets are involved or not, the presence of the Mashers has added another wrinkle, hasn't it?"

"Yes, Doctor." Taggart nodded. "And a damned hostile one at that."

"Captain?" Frost broke in. "The pickets have been deployed, and I've got the platoon settled in for the night. Anything else?"

"No, Gunny, thanks." Taggart sighed. "You go get some sleep, and we'll all go home in the morning."

Thomas S. Gressman lives with his wife Brenda in the foothills of Western Pennsylvania.

When not writing science fiction, he divides his time between leathercrafting, Civil War and Medieval historical reenactment, Irish folk music, and a worship music ministry.

Operation Sierra-75 is his fifth book. His previous works include *Sword and Fire* and *Shadows of War*, the Battle Tech® *Twilight of the Clans* series, and *Dagger Point*.

THE VOR™ SERIES

Vor: Into the Maelstrom
by Loren L. Coleman
(0-446-60488-7, $6.50 U.S./$8.99 Can.)

Vor: The Playback War
by Lisa Smedman
(0-446-60489-5, $6.50 U.S./$8.99 Can.)

Vor: Island of Power
by Dean Wesley Smith
(0-446-60490-9, $6.50 U.S./$8.99 Can.)

Vor: The Rescue
by Don Ellis
(0-446-60491-7, $6.50 U.S./$8.99 Can.)

Vor: Hell Heart
by Robert E. Vardeman
(0-446-60492-5, $6.50 U.S./$8.99 Can.)

**AVAILABLE AT BOOKSTORES EVERYWHERE FROM
WARNER ASPECT**

1143a

Experience the terror of VOR firsthand with FASA's exciting *VOR: The Maelstrom* miniatures game.

Comes with everything you need to play including detailed metal miniatures of a Growler™ pack and a Union squad.

For further information check out our web site at **www.fasa.com**

VISIT WARNER ASPECT ONLINE!

THE WARNER ASPECT HOMEPAGE

You'll find us at: www.twbookmark.com then by clicking on Science Fiction and Fantasy.

NEW AND UPCOMING TITLES

Each month we feature our new titles and reader favorites.

AUTHOR INFO

Author bios, bibliographies and links to personal websites.

CONTESTS AND OTHER FUN STUFF

Advance galley giveaways, autographed copies, and more.

THE ASPECT BUZZ

What's new, hot and upcoming from Warner Aspect: awards news, bestsellers, movie tie-in information . . .

* 9 7 8 0 4 4 6 6 0 4 9 3 2 *